— THE RISEN —

D. W. Vogel

NIGHTFELL: THE RISEN
Copyright © 2021 D. W. Vogel. All rights reserved.

Published by Outland Entertainment LLC
3119 Gillham Road
Kansas City, MO 64109

Founder/Creative Director: Jeremy D. Mohler
Editor-in-Chief: Alana Joli Abbott

ISBN 978-1-947659-19-3 (Paperback)
ISBN 978-1-954255-35-7 (Ebook)
Worldwide Rights
Created in the United States of America

Editor: Alana Joli Abbott
Copy editor: Scott Colby
Proofreader: Lorraine Savage
Cover Illustration: Nicolás R. Giacondino
Cover Design: Jeremy D. Mohler
Interior Layout: Mikael Brodu

Printed and bound in the United States of America.

Visit **outlandentertainment.com** to see more, or follow us on our
Facebook Page **facebook.com/outlandentertainment/**

— CHAPTER ONE —

The bedroom of Dolen and Rayli's small house smelled of sweat and blood. Dolen's hand had long since gone numb under his pale wife's strong grip, squeezing harder with every contraction. At the foot of the bed, a midwife kept peering under the sheet draped across Rayli's legs. Her expression grew more worried every time she met Dolen's eyes.

"You're doing great, honey," Dolen said, prying his hand out of Rayli's and giving her his other hand to squeeze for a while. "It can't be much longer. You can do it."

A noise like a dying ghote tore from Rayli's throat as another wave hit her. She was beyond words, and had been for over a cycle, hours bleeding into each other in the unending darkness of Nightfell.

Just one more cycle. Twenty-four more hours of pale, interrupted moonlight before the Eyes of the Atamonen opened in the sky, eight blinding suns to warm the land and drive away the horrors of the dark.

"Don't push yet," the midwife said from between Rayli's legs. "The baby is breech. I hoped he'd turn, but he hasn't. I'm going to have to reach in and turn him myself." The old woman wiped a hand across her brow, leaving a streak of blood.

Dolen hadn't looked under the sheet for hours. He leaned down and forced himself to peer at the bed beneath his wife. Blood. So much blood. He turned back to Rayli, whose thinned lips were white, eyes squinted shut against the pain. "You'll be fine," he comforted. "Just a little while longer."

It wasn't going well. Rayli was a Lightshaper, and in the first hours of her labor, the lanterns in the room had flared with every contraction, her power to magnify and shape the light running wild as she strained. Now the tiny flames barely flickered. Her strength was failing with each wave.

The midwife stood and nodded for Dolen to follow her.

"Just a minute, honey. We'll be right back."

Dolen followed the midwife through the curtained doorway of their bedroom, out into the cottage's main room. One of the living ranch hands and three of the Risen were waiting at the long wooden table where Rayli served their meals every day. The Risen didn't actually have to eat, but they stayed stronger and needed fewer embalming herbs if they were well fed.

"How is she?" one of the Risen hands asked.

The midwife answered for Dolen, speaking in a whisper so Rayli wouldn't hear through the curtain.

"She's in trouble. The baby is sideways, and I'm going to have to try and turn him. She's lost a lot of blood already, and turning him risks tearing the sac inside. If she can't deliver him fast, she could bleed to death very quickly."

Dolen felt his face go white. "But you have herbs for that, right? Something to stop the bleeding?"

She shook her head. "I already used everything I have."

"Well, go get more!"

Her eyes dropped. "*Everything* I have. There is no more."

Mayla, the living hand, spoke up. "The caravan would have some, wouldn't they?"

Yes! The caravan!

"But where is it? Are they close?" Desperation clouded Dolen's voice.

"Usually passing over the high mountains around this time, if they keep to their usual schedule. It's almost Daybreak, and they'll be losing their Risen help. I know they leave them to freeze in the high pass so they'll stay fresh for next Nightfell when they Rise again."

The Risen ranch hands looked at the floor, obviously not keen to be reminded that when the Eyes of the Atamonen opened, they would fall, returning to the dreamless, timeless world of the dead until they rose again next Nightfell, some ninety years in the future. Dolen and Rayli would be long gone by then, but perhaps their son would live to see it, a very old man meeting these same Risen who were here for his birth. Dolen and Rayli would Rise as well, to meet the future generations of their family.

If their son was born. If he lived. If Rayli lived.

"I'll go." Dolen reached for his fur-lined boots and heaviest coat.

Mayla offered to go with him, but Dolen shook his head. "Stay here in case anyone needs anything." Of course the Risen couldn't go. Their undead bodies would freeze much more quickly than living humans. For ranch work, they stuffed the inside pockets in their clothes with heated stones, but they still had to come back to the house every few hours to reheat. Without the support of a caravan, Risen didn't last long in the mountains.

Dolen pushed through the curtain, avoiding the blood smear where the midwife's hand had touched it. He knelt next to Rayli's bed and took her hand again.

"We need some herbs that will make it better," he said, smoothing away blonde hair glued to her sweaty forehead. "I have to go find the caravan to get what we need, but I'll be back just as quickly as I can. You just try to rest. Don't push. Just wait for me. I promise I'll be back. I love you so much." Tears filled his eyes. "I promise, Rayli."

She nodded, too exhausted to speak.

When Dolen kissed her cheek, it was cold and clammy. As if she were already dead and Risen herself, a walking, talking corpse held together with embalming herbs and the grace of the Atamonen gods. Dolen clutched the large, smooth stone that hung from his neck, whispering a prayer to Ata Lashka, whose eye was etched into its surface.

He paused at the curtained doorway, averting his eyes from the crimson stain that seeped into the bedsheets at Rayli's feet. Her eyes were closed, breath coming in short, quick pants.

Go now.

The midwife hurried past him, back into the bedroom. She would do what she could while Dolen was gone, but he had to hurry. The caravan wouldn't be easy to find in the northern passes. And Rayli didn't have much time. He had seen it in the midwife's furrowed expression.

"Any clue where to start?" he asked Mayla, filling a travel pack with some chitin scarab coins; a canteen of water and a hot rock to keep it from freezing; a few dried strips of ghote meat; and a small, hard loaf of bread. He wouldn't need the food. He'd be back long before he got too hungry. Surely he would.

Mayla shrugged. "No one knows for sure where they leave their dead, but I'd try Zigzag pass first. It opens up to some flatter land up top. Prob'ly a good place for them to camp at Daybreak."

Dolen knew Zigzag well enough. His father had died up there, chasing down a lost ghote in a storm. No one ever found his body, but whenever Dolen had to secure one of the flock from the twisty passage, he looked in vain hope of finding his father's corpse in the snow that never melted.

"Take this." Jak, one of the Risen ranch hands, held out a long, curved knife made from the sharp mandible of a skitter. A weapon of metal would have been better, but metal was a luxury few could afford. It was the most formidable weapon he had, and Dolen buckled the sheath around his waist gratefully. There were worse things in the high passes than ice.

He strapped the travel pack over his shoulder as another moan came from behind the curtain.

Hang on, Rayli. I'm going for help.

— CHAPTER TWO —

I ce crunched under Dolen's boots as he climbed ever higher. Snow fell hard in the moonlight, obscuring his tracks almost as fast as he made them. He poked ahead of his feet with a long staff before each step he took. The pass was a labyrinth of crevasses and drop-offs, invisible in the meager light of what passed for midday during the long years of darkness, when even the pale moon dimmed to shadow in the gray sky. Far below the ledge on which he walked, a river flowed beneath a thick coating of ice. One wrong move and he would tumble down. Even if he survived the fall, he would never make it back up the sheer cliff face.

One more cycle till Daybreak. The Eyes would open; the Risen would fall, but the terrors of Nightfell would be over for the rest of Dolen's lifetime.

Poke, step.

Poke, step.

He thought about his life as he crept along the ledge. For his first fifteen years, Ert had been bathed in constant light. The Eyes of the Atamonen shone down upon the mountains all the time. Some blinked closed for a time, leaving them in Dimlight for a few cycles, but even that was bright enough to keep the worst of Ert's horrors underground. Dolen loved hearing stories of Nightfell as a child, knowing the worst would never come to his mountain home. All the adults gave the same descriptions of what happened during the dark years. Predators emerged to stalk the lands, killing livestock and humans alike. Down on the flatlands, the Beneathers boiled up from great cracks in the soil, tentacles waving in delight as they feasted on the human dead. But the Atamonen were wise. When their Eyes closed, they called the dead to Rise and protect the living. Up here, they were a sleepless watch over the ghote herds and the village, fighting without pain or fear against the many-legged monsters that came out of the deep tunnels. No Beneathers ever came up this high. They weren't furred, and couldn't warm themselves like the ghotes and the other creatures of the mountain. Beneathers were all hard chitin, like the other monstrous insects and arachnids of the warmer climates.

Dolen had thought he knew what was coming. He was fifteen when the Eyes blinked shut, exactly when the astronomers said they would. He would be twenty-five when they blinked back open. Tomorrow, if the astronomers had it right again. The Risen would fall, and the caravan would come to take them down to Somteh, where the Embalmers would preserve them for the next ninety years, until they were needed again to protect the world of the living. So it had always been for the humans of Ert, and the Beneathers hated them for the gift of the gods that let them rise during the decade of Nightfell, when the hungry creatures of darkness crept to the surface.

Poke, step.

Poke, step.

The wind picked up, and Dolen burrowed deeper into his scarf, pulling his fur hat down over his ears. He had never been this far up Zigzag pass. If he stepped right over his father's body, he'd never know it in the swirling snow.

He and Rayli had married in the middle of this Nightfell, five years ago. This first son was set to arrive at Daybreak, the most auspicious day for a child to be born, but Dolen hoped he'd come tonight. Rayli couldn't hold out much longer. She was a strong rancher, but even she had her limits.

The moon overhead was still dim. It would rise and fall one more time before Daybreak. Time to find the caravan, buy the herbs, and return to Rayli while she lived.

Or if she didn't...

He shuddered at the thought.

If she didn't, he had to be home in time for her to Rise, if only for a few moments. If he failed her, at least he would have a chance to beg her forgiveness.

But he wouldn't fail.

Poke, step.

Poke, step.

The ledge widened and the river fell away to his left. The hard climb flattened out a bit. To his right, the edge of the mountain dropped in a sheer cliff face. Dolen couldn't see far in the storm, but surely this was the place. Surely the caravan would be here.

He squinted, peering into the darkness for any sign of a campfire. His ears picked up no sound over the wind howling along the cliff edge.

"Hello!" he shouted, cupping gloved hands around his mouth.

If anyone answered, he couldn't hear them.

The land was a gentle slope up now, with a shorter drop to the river on his left, and wide-open space ahead and to his right. Dolen had always been at home in the mountains. He'd grown up here, been born in the very bedroom where Rayli now lay waiting for him. His mother had died in that bed, just a few years after his father chased that ghote up the pass, never to return. Dolen's mother had been far too frail to Rise and fight or toil at Nightfell, so they burned her body, releasing her spirit to the Atamonen in the sky, the final death after a lifetime of hard work. His heart had bled as he stood in the smoke, knowing his mother was lost to him forever as well.

But Rayli wouldn't be lost. He would save her.

A lull in the wind let a sound through.

"Hello?" he called toward the noise.

It stopped for a moment, leaving him uncertain he'd heard anything at all. He called out again, and the sound returned— not voices, but a strange clicking noise. The wheels of a caravan plunging through snow? The legs of a furred beast pulling a heavy wagon?

Clouds parted overhead, allowing moonlight to shine through the glittering snowflakes.

Movement across the wide clearing caught his eye, and he pushed through knee-deep powder.

Wind swirled around him, and frost caked his eyelashes. He rubbed at them with heavy gloves, blinking the ice away.

Glowing red eyes blinked at him from across the plain. Twelve eyes, in groups of four, set far enough apart to freeze the blood in his veins.

Drillers. Three of them. The monstrous, shaggy beasts of Nightfell prowled the dark mountain passes in the bright years, hiding in the shadows. But since the Eyes had closed, leaving the land in darkness, the shadow creatures had grown bold, occasionally venturing near town, plucking ghotes from the herds. Dolen and his crew had killed two of them in the past few years. It took five men armed with ropes and blades to bring one down, and the last one had damaged one of the Risen farmhands beyond repair. Now Dolen was alone, poorly armed, and there were three of them. He pulled the knife from its sheath, feeling its pathetic weight in his hands. The length of his arm, it might just puncture the beasts' outer shells.

Run.

Dolen spun in the deep snow and bolted for the pass.

— CHAPTER THREE —

Dolen's heart pounded in his chest as he slogged through the snow, terrified to look behind him. The sound of his own breath masked the beasts' approach.

Drillers. They were named for the sharp points on their chins, used to punch holes in the frozen, lifeless lakes that never fully thawed in the high mountain passes. So much snow, but the liquid water was often beneath a foot-thick covering of ice. The bottoms of the lakes teemed with life, warmed by underground springs, but the surface was inhospitable to even the hardiest of Ert's creatures. Drillers carved great gashes in the ice for their own drinking water, and often waited in ambush for other creatures to approach the cold oasis.

Were they chasing him? Maybe they weren't hunting.

He risked a glance over his shoulder.

Three huge monsters, closer than when he'd turned. Gaining on him.

Wind swept across the plain. In places, the snow piled up past his knees, grabbing at his sodden boots. He burst through a snowbank and rushed out onto a flat, smooth surface, barely dusted with flakes, and picked up speed.

Dolen cursed the darkness. In the pale moonlight, the mountains hulked all around him, crowding in from all sides. Where was the pass he'd come up? The ledge was narrow, and the beasts behind him wide. If he could make it onto the ledge, they might have to give up the chase.

Another glance behind.

Two of the beasts were close enough to make out the thick, ropy hair that covered their six-legged bodies. The glowing eyes peered out from beneath it, in a face of hard, chitinous plates.

Where was the third one?

Dolen plunged ahead, breath coming in short, freezing gasps.

He stumbled, crashing to his knees. The knife fell from his fingers and spun away across the ice. Wind stung his eyes, freezing the lashes together as he struggled to his feet.

He could hear them now. So close behind.

Oh, Rayli. I'm so sorry.

The thought of her lying in their bed, counting on him to return with the healing herbs, spurred him forward, staggering in the blinding sleet. He crashed through piles of ice shards, careening forward.

From the darkness at his left loomed a huge white shape.

The driller crashed into him, throwing him across the ice. The sky above him spun as he skidded over the surface, scrambling to roll over and get to his knees. Before he stopped sliding, he managed to get a boot underneath him and lunged away from the approaching beast.

They were faster than he was. As tall as his shoulder, and so much stronger. Six legs made them surefooted on the smooth, snow-dusted surface. Dolen had no idea which way the pass was— and even if he did, he'd never make it.

He dodged another high snowdrift, limping forward across the white ground. It was rougher here, jagged and torn.

But the beasts had not grabbed him yet. He remembered the sound of the driller that had mangled his ranch hand. How his bones had snapped in the creature's mandibles. The Risen had not screamed. Impervious to pain, the man had fought back even as his legs were torn from his body and his chest crushed with a whoosh of dark, bloody foam. Dolen was alive. His blood would flow bright against the snow when the drillers tore him apart.

One of his gloves was gone, and his fingers were numb. Beneath his boots, shards of ice shattered as he staggered on.

He could hear them now. So close.

A gust of wind whipped into his face, and he lowered his head, pushing through a waist-high pile of jagged ice. Why was the ice so broken up here? There were no mountain ledges for it to have slid down from. Something must have churned up the tundra here. Something strong enough to hurl man-sized chunks of ice from the frozen ground.

Dolen's boot slipped on smooth wetness, and he plopped down backward, hearing a sickening crack.

Wet.

Oh, sweet Atamonen.

He sat up and peered ahead of him, squinting down at the ground. One step more and he'd have fallen straight into a wide pool dug into the surface of the frozen lake he'd been running on. Drillers. This was their oasis. They'd herded him straight into their trap. Just one more step and he would have plunged in. His heavy clothes would try to drag him down, but the drillers would pluck him out before he sank and eat him at the edge of the hole.

Get up! Run around it! Try!

But they were right behind him. Even as he stood, he heard their feet skitter to a halt just a few paces away. He turned to face his death. They flanked him on both sides, with one straight ahead. The only path open was back into the icy water.

They stood still, eyes red against their fur. Not white, as he had thought. This close, he could see the filth staining the long, twisted ropes of hair. Blood from their prey caked along their front legs under hulking shoulders. If they stood upright on their hind legs, they would tower over Dolen by a head, but they crouched now, all six legs poised to lunge. Gray drool pooled around the hard face plates, exposed to the cold. The thick pointy chins tapped against the ice as they bobbed their heads in anticipation of the meal that shivered before them.

Visions of Rayli swam before his eyes. She would live. Somehow she would survive and raise their child without him. They would never know what happened to him. Nothing would be left to Rise, and even if there was, it would be frozen solid, unable to animate and return to her. This was it. The final death, without even the cleansing kiss of fire to speed his soul to the Ata in the heavens.

Tap, tap, tap.

The beasts took a small step forward and Dolen shuffled backward.

Tap, tap.

Crack.

Dolen registered the sound an instant before he fell, the thin, battered ice at his feet giving way beneath him. He gasped a single breath as he plunged into the water, clawing at the ice shards shattering around him. He had a brief vision of one of the drillers plunging under with him, but the water closed over his head, and his eyes snapped shut at the sudden shock. A lifetime of cold in the mountains had never prepared him for the breath-stealing stupefaction of the frigid water's embrace.

Swim. Escape.

His ungloved hand was a useless claw, beating at the water that pulled him down. He kicked with heavy boots, straining toward the faint glow of the surface. *Pull. Kick.* One glove closed around the edge, and he hauled himself up, face emerging for a single intake of air before a sharp pull dragged him down, skidding along the underside of the ice.

The driller that had fallen in grasped Dolen's boot with one of its hairy legs. Dolen kicked and struggled, and the beast fell away into the depths.

Swim. Find the hole.

Dolen banged his fists against the underside of the ice, pounding at the jagged ceiling that kept him from moonlight and air. He clawed his way along, searching for the opening, lungs burning to breathe.

But it was so cold.

The ice water filled his ears, freezing his eyes and lips. His soaked clothing weighed like stones, sapping the will from his muscles.

Each pull was like climbing a mountain, every second pulsing in his throat. His movement slowed.

So close.

He could see the hole in the ice just a few feet away. If only he could reach it. Just one breath. He flung an arm forward, his heavy coat catching on a sharp edge of ice.

So heavy.

He hung there in the freezing water, struggling to free his coat, desperate to breathe.

Rayli. I'm so sorry.

The dim light of the moon wavered through the thick ice above him, and Dolen's vision went black.

— CHAPTER FOUR —

L anterns flickered as a gust of hot wind blew through the network of small tunnels that ventilated the carved-out warren of Somteh. Sorreg looked up from her writing and stretched. Her new laboratory was one of many in the great city-under-stone, the hub of all science on Ert, and she blinked to clear her vision, rolling her neck in circles.

"Sit too long. Sorreg pops."

On the other side of the long, narrow space, her assistant Kratch gave her a reproachful look. Sorreg wasn't sure how he managed the humanlike facial expression in his hard-plated, insectoid face, but he peered at her from beneath his hood, eyes glowing in the shadow.

He was right, though. Her neck gave audible pops and cracks as she stood up and rolled her skinny shoulders back.

"Yes, I sat too long. But we're onto something here, Kratch. I can feel it."

The Beneather blinked at her.

Berunman. They prefer to be called Berunfolk. She never called him a "Beneather" out loud, but forty years of humans looking down their noses at the other intelligent life form on Ert was hard to break in her mind. She'd been raised to think Beneathers were animals, ravenous beasts who lived with the other monsters underground, just waiting for Nightfell to come to the surface and kill anything that moved, human or otherwise. But Prime Embalmer Zarix, her boss and the head of Somteh's Guild of Medical Embalmers, had brokered a truce twenty years prior. Though the Berunfolk were hardly accepted, Sorreg had to admit it was a genius move. While Kamteh and the other great cities of Ert had been besieged by Beneathers and beasts of the deep this Nightfell, Somteh had flourished, safe from attack, secure in their alliance with those that dwelled underground. And before that, no one even knew they could talk.

But they sure were challenging to look at. Fortunately, the short creatures hated the light and stayed hidden in the folds of long, hooded cloaks. Sorreg didn't have to see the pink brain pulsing with its hideous glow under a clear chitin skull, and the slimy tentacles only poked out the sleeves when Berunfolk needed to use them. Kratch had been with her since the start of this Nightfell. No one could handle delicate equipment like he could, and he was far from stupid. With no small thanks to his deep knowledge of the incredible diversity of fungus growing in the depths, Sorreg had been able to synthesize the green-lung cure that won her the promotion to Senior Embalmer Scientist: Medical, and this big, airy laboratory.

She edged around her desk and joined Kratch at the long, smooth countertop. Glassware littered the surface, tiny flames dancing under beakers bubbling in glowing colors. This new lab was bright and airy compared to the one she'd shared with three other researchers before her promotion. The carved-out stone walls were smoother and the ceiling higher to let in the breeze through ventilation tunnels. It smelled more of fresh air and less of chemicals and damp fungus, though the lab animal room at the back emitted its own earthy scent.

"Is the new culture growing?" She pulled a small plate of blood gel from the warming oven and looked at the underside. "Looks pretty dead."

Kratch shrugged, a human gesture he'd picked up over the years. "Kratch told you. Only grows on rock."

The lichen in question gave a powerful sedative fume when grown on porous stone. It worked on almost everything except humans, and Sorreg hoped she could harness it to enable her surgeon-embalmer colleagues to perform procedures on the living that were currently reserved only for the Risen. At the moment, the end result was typically the same—whatever live human the surgeon was working on usually died during the surgery and was Risen by the end anyway. If she could tailor the lichen to work on living humans, they could save so many lives. Had it grown on the human blood gel plate, she might have been able to mutate the fume to affect humans. But it hadn't.

She sighed. "Well, we know another way to not make a sedative."

Kratch eyed the plate as Sorreg scraped its contents into a trash can. "Try again."

He was a creature of few words. At least, she assumed Kratch was a "he." He had the wide eyes and larger body typical for the males of the other insect species she'd studied. If Berunfolk were similar to the rest of Ert's life, then all the females Sorreg had seen would be nonbreeding workers. Somewhere in the bowels of the land, there was surely a Berun queen. Despite her comfort with Kratch, the thought of a huge Berun female pumping out thousands of eggs somewhere below them in the darkness made Sorreg squirm.

A voice echoed in from the open doorway. "Delivery for Medical."

Kratch scuttled into a corner while Sorreg signed for the delivery. Those in the sciences were used to Berunfolk, but not all humans felt the same way. Even here in Somteh, trust ran thin.

She looked over the deliveryman's shoulder. A large, wheeled trolley sagged under heavy weight. Long, flat stones of various colors and textures made the trolley squeal when the Risen man pulled it into the lab.

The man's skin had the telltale gray cast, and his eyes were like dull granite. He gave her the traditional salute of respect, with three fingers pressed over his lips. It meant "your words are more important than mine," and Sorreg responded with a similar gesture with fingers touching her chest instead. It was intended to reply "I speak from my heart." He was very well preserved. Probably his first Nightfell, from the looks of him, and he carried the faint herbal scent of the unguents used to keep his skin supple. He wore the plain brown uniform of all Embalming Guild staff, but when he turned around to start unloading the stones into a pile at the far corner of the lab, she saw the side of his head was blackened, hair singed off right above the identification tattoo on the side of his neck.

"Are you all right?" Sorreg asked. "Did you get burned?"

The man shook his head. "Not a Riser. Don't hold with that."

Sorreg searched her memory. Riser. What was he talking about?

"And look, you're injured. One of the stones cut you."

The Risen looked at his arm, from which oozed the dark blood of the undead. A couple of the sharp stone's edges had stains already drying from where he had bled on them.

"No matter." He rolled down the sleeve of his uniform shirt, covering the cut. "Doesn't hurt. Sorry I got them dirty. Do you want me to wash them off?"

Sorreg shook her head. "No, it's fine. We always clean everything before we use it."

On the bottom shelf of the trolley, a row of large eggs sat nestled in beds of straw.

Sorreg peered at them. They were soft-shelled, and once the embryo inside was liquified, some of Sorreg's colleagues had been able to do some interesting research with the protein gel that remained. "Are those for us? Kratch, did you order those?"

A voice from right behind her made her spin around, heart pounding.

"Eggs not yours. Eggs mine. Eggs late."

A Berunfolk—Sorreg guessed female by her size—stood just behind Sorreg in the open doorway to the lab, tentacles writhing under her cloak, which bore the emblem of the Prime Embalmer.

"Oh, you scared me," Sorreg said. "It's Orchadonatz, right? My apologies for delaying your supplies."

Orch flashed an annoyed glance at her. The Risen deliveryman paled even further, and doubled his efforts to get Sorreg's stones off the cart. When the unloading was finished, the Berunwoman stalked out without another word, and the Risen man hurried away behind her.

Kratch emerged from the corner where he'd pretended to be very busy while Orch was there. *Apparently there's a hierarchy among Berunfolk as well*, Sorreg thought. And apparently Orch ranked well above Kratch. Was it because Orch was female? Were females higher in their society? So much she didn't know.

She wanted to ask him more about it, but his posture stayed her questions about his people. Instead, she asked about the term the Risen man had used.

"Riser? What did he mean by that?"

Kratch gave her a side-eye from beneath his hood. "Riser. Dead humans think dead are better than living. Want to be like living again."

She knelt in front of the pile of stones, running long, thin fingers along the edges of a few likely candidates. "Is that a real thing? I thought I heard something about a few Risen starting trouble down in the merchant district. But it's just people talking. And it will be over anyway when Nightfell ends and they fall. I heard the Embalmers have some great new techniques to preserve them for next Nightfell. They should be grateful they'll Rise again next time." *As will I, most likely*, she thought. Assuming that by the time she died, she was still in good enough shape to preserve for the rest of the century so she could Rise and serve a new generation of the living.

"Long time before next time," Kratch said. "Long time for dead."

"Huh. Well, it hardly matters to us, does it? Sorreg and Kratch, the dream team of science...we don't need Risen. We've got each other."

The glow in Kratch's eyes brightened for a moment in a Berunfolk's stiff-faced grin.

"Team of dreaming."

They laid a few of the stones in a line down the workbench under the drafty ventilation tubes.

"Stay back, now. Let's try the lichen on a couple of these and see what we can do."

Kratch backed away while Sorreg worked. Dream team, indeed. And if she could ever get this stuff to work, she'd share her dream with all of humankind. She glanced back at Kratch. Berunkind as well, perhaps. And why not? Centuries of hatred had to end somewhere. This lab in the carved-out stone tunnels, in a cliffside overlooking the vast desert plain, was as good a place to start as any.

— CHAPTER FIVE —

Sorreg crouched in front of her long row of specimens. Palm-size squares of rock specimens from every corner of the continent sat under small glass domes. Some of the domes held other substrates: chitin plates from the armor-plated beasts of Berun, dried strips of various fungi, even some precious wood from the small trees that died off during Nightfell.

Lichen grew on several of the rocks but on none of the organic matter. Sorreg peered down the row, noting the growth pattern of the light green plant. In the dim torchlight, most of the powdery specimens appeared to be thriving. None were mature enough to produce the sedative fume, but they were coming along. She sidled down the long table, making notes as she went. The last two domes contained a smooth, shiny stone, and the lichen on it was a different color, red-brown and thriving.

"Kratch, did this get the wrong culture on it?"

Her assistant shuffled over and peered under the dome with her. "Same as rest. Color wrong. What rock?"

"They call it mirrorstone. Usually it's polished up for jewelry and such. This one looks raw, but it flakes off smooth like this, in layers, if you do it right. So the geologists tell me, anyway."

Kratch lifted a clawed hand for the dome, but Sorreg waved him away.

"Not yet. This one's different. Not sure we should open it in here. And not yet. We'll give it some time." She looked more closely at the stone. "It's not all that color, though. Look how it's greener around the edge here."

The stone was darker in places, mottled with a deep brown color. Where the lichen grew on the dark patches, it took on that ruddy hue. Where it grew on the smooth, silvery surface elsewhere, it was the normal green.

"Interesting," she said. "Let's get some more of this stone. And we'll need some scrits to check for toxicity when we open it."

From the doorway came the sound of someone clearing his throat. Sorreg turned to see her boss standing just inside her laboratory.

"Prime Zarix, you honor me." She laid her hand across her lips in greeting, and the older man responded with hand over heart. Sorreg was not a short woman, but the olive-dark Zarix towered over her, and she shrank back from his presence.

He smiled, revealing long, yellow teeth under a heavy mustache that grew into his thin, silver-streaked beard. "I like to visit my scientists when my own work allows a break. How goes your latest miracle?"

Sorreg gave a nervous laugh. "Well, I know many formulas that do not make an effective sedative. I'm certainly narrowing down the options."

His smile faded. "I can see you are working hard. Are you eating well?"

She nodded. "I am, sir."

"And sleeping? Sleep is most important to keep functioning at a high level. We accept only the best."

"Fine, sir," she lied.

Zarix's bushy eyebrow raised at the sight of Kratch in the corner. "Ah, I see you have a Beneather working for you." He leaned in, and Sorreg forced herself not to flinch from his breath. "They're really quite docile. All they want is food, so hard to come by in their natural underground habitats. They'll literally do anything for a meal. A hardy folk, to be sure."

"Kratch is very valuable to my work," Sorreg said.

"I'm sure it is. I have several in my own lab as well. Great knowledge of the underground plant and animal life, but of course no idea of the potential. No imagination, but good with the lab animals—as long as they aren't too hungry."

Zarix straightened up and smiled again. "Well, I do look forward to your progress and success. Do let my office know what resources you might require. My door is always open." He turned and strode away down the torch-lit corridor.

"Mean man," Kratch said from behind her. "Smells."

Sorreg turned to him and sighed. "He's a brilliant scientist. Maybe not the best communicator, but his work is legendary." She gave a weak grin. "And without him, I wouldn't have you."

Kratch shrugged. "Maybe no. Maybe yes. Much work to do."

Wasn't there always?

She took her notebook to her desk to start transcribing the day's data. Forms and requests. So many forms. She filled in the requisition for more of the mirrorstone and sent a repeat request for workers to patch the hole in the back wall of her lab where the stone was crumbling over the doorway that led back into the animal room. And she could use a couple more strong hands to help with the lab animals as well. Risen were growing scarcer this late in Nightfell, but they were so much better at handling some of the larger creatures. The ones with the sharp claws and needle teeth. Only Berunfolk were better, but she'd given up asking for another assistant like Kratch. She should have asked Zarix directly, but his offer of help had sounded empty, and she wouldn't want to bother him with trivial matters. Not until she had another triumph to prove she wasn't a one-off scientist.

Hours later, Kratch stood in front her desk.

"Done?"

She waved him away. "If you're finished, go on. I've still got some paperwork to finish."

"Stay too long. You get sad."

She looked at him. Sad? She wasn't sad. Tired, yes. Under pressure to deliver. But not sad. No, she had nothing to be sad about.

"I'm not sad. Are you sad, Kratch?"

He gave his odd shrug. "Not sad. Not happy. Fine."

Yes, fine. He was fine. She was fine.

"Sometimes that's the best we can do, isn't it? Goodnight, Kratch."

He shuffled away.

For a moment, she wondered where he went. She assumed he lived somewhere underground. Only humans were allowed to live in the hollowed-out cliffs, or the mud-brick homes that dotted the plain in its shadow. Berunfolk always lived underground. Did they live in families? Did Kratch have a wife? Children? She had no idea how old he was. Could he be a grandfather? Should she ask?

A yawn escaped her lips. Questions for another day.

She packed up some papers to take home and work on later and extinguished the torches in the lab. Her tiny apartment was high in the cliff face, internal with no windows. The whole system was designed with ventilation in mind, so it wasn't stuffy, but she had to admit it was depressing. There would be a meal waiting for her just outside her doorway, left by one of the faceless servants that provided for the Embalming Guild's scientists and doctors. Preservation embalmers, who kept the dead preserved in Nightfell and during the long years of light, got the best of everything, of course. She assumed Prime Embalmer Zarix, who oversaw the whole guild, got even better than the Preservers. Surgeons were next, then research scientists like her. But she was a Senior now, and although she hadn't gotten a better apartment with the promotion, she had noticed the improvement in her rations.

Up and up and up the stairways she climbed. During the light years, windows on the front of the cliff kept the stairwell cheerful with sunlight. Now everything was gloomy. She paused on the final landing, looking out over the long plain toward the mountains in the far distance. The moon was high, half-full and red from the light of the distant, dim sun which barely cast any shadow. When the Eyes of the Atamonen were open, shining down on everything, the moon and that distant Eye were invisible. Or gone. The astronomers seemed to believe they were still up there somewhere, overshadowed by their bright cousins. But now everything was darkness.

It wasn't healthy. She knew that much. Her skin had become pale since the Eyes had closed almost ten years before. Not that she'd had much time to be outside lately, even if there had been any reason to go. But all her life until Nightfell, she had never appreciated how uplifting it was to see dust motes dancing in beams of light. She envied the Lightshapers who could use even torchlight to make bright images in the air, sending their glow around an otherwise dark space. The most talented could make tools with it... knives of light that burned through meat. Swords that cut through flesh. But that was not Sorreg's gift.

She turned away from the window and finished the long climb to her empty, spartan home.

— CHAPTER SIX —

Bright shapes flashed in Dolen's vision, a blur of starbursts and shadow.

"Get him out! Hurry!"

Voices reached his ears, but he had no strength to move.

I'm here, he thought. But his arms were numb, legs stiff as stone. He felt nothing as someone dragged him across the frozen lake's surface.

"Hurry up and get him warm."

The words had no meaning in his mind. Warm. What was warm? For Dolen, there was nothing but cold. There had never been anything but cold.

A few stars flickered in the darkness overhead.

Darkness.

Nightfell, not yet Daybreak.

Rayli.

Dolen strained to move, but his sodden clothing was ice all around him. A small grunt escaped his lips, and his rescuers looked back.

"You're all right, friend. We got you."

One of the men's eyes widened for a moment from beneath his heavy fur hood, but Dolen barely registered the glance.

Rayli.

He was saved, pulled from the freezing water by the caravan's people. Who else could it have been? The ranch hand had said they would be here. It was why Dolen had come into this forsaken place: for herbs that would stop his wife's bleeding and bring their child safely into the world. He hadn't found the caravan, but they had found him. They had saved him. And with their help, he would save her.

Once more he tried to grunt out a word, but the effort exhausted him, and the stars winked into darkness once more.

When next he awoke, he was wrapped in dry, warm blankets and lying in front of a fire.

"Not too close, now," came a soft voice from above him.

He could move again. His skin was still numb, barely tingling, but the fire warmed his face. He blinked as his vision cleared.

The walls of a tent surrounded him. He lay on a fur rug in front of a campfire ringed with stones. The heat brought life back to his mind, and he struggled to sit up.

"Careful," came the voice again. "Don't try to do too much too fast. You've had a difficult time."

Smoke from the fire drifted up through a hole in the tent's roof. Blurry darkness beyond. Stars.

There was still time.

"Still...Night..." he croaked, his words sounding like echoes from the bottom of a well.

"Yes, it's still Nightfell."

Dolen craned his neck to see who was speaking. An old woman sat next to him, bundled in warm furs. Only her face poked out, dark eyes lined with wrinkles. She smiled at him, thin lips parting to reveal worn teeth.

"Have to...go."

The woman shook her head. "You're in no shape to travel. Let Naren'da work her magic. There's plenty of time."

But she didn't understand.

"Wife...needs me. Herbs."

She smiled again. "Don't worry. You're no good to anyone until your strength is returned."

His skin was still numb from the freezing water, and his brain felt fuzzy. He might be no good, but he had to try. He shrugged off the thick blanket and struggled to his feet.

Strong hands steadied him from behind. He swayed in their grasp, struggling to stay upright.

"Come on, then, if you're ready," the old woman said. Naren'da. The healer, leader of the caravan. She had to be.

Dolen looked around the large tent. Chests and traveling trunks were stacked around the edges, some open to reveal cloth-wrapped packages. Herbs. Healing herbs. A slight floral scent reached Dolen's nostrils. Naren'da would have what he needed. The midwife had told him what it looked like. Bloodwort, she called it. Dried spores from a fungus that grew in the south. One of those packets was sure to have it.

The strong hands guided him to a large canvas trough, supported by a thick wooden frame. Steam rose from the water that filled it. A younger woman wrapped in a thick cloak ladled ground leaves into the water.

"Here you go," Naren'da said. "Get into the tub and warm yourself up. You'll feel better for it."

Dolen's knees popped as he struggled to lift his feet over the edge. The men at his sides pulled the cloak from his shoulders and helped him flop into the water. Dolen lay back in the warm bath, breathing in the moist air rising from the surface.

"Good." Naren'da turned away. "Let me make you some soup. Warm you from the inside."

Dolen lay back, feeling his muscles unknot. His mind whirled, but he forced himself to breathe slowly. Rayli was waiting. Suffering. And so far away. But he had to be strong enough to reach her. Just a few minutes more in the tub and he'd be ready.

One of the men approached with a steaming bowl. He knelt next to the tub and held out a spoonful.

"I'm not a baby." Dolen reached for the spoon. "You don't have to—" But his hands were shaking, and the spoon slipped in his grasp, falling to the carpeted floor.

The man reached for it with a sigh. "You're not ready to feed yourself. Just be patient and let us help you."

Dolen let the man feed him a few bites. The broth was faintly yellow and had very little scent, but the heat warmed Dolen from the inside, filling him with energy. In a few minutes, his hands were steady, and he took the bowl from the man, slurping down the contents in greedy gulps.

From the far side of the tent, he heard whispering. Naren'da was talking with another man. Dolen thought it might be one of the men who had pulled him from the ice. His rescuer, arriving in the nick of time.

"...tell him..."

"...healing, and then..."

"...wife."

The last word jolted Dolen from his warm haze.

Wife. Rayli.

He struggled from the tub, and the man handed him a thick towel. Dolen dried himself in the cool air and pulled on the dry clothing that sat on a trunk next to the tub.

When he had finished dressing, Naren'da approached with a large, wrapped packet.

"Keep this with you," she said, handing him the packet. "It will help you heal. Dissolve it in hot water to make the broth, and drink it while it's still steaming."

He tucked it into a pocket.

"Thank you." He reached for her hands. "I cannot thank you and your people enough for saving me from drowning. Truly, I am in your debt forever."

She nodded. "It was fortunate that we found you at all." The old woman pulled down the hood of her heavy cloak. Her hair was thick and gray, knotted in lengths with glass beads that clinked as she moved. Tattooed runes adorned her cheeks, the signs of the Atamonen blessing her face in dark blue and black ink.

Dolen smiled at the symbol of Ata Lashka.

He reached into his shirt and pulled out the stone he wore, emblazoned with the same rune. "May the Ata watch over us all."

Naren'da smiled. "They do. They surely do."

She turned away and exited through the tent flap, snow blowing in as she left. One man stayed behind, the one she had been whispering with earlier.

"How are you feeling?"

The voice. It was darker. More gravely. But Dolen would know it anywhere.

He stepped forward as the man turned around.

Dark eyes like his own, and a sad smile.

Dolen struggled for words as he looked into the face of Marten Roald, his father.

— CHAPTER SEVEN —

Dolen rushed into his father's arms. They clung together for long moments, parent and child again after so many years. When they finally stepped back, Dolen scrutinized his father's face.

"I can't believe you're here. It's been..." He thought for a moment. *Twelve. I was twelve.* "It's been almost fourteen years."

Marten smiled. "Such a long time. I thought I'd never see you again, son."

The fire in the middle of the tent crackled. Dolen's joy on seeing his father curdled in the hazy room.

"Why? Why didn't you come home?" He turned away from his father and plopped down on a thick pillow near the fire.

"Careful," Marten said. "Not too close."

Smoke wafted up from the flames, swirling out the hole in the roof. The canvas fluttered in the wind, but no snowflakes fell in.

"All this time we thought you were dead, but Naren'da saved you, too?"

Marten sat on the cushion next to his son. "All this time I was dead." He turned to face Dolen. "I died in the pass. I'm Risen."

Dolen leapt to his feet, backing away from his father. "You aren't. You're fine." His eyes took in the familiar features, the smooth skin and strong build. "You can't be Risen."

The Risen ranch hands all showed wear. Though the gift of the Atamonen allowed them to reanimate after death, decay swiftly set in. Traveling Embalmers used oils and secret potions, along with holy words and rituals, to keep the Risen fit for work. When a limb was damaged, another could be sewn on in its place. Properly treated, they didn't smell of death, but even in the freshest, one could always tell in the pallor of the skin, the slight graying of the eyes. Those who had Risen many times over the centuries eventually fell into a decay that even the most skilled Embalmers couldn't fix. When they fell at Daybreak, going dormant for another ninety years until the next Nightfell, they were released to the Ata with fire, their souls journeying to the heavens for their reward. A talented embalmer could hold off that journey for centuries.

A talented embalmer. A traveling embalmer.

Like the one who ran this caravan.

No. Not possible.

But when he looked again, really looked, he saw the truth he'd ignored at first glance.

Gray eyes. Pale skin.

"Oh, father."

Dolen wanted to cry, but tears didn't come. Grief warred with relief in his heart. His father was dead, and had been lost all these years. He couldn't have returned to Dolen.

At least, not until Nightfell.

"When did she find you?" he demanded. "What happened to you?"

Marten sighed, still seated on the cushion. "I don't remember falling, but the caravan found my body, saw it at the bottom of a ravine. I was frozen solid, of course. Didn't Rise down there. But they hauled me up and replaced my broken arms and legs." He pushed up the sleeve of his shirt, revealing an arm that didn't quite match the skin tone of his face. "Nearest we could figure, it was about ten years after I died. I've been with Naren'da ever since."

"But you can come home now." Dolen's face lit with new hope. "You can come home with me. I came here to get herbs from the caravan. My wife is..." he paused. *Father doesn't even know I got married.* "Rayli is my wife. Remember her? The adorable little blonde girl with the freckles? Well, she grew up. We got married a couple of years ago, and she's pregnant." He glanced at the sky through the tent hole. "She's in trouble, and I have to get back to her. The midwife needs herbs. I have to take them back. It's still Nightfell, so there's still time." *Please let there still be time.* The midwife hadn't said how long Rayli could last. Hours? A cycle? He'd have to hurry to get back to her before Daybreak.

When the Risen would fall.

"I don't think we'll make it in time," he finished. He wasn't sure if he meant before his father would go dormant, dying again until next Nightfell, or in time for Rayli and the baby.

Marten shook his head. "There's time yet. But you know the laws. Risen can't go home. Can't own their property or live with their families. We're dead, and it's far too disruptive. We must serve elsewhere as long as we can, until it's our time. This is the way it's always been."

The wind picked up, rippling the walls of the tent all around them.

"I know, father, but—"

"But nothing," Marten said. "I can't go home. But we're here now. We're both safe, and Naren'da is the best healer and embalmer anywhere. Everything will be all right."

A voice came from outside the tent. "Marten! We need you."

Marten stood up. "Probably a tent down. Stay here, son. I'll be back in a few minutes." He grabbed a couple of stones from near the fire, warmed from its heat, and tucked them into pockets in his shirt and pants.

Dolen watched his father disappear out the flap.

It's now or never.

He rushed over to the trunks, pulling them open one by one. Herbs of all kinds were wrapped in pouches.

What had the midwife said? Bloodwort.

He searched until he found a large packet of dried fungal gills with the correct label, and pinched off a large portion, wrapping them in another cloth packet. *How much money should I leave?* A couple of scarabs should be enough. He left the money on the trunk lid, tucked the packet in with the healing herbs Naren'da had given him, and grabbed a thick coat and gloves from a pile near the flap. Icy wind blew in from outside when he peeked out.

Stones. They kept the Risen warm. They'd keep him warm, too. He tucked a few into his pockets before he left.

After all this time, he'd found his father, and now he was leaving without saying goodbye. But Rayli didn't have time to waste. They wouldn't want him venturing out into the dangerous pass again, but he'd be more careful this time. He had to make it home.

Rayli was waiting.

— CHAPTER EIGHT —

Dolen stayed low as he crept across the icy plain. He wouldn't actually *be* safer in a narrow pass, but he would *feel* safer. Moonlight cast weak shadows, and he paused, looking at the sky. Over the past nine years, he'd learned to read the stars that came out of hiding when the Eyes were closed and the heavens turned black.

Long ago, people had looked at the glittering dots in the sky and grouped them into clusters, shapes drawn by the gods. The Swordsmen crossed low in the sky from east to west. By this point in Nightfell, it would barely be visible, peering over the mountains. Next to it, just above and to the east, shone the Three Daughters. Dolen never really saw the pictures the stars were supposed to represent, but he knew the constellations, and by these, he knew his way. South and down. Home.

The caravan hadn't moved far, and the top of Zigzag pass came into view. Its high walls closed around him, and he began to pick his way down, clinging to the narrow ledge.

Just a few more hours, Rayli. Hang on. I'm almost home.

His fingers already felt stiff from the relentless cold, and the wind rang in his ears, hollow as it whistled down the pass. He paused at the opening to a cave, part of the vast system that cut through the mountains and down to the wide, hot plains below. Ert was riddled with them, a labyrinth of death beneath its surface, where the horrors of the night bided their time until darkness set them free. The entrance shone faintly green, phosphorescence from the hardy fungi that thrived in the cold making it hard to focus on the cave walls. He peered in, checking for predators, and scuttled past.

"Atamonen, guide my steps," he prayed quietly. Once inside, he slowed, testing each footfall before placing it.

This was Ata Lashka's time. As he walked, he remembered the old story, just as his father had told him when he was a small child, sitting by the fire with cold light streaming in the windows.

"Long ago," his father would say, "longer than any human can remember, before the snow and the hills and the sky, the Atamonen lived in the heavens. Shining in the darkness, they searched the empty, cold space to find a home where they could thrive.

"You must understand that Ert then was nothing like it is now. It was dark and cold, for the Atamonen had never been here to share their light. It was full of giant mushrooms, taller than our house, and all manner of small creatures that ate the mushrooms and lived in peace. The Ata saw that it was good, and formed their bodies from the very mud, shining their brilliant light through the cracks as it dried."

Dolen, the youngest, would snuggle back against his sister's lap, and she would wrap her arms around him.

"They warmed the land and brought forth many children, who filled the plains and the mountains and the wide, windy deserts with joy and laughter. Those children were humans just like us, and though they had no light of their own, they were happy in the glow of the Ata parents who traveled the land, spreading wisdom. There were no monsters in those days, and nothing beneath the surface but clean dirt and solid rock.

"The youngest of the Atamonen were twins, Ata Runi and Ata Lashka, and they loved to play with their human cousins. Runi was the brightest of all the Ata, and Lashka the dimmest, and over time Lashka became jealous of her brother's shining glory. She started to dig in the ground, boring great tunnels where her dim light felt bright and warm.

"That's where she met Kisamon."

Dolen and his sister shuddered at the name, and his sister would cuddle him closer.

The path widened under Dolen's feet as he strode through the snow, steep drop off giving way to a gentler slope. Another hour and he would be home to the heat of his fire and to Rayli. He patted the pocket that held the herbs he'd bought from the caravan. They would be enough to save her and their child. They had to be. Pushing aside the pain of leaving his Risen father behind at the caravan, he lost himself back into the old memory.

"Kisamon lurked in the tunnels," his father had said, "feeling his way with the great tentacles that grew from his back. He walked on two legs like a human, but his face was stiff and rigid and only his eyes glowed. His head was clear chitin, and inside Lashka could see the pink flesh of his brain. If only she could have read that mind, we would still be safe, with the Ata walking among us." Dolen's father sighed. "But Lashka was so lonely, and Kisamon was full of guile.

"He guided Lashka's digging to a deep well, far inside Ert. Steam rose from its surface, and a pale green light glimmered deep in the water.

"'Dive down and bring me that stone,' Kisamon said to Ata Lashka, 'and we shall be best friends forever.'

"So Ata Lashka dove, and with every stroke she felt her tired lungs burning to breathe, until finally her hands touched the glowing stone. She pulled it free from the bottom and swam with all her might, pushing it to the surface. Kisamon danced with joy. 'Finally, I have the power!' He swallowed the stone in one gulp, and the green glow burst from the hard plates of his skin. 'Awaken!' He cried into the tunnels, and all around, Lashka watched in horror as the rocks and fungus took form. The stones rose, shaped into hideous beasts with claws and teeth that would crush a man. The fungus grew legs and skittered off into the darkness. All through the deep ground, Lashka heard the bowels of the Ert respond to Kisamon's call, living monsters waking from the very stones and the deep root rhizomes that snaked through the tunnels Ata Lashka had dug for her friend.

"Ata Lashka ran. She bolted to the surface and saw what she had done. The monsters terrorized the humans, tearing and eating them, killing and never tiring, for their power came from Kisamon with his pale, sickly glow."

When his father had told the story, Dolen had been a small child. The Eyes of the Atamonen had shone in the sky every hour since his birth, eight golden suns beaming down. Sometimes one or another would fall asleep and wink out for a few days at a time, but in his youth, Dolen couldn't imagine them all going to sleep at once, as his father told him would happen.

"When Kisamon emerged from the tunnel," his father would say, "Ata Lashka was enraged. She chased her treacherous friend from one corner of the Ert to another, and where Kisamon tread, the Atamonen fell asleep. Only Ata Lashka could withstand the power of sleep, for she had been the first to touch the stone, and she chased Kisamon into the sky and far into the heavens. But the damage was done.

"The Atamonen no longer burned without sleeping, and though their light dispelled the beasts of darkness, they could not be everywhere at once. 'We must flee to the sky,' they said, 'so that we may watch over our world and keep it safe.' So they flew up into the heavens, shining their light over the whole world, and only napping in turns so that some were always awake and alert for the treachery of Kisamon.

"For ninety years, they protected the world. Kisamon's monsters, the Kisamonen, hid in the dark tunnels, and only the very foolish ventured into the depths, never to emerge. But one day Kisamon returned, with Ata Lashka close behind. The Atamonen felt sleep overtaking them, and they knew the Ert would soon fall to darkness. So Ata Runi, brightest of the Atamonen, leapt from the sky and crashed into the Ert, scattering his light for the humans, who took it into themselves and learned to shape it to dispel the darkness. Only a few could control his power, but it survives to this day, the final gift of Ata Runi, given for us in our time of need.

"And as Kisamon approached the remaining Atamonen in the sky and they fell asleep, closing their eyes and leaving the world in darkness, Ata Lashka knew she must share her gift with the world, as her brother had done. She poured her power into the land, and the dead arose to protect the living when the night fell, and the monsters emerged from their tunnels to stalk the land."

Dolen's father had smiled at his children. "After ten years of Nightfell, Ata Lashka finally chased Kisamon away, and the Atamonen's Eyes reopened. And this how we live to this day. For ninety years, the Atamonen in the sky look down upon us, the light from their Eyes a never-ending brightness in which we are safe. And when Kisamon returns, the Atamonen fall asleep. Then we can see Kisamon, the moon in the dark heavens, his pale sleep-glow casting shadows that his monsters shape as we shape the light. Ata Lashka's dim glow is always behind him, awakening our dead to protect us as Kisamon once awakened the monsters, and she chases her former friend around the sky for ten long years, until they leave our heavens and the Atamonen awaken to shine upon us again."

Dolen shook himself back to the present as he rounded a bend. His fingers were frozen to claws and every muscle was stiff. The heated stones had long since cooled against his skin. But Marskateh lay just below him, and watch fires around his ranch glowed just ahead. He looked up to the sky of his familiar valley home. Kisamon was a waxing crescent, his pockmarked surface glowing faintly. And in the southern sky Ata Lashka was a small red spot, chasing her treacherous friend away so her brothers and sisters could awaken tomorrow.

No one was out in the fields waiting. He'd expected Mayla or even Jak to be keeping watch up the pass, but only the occasional bleat of a ghote greeted his return to his lands. Was it good or bad that there was no watch fire? He stumbled across the fields, kept clear of snow for the ghotes to graze. Cold wind blew their shaggy fur into dirty white clouds around them as they browsed the hardy fungus. They raised their flat, chitin-covered faces to stare at him for a moment, skittering away from him, and he staggered up to the front door.

Rayli, I made it. He prayed he was in time. That she would still be alive, and not newly Risen.

Warmth hit his face as he burst through the front door. He longed to pause at the kitchen fire, but the large room was empty. Everyone must be in with Rayli.

He ran face-first into a door. A door? They only kept a curtain hung in the doorway to their bedroom. Who had hung a door while he was gone? And why? Stumbling back, he pulled the handle open.

Their bed was empty.

Oh, sweet Ata. I'm too late. He fell to his knees, reaching out to the clean white sheets.

From behind him came a small voice, and he turned to look into the face of a little girl. A strange man stood behind her, holding onto her shoulders.

Who are these people? And where is Rayli?

He started to speak, but the girl cut him off.

"Daddy, why is there a dead man in the bedroom?"

— CHAPTER NINE —

Dead man.

The words echoed in Dolen's head as he looked to the man who had moved in front of the girl. He didn't look Risen. His eyes were clear and brown, just like the little girl's.

The man spoke. "Are you a new ranch hand? I didn't order any more Risen. I think you must have the wrong house."

Risen?

They were looking down at him where he knelt on the floor next to the empty bed, and they were speaking nonsense.

"Who are you? This is my house," Dolen said. "Where is my wife? Did she have the baby already? Did you come to help?"

The man and his daughter backed a step away into the kitchen.

"I'm Allom, and this is my house. Are you new-Risen? I think you're confused, and I'm sorry I don't know where you belong, but you need to go now. Someone must have paid for you, and they'll be wondering why you haven't shown up yet."

My house. Sweet Ata, am I that confused? So worried about Rayli that I walked into the wrong house? The bed looked different. And the little lanterns on the bedside table weren't ones he recognized. Nor were the tables, now that he really looked. But no, the stain in the wood floor where Dolen knelt was faintly evident, from where he'd cut himself when he dropped a tray bringing Rayli breakfast in bed late in her pregnancy. And there in the doorframe...the little chip out of the wall where they'd knocked it bringing in the wide bedframe. This was his house. So where was Rayli?

"Look, I don't know who you are, but this is my home, and when I left here yesterday my wife was in labor in this bed." This bed? Was it this actual bed? This one was wider than he remembered, and the headboard was carved in a different pattern, floral spores with their faces turned toward the suns.

A creeping dread wormed its way up Dolen's spine.

"How long have I been gone? How long is left in Nightfell?" *One day. When I left, it was just a day away.* The suns would shine any moment.

"A couple of months left," the man said. "Plenty of time to figure out who owns you and get you back to them."

A couple of months.

Dolen patted his pockets where the heated stones he took from Naren'da's tent were now cold in his pockets. Where the packet of herbs for Rayli sat against the other packets that the old woman had given him. *Dissolve it in hot water and drink it,* she'd said. He'd drank a lot of it while he lay in the bath, submerging beneath the steaming, herbal waters as she'd instructed.

A healing bath in steaming herbs that barely felt warm against his skin.

No. It can't be true.

Dolen lunged to his feet and lurched over to a small mirror that sat on the dresser. The dresser that wasn't Rayli's.

His dark hair was crusted with frost. He looked deep into his own deep brown eyes.

Gray. They were gray. His brown skin also had a slight grayish sheen.

Risen. I'm Risen.

The herbs weren't meant to heal him; they were meant to embalm him. Naren'da was an embalmer, and very skilled from the looks of Dolen's skin.

And there were a couple of months left in Nightfell.

This Nightfell.

I didn't make it back. I died up there in the mountains. I drowned in that lake, where the drillers couldn't get to me.

How long had he been dead, frozen in the ice?

His father must have known. Dolen thought back to their conversation. He'd said he couldn't go home. Risen weren't allowed to live with their families, even the newly dead. Too complicated. And he'd said they wouldn't make it in time to save Rayli. He knew, and he didn't have the heart to tell his son, returned to him after so much time.

Even if she'd survived the birth, that Nightfell was almost a hundred years ago. She would have aged and died long before Naren'da's people pulled Dolen from the ice.

I left, and I never returned. I promised I'd come back to save her, and I failed.

He wanted to weep, to feel the hot tears of grief coursing over his cheeks. But Risen didn't cry. Dolen hadn't paid much attention to his undead ranch hands, but he knew that only some of their systems worked. They couldn't reproduce. They could eat and eliminate, but they didn't have to, and they said nothing had any flavor anyway. Stronger than any living man, they didn't flinch when their skin was cut, or their bones were broken. They healed slowly, and usually just had the Embalmers replace a damaged limb rather than trying to save it. There was always a good supply of spare parts available in the markets of Somteh, miles away over the desert.

I left. I left her to die, along with our child.

The man behind him cleared his throat, and Dolen turned to face him.

"I'm so sorry," Dolen said, conscious now of how his voice sounded like it was coming from far away. Everything felt that way. Distant, and hollow. Real, but...less so. How had he missed it? "I was looking for another ranch and got turned around."

The man nodded. "Easy to do if you're not from the mountains, especially in the dark. You know where you're supposed to be?"

Where he was supposed to be.

Nowhere.

Dead. Gone. Risen to protect the living, to work as long as he was able while Ata Lashka gave him life, and to fall again when the Ata opened their Eyes in the sky, hoping someone would keep his body frozen or embalmed so he could Rise again in another ninety years.

Rise again.

Rayli was long dead, but so was he.

"Yes," he said. "I know exactly where I need to go."

He pushed past them and bolted out into the night.

— CHAPTER TEN —

T he smell of smoke drifted up the stairwell as Sorreg headed to her office. Carved out of the rocky cliff-face, Somteh was in no danger of burning. The ancients who had begun the extensive tunnel system connected every room with ventilation shafts, ensuring plenty of fresh air even at the lower levels. Somteh couldn't burn, but by the time Sorreg reached her lab, her eyes were inflamed from the fumes.

Kratch was already there, along with a small team of Risen repairing the hole in the back wall.

"Good morning, everyone," Sorreg said, setting down her bag. She hadn't finished her paperwork last night, and her desk was already piled with more. With her Senior Scientist status came supervision of labs full of Junior Scientists, approval of their experimental designs and requisitions, along with their personal complaints and requests. All Sorreg ever wanted was to pursue her own research. Now she was half scientist, half bureaucrat, buried under mountains of forms.

Kratch sidled past the Risen, who cast sneering glances at him. "You look bad," he said to her.

They can learn to talk, Sorreg thought, *but social niceties seem to elude them.*

"Thanks," she replied. "You look bad, too."

That seemed to confuse him for a moment. He pulled up his sleeves, examining his claws and arms for defects. Within his loose cloak, Sorreg saw the writhing bumps of the tentacles that grew from his back probing his skin. She had to turn away until he was finished.

"No, Kratch fine." He pulled his sleeves back down.

Sorreg plopped down at her desk. "Did something burn last night? It smelled like smoke in the hallway."

Kratch nodded. "Dead people fight live people. Fire in big storeroom. Many die." He gave the little snort-laugh. "Now more dead to fight. Live never learn."

So the whispers were true. Risen revolting against their owners, forgetting their duty to protect the living, as Ata Lashka commanded. "It's a fool's fight. What do they hope to accomplish? In a couple of months, they'll all be dead again. And without Embalmers, they'll just rot away."

She realized the Risen working on the back wall had stopped to listen.

"Risen and living have always been two sides of one scarab. They protect us in Nightfell. We protect their bodies over the long years of light. It's what the Atamonen demand of us all." She smiled at Kratch, aware of the Risen eyes on her. "I'm sure it's just a few angry folks who haven't been treated well. I'm sure the Guild masters will make sure it's all settled."

The Risen didn't look impressed, but turned back to their work, pounding at the far wall with strong blows.

Three hours later Sorreg's head was pounding. The Risen had chipped away all the loose scree around the hole, each hit of their stone tools drilling into Sorreg's ears. Her temper got shorter with each ringing blow.

"That's it," she finally muttered, standing up from her desk. She crossed the lab to where the workers were pounding at the wall and stood out of range of the flying chips. "Enough!" she yelled over the noise. "You're done for today. Everybody out!"

The Risen crew leader turned, eyebrow raised. "We have an assignment here. We'll stay until it's finished." The dead woman turned back and raised her hammer, which Sorreg snatched out of her hand on the backswing.

"You're done for today," she repeated, feeling heat rise in her face.

The other three Risen stood behind their crew leader, gray eyes watching Sorreg.

"We finish the job. If you have a problem with our work, take it up with Maintenance." The woman pointed to the number tattooed on her neck.

"I don't need to take it up with Maintenance," Sorreg said, rubbing her temples. "This is my laboratory. When I say you're done, you're done."

The four Risen just stared at her, holding their heavy tools. All of them reeked of the smoke she had smelled on the way into the lab that morning. Whatever the fighting was last night, these Risen had been there. Sorreg was suddenly aware of how strong they were. Risen didn't feel pain, didn't sleep, and never stopped working. Nothing slowed them down except the loss of a limb, easily replaced by a skilled Embalmer. And almost nothing completely stopped them except fire.

"What happened last night?" Sorreg asked the crew leader.

"Just a few angry folks that haven't been treated well," the woman replied.

"I see." Sorreg took a tiny step back, hating herself for the show of fear. "And did they burn in the fighting?"

"Some did. Some did not."

Kratch was right that the odds favored the Risen, should they truly revolt against the living. When a living human died, they would almost immediately find themselves on the other side of the battle, suddenly without the rights of the living that they had fought to conserve. And Somteh had so many Risen. Small villages from all over Ert sent their dead to Somteh for embalming and storage. Here, their labor was bought and sold as needed, most heading to the larger cities to be soldiers in the fight against Kratch's people and the beasts from Beneath. Sooner or later, everyone that died intact would join the Risen, protecting the living in all those places where the truce of Somteh didn't exist. She gave silent thanks once again to the vision of Zarix, for bringing peace to this great city by his treaty with the Berun. *Everywhere else, they fight Berunfolk. Here, we fight our own ancestors.*

There was only one threat that held any power over the Risen.

"And those that didn't burn—they'll be left out to rot at Daybreak?"

The words hit home, and the Risen shrank back. It was the worst thing anyone could imagine. When a body was consumed by fire, the Risen soul was freed into the arms of the Atamonen. That's what the living did with unfortunates who died in such a way that they couldn't be allowed to Rise. Children and babies. The very old and frail. Even criminals were given the final death, released straight up to the gods. But when a body wasn't burned, the soul rotted inside it, forcing that soul to climb free and traverse the heavens until it found the Atamonen on its own. All Risen worked tirelessly with the promise of the fire when their bodies couldn't be preserved any longer. And they worked under the threat of being set out to rot away when Nightfell ended, their lifeless corpses at the mercy of the living who could dispose of them as they wished.

"No one should rot," the crew leader said.

"I agree." Sorreg straightened her shoulders. "And no one has to. Tell your supervisor that you were asked to return overnight and finish outside laboratory hours. Thank you for your service."

They started to argue, but Sorreg cut them off.

"Just bite off your tongue, all right? Stop talking, be silent, and get out of my lab."

The crew leader gave a reluctant salute and strode away, jaw set, and her team followed with backward glances.

Kratch sighed. "Sorreg angry. No sleep makes temper small."

She massaged the back of her neck, willing the headache to go away. "You're right about that."

"Dead angry, too. Tempers small."

No sleep did indeed make tempers small. Sorreg's fingers stilled as a thought struck her. "They don't sleep at all, do they?" she muttered to herself. "Almost ten years awake, working all the time. No wonder they're angry."

She looked over to the long stone table where glass domes covered rocks growing the lichen that made spores that put Berun creatures to sleep.

"We have so much work to do."

— CHAPTER ELEVEN —

Dolen stumbled down the path from his ranch toward the little village that had been his family's home for generations.

Rayli. I failed you.

Almost a hundred years had passed since he set out that night, searching for the caravan that would have the medicine she needed. Questions flooded his brain as he slogged through the snow.

Did she survive childbirth? Did the child survive? It hadn't looked good when he left. The midwife wouldn't have sent him on such a dangerous mission if she thought Rayli had a chance without the herbs. Did she die calling his name, trusting him to return and save her? How long did she labor in agony, waiting for a husband who never came home?

Watch fires burned around the edge of town, tended by the living. He paused near one, warming himself for a moment as the reality of his situation settled around him.

I'm dead. Risen.

In his past life, he'd wondered how it would feel. The Risen ranch hands had said there was a hollowness to everything, and Dolen hadn't understood. But they were right. Hollow was the best way to describe it. He could see, but the edges of the world were blurry. He could hear, but somehow everything sounded both clear, yet far away. His mind worked, thoughts racing through his head, but the images were harder to catch and hold onto, and his memory felt thick, like soup cooked too long on the stove. Everything was in there, but it was harder to fish out. Cold air seeped into his bones but didn't bite his skin as it had when he was alive. The cold made him stiff and clumsy, but the sting of icy wind on his face was distant and unimportant.

"Careful there, not too close."

He backed a step away from the fire at the living man's advice. Fire had always been his friend, especially since Nightfell, keeping the monsters at bay. Now it threatened to consume his preserved flesh.

The heat loosened his muscles, and he trooped on into the village.

All the records were kept at the Atamonen Temple that dominated the square. Births, marriages, deaths, all recorded in logbooks kept by the young scribes. His sister had been a scribe in the early years of her novitiate, when she'd pledged her life to serve the gods. Not here in Marskateh, but down in Lonteh, one of the bigger cities on the plain. She'd been so excited to go and had written letters home describing the amazing things the city had to offer. The letters had stopped when she became a full Sister, as was proper. Time to let go of her old family and ascend to the family of the Atamonen. Dolen thought there must have been a ceremony of some kind, but she couldn't write to tell him about it.

So long ago in his own lifetime. And a whole lifetime ago now.

She was long dead.

Everyone he had known was long dead.

But it was Nightfell for a few more months. Some of them might be Risen.

Rayli might be Risen.

And the Temple was the first step toward finding her.

He slogged through the slushy streets. Risen worked day and night, shoveling snow from the paths to keep the way clear. None of them looked up as he passed.

Nothing was familiar. Shops he'd known were renamed, buildings torn down and rebuilt. He weaved his way down the darkened streets, pulled by light beckoning from the square. The Atamonen Temple lights burned nonstop, tended by acolytes. All were welcome in the house of the gods.

Homes and shops were mostly dark in the hours that passed for night. If his child survived, might one of these houses belong to a descendant? The child would be gone by now, but perhaps a grandchild? A great-grandchild?

Assuming the child had lived. Assuming Rayli had lived to raise him.

And what did Dolen hope to find at the Temple? He wrestled his thoughts as he crossed the little square, looking up at the small statue of Ata Marska, the goddess who gave the town its name.

If Rayli survived, she would have delivered their child, raised the baby. Perhaps she would've married again, which caused a squeeze in Dolen's heart. She might have lived to a happy old age, surrounded by loved ones. *Did she remember me? Did she smile at my name, or curse me for abandoning her?* And when she finally died, old and spent, her body wouldn't have been useful. Her loving family would've put it to the flames, sending her soul to the Atamonen's reward. How could he hope for anything else for his beloved wife?

But if she died in childbirth, she would have Risen shortly after her death. Young and strong, she would have been sent away to serve the living in some other town. If she'd worked well, she would've been embalmed, preserved through the long years of light. She would have Risen again at the start of this Nightfell.

She would be out there somewhere. And Dolen could find her. He could fall to his knees and beg her forgiveness. She might spurn him, kick him away for letting her die.

Or she might welcome him into her arms, cold in death, but warm in love.

What kind of man hopes his wife died young?

He paused at the door to the Temple.

A man who craves forgiveness.

The Temple stood three stories high, dominating the little town square. Light poured through windows that usually let the sunlight stream in but now allowed a warm glow to escape, illuminating the night around its smooth stone walls. Carved runes framed an arched doorway, proclaiming the glory of the Atamonen gods, and praising their sacrifice to protect their children.

The heavy door squeaked open, and Dolen squinted in the bright interior. Lanterns hung around the tall entryway. Light streamed up the walls and glowed from a ten-tiered chandelier hanging two stories up in the high rafters. Low, padded benches allowed worshipers to kneel in comfort before a gleaming image on the back wall, the Atamonen Eye, open to watch over all of Ert. No one knelt in prayer, and Dolen paused only a moment to pay his respects.

"Ata Lashka," he whispered, "I pray you guide my steps. If she walks the land with your gift, as I do, please let me find her. And please, Ata Lashka, let her find a way to forgive me."

He stood and glanced around the chamber. Doorways on the side walls were marked with official runes. He chose the doorway to the Records department and silently walked under the arch.

"How can I help you?" asked a young man dressed in acolyte's robes.

"I'm looking for birth and death records from about a hundred years ago," Dolen answered. "End of last Nightfell. At least, that's where I'll start." If Rayli had died around the same time as Dolen, the record would be here.

The young man nodded and turned back to a long row of shelves. Bound books of valuable paper were labeled with dates going back centuries. Some of the oldest had recently been rebound, probably recopied entirely as the pages disintegrated over time. The man selected a book that was obviously original, and it released a musty odor when Dolen opened it, scanning the dates at the top of each page.

He paused a few years before his own death when a name jumped out at him.

Marten Roald, missing, presumed deceased. It was dated a year after Dolen's father disappeared, the appropriate time to wait before declaring someone dead. The entry listed Dolen and his sisters with their dates of birth, but Dolen would have to find either their established dates of death or go back and find their birth dates earlier in the book to see when someone had gone back and filled in their dates of death.

He flipped forward to the last day he'd seen Rayli, scanning down the page.

His heart stopped for a moment when he found it.

Rayli Roald (Branton), died in childbirth. Preserved for transport to Somteh. A later date was scratched in with the day Rayli's body had been embalmed for transport to the desert city.

Emotions warred in Dolen's hollow soul. She died waiting for him. She died not knowing he would cross a century to return to her. He fingered the small bag of herbs in his pocket, taken from Naren'da's caravan. *I tried to save you. I tried to save us both.*

Son unnamed. Father missing, presumed deceased. No family to claim. Sent to Kamteh Orphan Care. The last entry had a date three months after the baby was born. Three months that Dolen's dead body had been frozen in the ice of a lake in the mountains.

A son. I have a son.

Had a son, he corrected himself. Even if the child had lived to be a very old man, he wouldn't have lived to approach his hundredth birthday. But the baby had lived. He had been sent to the biggest city on Ert, Kamteh, to be raised by the priests and priestesses there. Or adopted by some childless couple, perhaps. A family of his own. Those records wouldn't be here. If Dolen found Rayli, they could go to Kamteh together and search the books there. Find the people who had cared for their baby, and maybe find their great-grandchildren still alive today.

If he found Rayli.

She hadn't lived a long, happy life. But she was preserved. And if the Atamonen smiled on Dolen, he might find her again.

"Thank you so much," he said, sliding the book back to the acolyte.

He paused in the Temple's lobby to grab a few fire-warmed stones, kept there for the Risen that came to worship. He'd need to make fires to re-warm them on the journey south, but Risen didn't sleep. If he pushed hard, he could make it to Somteh in a week or two at most.

Again, the dead man spoke the words he'd uttered a hundred years before, when he and his love had still lived.

"I'm coming, Rayli. I promise."

— CHAPTER TWELVE —

Rayli stood in the darkness of the tunnel, listening to the chanting voices on the bright side of the archway ahead of her. Barely dressed in strips of animal hide, with fresh red dye dripping like blood from her face and hair, down her arms and over her torso, she rubbed her hand across the deep scar on her belly, where her child had been cut from her dead body a century before.

"Ata Lashka, protect us," she prayed. "This was never your plan."

Rayli didn't remember dying. The last memory she had of her life was of watching her husband disappear through the curtain from their bedroom, heading out to find the herbs that Rayli already knew wouldn't be enough to save her life. She'd been angry that the midwife let him go on such a dangerous journey when the cause was already lost. But the woman said there was still hope. Rayli knew otherwise, but even through the haze of her imminent death, she recognized the wisdom of sending Dolen away so he didn't witness what would have to be done. The midwife was a quick hand with a knife, and in the moments after Rayli breathed her last, that knife had opened her belly to allow the midwife to pull her child into the world. It had to be fast, but the midwife knew her business. To save the baby, she had to be quick. Best that Dolen not be present to see it.

There was pain. So much pain. When it eased into a mellow golden swirl, she knew it wouldn't be long.

"Dolen," she mumbled, but the rest was lost.

When she awoke, her mind was a deep valley covered in clouds. She looked into her memory as if standing on a mountain, knowing her thoughts were down there somewhere, beneath the layer of mist, glowing in the darkness in pinpoints of hazy flame. Her hand reached down to her belly, so recently pulsing with the life of her baby.

Flat.

A line of neat stitches closed the rent where the child had been taken, the skin edges raw but painless.

"Welcome back, Risen. Praise to Ata Lashka."

The voice sounded far away. Rayli forced her eyes to focus. She lay on the floor of a dim room, surrounded by dead bodies. One by one, they started to shudder.

Rayli sat up. "Praise to Ata Lashka."

I died. I knew I was dying, and I died. There was scant comfort in being right.

The Embalmer chanted over the bodies, gliding around in a gilt-edged robe, wafting floral-scented smoke from a burner he carried on a chain.

All around her, the newly Risen lurched to their feet. They ranged in age from their teens to perhaps sixty, and in varying states of freshness. Some looked like it was their first Rising, with clear, supple skin and bright gray eyes. Others had clearly been around for centuries, with mismatched limbs and patchy flesh.

Rayli raised a hand to her face. Felt pretty good. Whoever had embalmed her had done a nice job, from the feel of it.

The thought settled around her. *I'm evaluating my embalming.* But the rest was too painful to think about.

Daybreak had been only a day away when Dolen left her in their mountain home. She must have held on long enough not to have Risen then. Did she die in sunlight, under the watchful Eyes of the Ata? They would have frozen her body in the high, solid ice until the regular patrol came to pick up any suitable bodies. A hasty application of herbs would have gotten her down to the plains, a journey of several weeks, and the Embalmers here would have finished the job, storing her for ninety years until the next Nightfell.

Now.

All of Marskteh's bodies came to Somteh for storage. So that's where she must be. Her pragmatism wouldn't have surprised anyone who knew her. Rayli was a mountain girl and a rancher's wife. She could kill a ghote with one precise knife cut, butcher it for dinner, warm and feed an orphaned ghote kid at her cooking stove, and weave a coat with wool from her own flock. Ranchers did what needed to be done. In a way, she'd been training to Rise her whole life. Now it only remained to see where she'd be placed.

And in that, she was lucky. With her Risen number freshly tattooed on her neck, her labor was purchased by a woman who lived in one of the mudbrick houses on the plain around Somteh. An accountant who worked for the mushroom merchants' guild, Carrol became a fast friend. She treated Rayli like a daughter, having no children of her own, and Rayli kept the house in repair, joining the other Risen to fight off the occasional beast that wandered across the desert, drawn to the light of the city. Rayli's Lightshaper power wasn't strong enough to frighten the monsters away, but she could manage to edge a blade in hot fire, or light an arrow shot by an archer into a hungry creature's throat. Her gift of light had always been a joy in her life, but since Rising, it had been tinged with fear. Risen like her were highly flammable. Where once she tossed the bright glow carelessly in the open fields, now she kept her tiny fires at a safe distance.

Still, she longed for the days of bright light from the Eyes. Lightshapers didn't make their own light, only shaped it into other forms, and the long years of dark skies left her little to work with on the rare days when danger approached. Somteh's truce with the Beneathers meant Risen weren't needed to fight much here. Many were sent to the other cities besieged by monsters, but plenty were left to ease the daily labor of the living.

In the nine years of Rayli's service with Carrol, she'd had a lot of time to think about her life. She'd grieved for her losses, and her heart had broken anew every time she thought about how devastated Dolen must have been when he came home to find her dead. How he must have wept over her. He would have blamed himself. That was Dolen's way, and Rayli wished she could cry real tears over the misplaced guilt he must have lived with. But he had the baby. She never doubted for a moment that the baby survived. Dolen would have raised their son to be a strong, kind man, just like him. Rayli prayed every night that Dolen lived to forgive himself, enjoying their son and grandchildren, living to be an old man surrounded by the love of family.

For nine years she'd worked for Carrol, secure in her place.

Then a week ago, the knock came at the door. Somteh guards in uniform stood outside, and Rayli's heart sank.

Carrol was dead, a bystander killed in a protest by Risen inside the cliff city. She would Rise shortly, but Risen didn't own property. Risen *were* property. And now, since she had no descendants, Carrol's property was owned by the city.

Carrol's property included Rayli.

— CHAPTER THIRTEEN —

They hauled her into the city and shut her in a room with other Risen. Some were freshly embalmed, and others showed the wear of Nightfell in scarred skin and weary faces. The next morning, armed guards marched them into a torchlit room crowded with crates of goods for sale. Rayli stood against a wall with a dozen others, looked over by potential buyers the way she would once have evaluated a ghote bull for breeding.

Carrol was there.

Rayli's former employer stared around her, obviously still in the shock of Rising. She looked frailer than she ever had in life, and her head was slightly misshapen, though the Embalmers had clearly done what they could to repair the damage that had killed her. The woman trembled, wrapped in the same plain brown robe as the rest of the Risen, tattoo fresh on her neck. Rayli called down to her but was shushed by the auctioneer.

A couple of men moved down the line, examining the wares. When they got to Rayli, they pulled her robe open, shaking their heads at the scar that crossed her belly.

"Good shape, this one. Pretty," one of the men said. He had a sharp nose and wore polished chitin earrings all up and down the edges of both ears.

"Yeah, shame about the big scar. But she'll do for a last-standing." The other man was shorter and fatter, with blubbery lips and a bald head.

Earrings nodded. "Yeah, we'll get some good bets there. How many more we need?"

Blubberlips thought for a moment. "We got six, right? This one makes seven, and..." he trailed off, looking down the line. "How about that one?" He pointed to Carrol.

A laugh from Earrings. "Yeah, that will do fine. Somebody's gotta go down first."

Scarabs changed hands, and Rayli found herself next to Carrol again.

"Are you all right?" she said to her former employer.

"I... I think so," Carrol said. Tufts of her gray hair were missing where her skull had clearly been smashed in and reconstructed by the Embalmers. "Everything just feels so...strange."

Rayli smiled. "I know. But you get used to it." She took the older woman's hand as they followed their new employers out of the auction hall.

Down into the bowels of Somteh they went, past the huge ware-houses of goods, through the dark workrooms where Risen and living toiled side by side at looms and workbenches. Fumes from the chitin tanners made the living men cough, and Rayli held her breath as they wound their way deeper. The air thickened with smoke, and the tunnels narrowed.

"I don't think—" Carrol began, but the men shushed her.

"Quiet, you," Earrings snapped. "You're not here to talk."

What are we here for? Rayli wondered.

Finally, she and Carrol were pushed into a barred chamber with several other Risen. None of the others were in particularly good shape. Shoddy Embalming or simple neglect had let decay set in, and the cavern smelled of rot.

They waited a week. No one fed them, so there were no messes to clean up. Risen didn't need to eat, but wounds healed faster if they did, and muscles stayed stronger.

Whatever we're here for, we just have to hold out for a few months. When Nightfell was over and they fell again into death, they'd be returned to the Embalmers for storage until the next time the Eyes closed. Whoever had bought their service would be long dead, just like them, and someone new would take over their contracts. Rayli had been lucky for nine years with Carrol. She could last through a few months of wretched conditions.

Blubberlips returned for them a week later. He tossed them each a garment made of thin leather strips that barely covered the important parts. When Rayli balked, he laughed.

"Don't worry, Rotten. Nobody's interested in getting near your nasty dead body. But our audience likes to see all the details, so put it on and shut your mouth, or I'll sew it shut for you."

Rotten? What a horrid thing to call her. She wasn't rotten at all. But after a week in the cell with some of the others, she had to admit she didn't smell fresh anymore.

They trooped out of the cell at Blubberlips's direction, crowding together in a wide chamber lit with smoking torches. From a long, echoing distance, Rayli heard the sound of a large, raucous crowd.

"All right, Rotten, listen up," Earrings said. He handed each of them a short chitin knife. "Praise to Ata Lashka, thanks for your service, and all that. The folks out there paid a lot of money, so give them the best you got." He paused in front of Rayli. "I got a lot of scarabs on you, so do me proud out there."

What in the bowels is going on?

A couple of huge Risen men emerged from the tunnel. They were barely dressed in leather strips like Rayli's, and each had a stylized whirlwind tattooed on their left cheek. One carried a basket of pots, and the other pulled a pot out, standing in front of the first of Rayli's terrified line.

The Risen man opened the pot, pouring purple dye over the head of the thin old man.

The next Risen was dyed yellow, and Carrol got orange.

Red dye dripped into Rayli's eyes when the huge man dumped the pot over her blonde hair. He paused for a moment. "Be smart out there. It's not unheard of for bait to survive. If you make it long enough, they'll call the beasts off, and you'll join the ranks." He touched the whirlwind on his cheek. "Hope to see you again."

Down the line he continued, until every Risen was coated in a different color dye.

The living and the huge, tattooed Risen prodded them down the corridor, and the sound of the crowd got louder. They waited in the dark, peering out to where the crowd noise echoed in.

A man's voice boomed through the tunnel.

"Hello, Somteh!"

The out-of-sight crowd roared.

"We've got a special treat for you tonight, folks," continued the voice. "Clan Tornado brings you a Last Man Standing, with twelve Risen looking to go the distance against three full-grown skitters!"

Another roar.

Oh, Ata. Rayli gripped Carrol's arm in one hand, the other clutching the small chitin knife she'd been given.

"First call for bets. Which color will last the longest? Well? Do you want to see them before you lay your scarabs down?"

Oh, yes. They certainly did.

"Well, let's get them out here! Welcome to the Last Man Standing for Clan Tornado!"

The crowd went wild as Rayli and the others were shoved out into the torchlit arena.

— CHAPTER FOURTEEN —

Rayli blinked in the sudden light. Torches lined the rim of the huge, flat-bottomed bowl in which she stood surrounded by the other dyed Risen. The edges of the bowl were ten feet high, and all around them, rows of people disappeared into the high darkness beyond. Roars, applause, and the stomping of hundreds of feet on stone pounded into Rayli's ears.

"And here they are! Clan Tornado brings you a brand-new batch of corpses, fresh from the auction houses. Ata Lashka would be proud of this lot, don't you think?"

The crowd erupted in laughter at the unseen announcer's amplified voice.

"Stay together," Rayli shouted above the din. "I don't know what this is, but it's bad. Stay together and keep your eyes open."

A ladder appeared on one edge, and a man climbed down to their level. The crowd above quieted at his gesture.

"Let's meet them, shall we?"

Two burly men followed the first one down the ladder and stood nearby, glaring at the Risen. The first man approached the little group, who huddled together near the doorway through which they'd entered, now barred from behind.

No exit. We're trapped in here.

The man wore brown pants and a bright red shirt that reflected the torchlight. Black hair and dark eyes searched the terrified Risen. He grabbed Carrol by the arm.

"So tell the fans a little about yourself, Orange," he said. "Come on. Don't be shy."

Carrol peered up into the stands, open-mouthed.

The man grinned at the crowd above. "Aw, she's a shy one, isn't she, folks?" He turned back to Carrol. "You look pretty fresh. How long have you been Risen?"

She focused on him. "Um...I think...six days? A week?"

"A week!" he yelled, holding Carrol's arm up. "A week! Not long to honor Ata Lashka, but we're sure happy to have you here, Orange. Best of luck to you." He shoved her back toward the group and pulled on a young man dyed blue. The kid was skinny, and he limped as he was dragged to the middle of the arena. One of his legs was shorter than the other, with big scars where each had been sewn on.

Not his original legs. *Poor kid.*

"And here we have Blue," the announcer said. "Looks like this little guy's been through it already. Blue, how did you lose your legs?"

The kid straightened up. "I work for the city. I'm a miner, and..."

The announcer cut him off. "Not anymore, kid. You're bait today."

Bait. The tattooed Risen had used that word. Rayli knew what it meant in normal life. She feared what it meant for her today.

The murmuring of the crowd got louder, and all around her, Rayli heard people in the stands calling for bets.

She lost her footing as the announcer grabbed her next.

"Well, here's a pretty one," the man said, beaming a smile at the appreciative crowd. "Sure would be a shame to see these parts scattered all over the sand."

Even through the distant, hollow haze of her Risen state, Rayli felt her blood heat.

"You, pretty thing, how long have you been a corpse?"

She gripped the chitin knife in a hand slippery with red dye. *You can't hurt the living. Ata Lashka gave her power so you could protect them.*

And in return, the living were supposed to protect the Risen.

Bait. She'd show him *bait.*

Her knife whipped around, aimed straight for his chest. It shattered against his red shirt, and he jumped back, releasing her arm.

His eyes widened for a moment, then he laughed.

"We've got a lively one here!" The crowd roared approval.

Rayli stared at the broken hilt in her hand. The announcer lifted his shirt, showing the stiffened chitin mail beneath. "Not my first time in the arena, sweetheart," he whispered with a wink, and his guards dragged her back to the group.

The announcer strode toward the ladder, guards behind him.

"All right, folks, just a couple more minutes to place your bets. We've got three full-grown, hungry skitters just waiting to make a tasty meal of these corpses. Which one will be the Last Man Standing? Do you bet on Orange, who will hide behind the others? Or do you bet on Red, who's got a knife and isn't afraid to use it?" He paused and smiled. "Who *had* a knife."

Crowd noise thundered and the foot stomping began again.

"Place your final bets, and let's see who from Clan Tornado is the Last Man Standing!"

As the announcer and guards raced up the ladder, Rayli returned to the group. "Okay. What's a skitter? How big?" She'd just lost her only weapon, pathetic as it had been.

An older man dyed green spoke up. "They're big. Head-high. Some of the people in the wilds ride them, use them for pack beasts."

"Are they venonous?"

The man shook his head. "No. Just strong. Six legs, no tail. Big, glowing butt."

Could be worse.

From all around them, the crowd noise grew to a deafening echo. The pounding and yelling drowned out anything else the green-dyed man was going to say.

By unspoken agreement, the group of Risen moved back to the doorway through which they'd entered. Rayli and the others pulled on the bars, expecting no escape. The bars didn't budge. But from out of the shadows, the whirlwind-tattooed Risen scuttled into view.

"Here," he said, shoving another knife into Rayli's hand. "Go for the neck."

The new knife was heavier than the one she'd broken against the announcer's armored chest. Before she could thank him, the man was gone.

"The neck," Rayli repeated down the line. "Go for the neck."

They all turned around.

At the far end of the arena, a huge door rose an inch off the ground. Supported by thick rope that ran up to pulleys high above, it was hauled open by Risen on each side, straining against the weight.

A foot. Two feet.

Behind the door was darkness. Rayli couldn't see anything under the door, nor hear anything over the screaming of the crowd.

Three feet. Four.

The door locked into place, wide open, a black mouth in the smooth stone of the arena walls.

From behind it, a bright light flared. Silhouetted against it were three enormous shapes. They fled from the sudden brightness, surging into the arena, and Rayli got a good look at the monsters sent to kill and eat them for the amusement of a bloodthirsty crowd.

Shoulder high. Six legs, with huge mandibles. A jointed body with glowing red eyes, and a blue phosphorescent rear end, clear chitin that revealed the monster's guts inside.

The creatures skittered away from the bright light in their tunnel, stopping in the middle of the arena, as far as they could get from the torches around the rim.

Rayli gripped the heavy knife.

"Stay behind me," she yelled to Carrol, "and may Ata Lashka protect us."

— CHAPTER FIFTEEN —

"S o what do we have?"

Sorreg and Kratch peered down the long workbench. Glassware was stored at one end on high shelves. A couple of soft egg-balloons full of flammable gas were carefully laid in baskets, padded with dried grass. When controlled fire was needed, the balloons were punctured with tubing made from the hollow tentacles of a blackslug, plucked from the mushroom forests where they dwelled. Gentle pressure on the balloon allowed a metered flow of the gas, which could be ignited to heat chemicals in a beaker or flask. It was how the gaslights worked, tubes crossing all through the upper levels of Somteh. They had Prime Embalmer Zarix to thank for that invention. His work with the egg-balloons was the push that got him named Prime, back when Sorreg was just a child. She dreamed of creating something as important as that, lying awake nights pondering what her contribution to science would be.

Farther down the table, jars of embalmed specimens teetered in stacked pyramids. Bizarre creatures from the depths of Beneath, their phosphorescence still glowed in death: fish plucked from murky lakes and rushing streams; furry things; and things with scales. All gaped wide-eyed from their glass coffins. Some had venom that would kill a human in five paces. Others were deadly to Berunfolk, yet harmless to humans. Lifetimes of study hid in the deep fungal forests, the rich grasslands that withered in Nightfell—even the desert around Somteh teemed with life if one knew where to look.

The end of the long bench held a similar variety of plant life. Most of Ert's foliage was rhizome-based, spreading beneath the ground in huge colonies. Lichen grew on every kind of rock. The grasses and trees were already dead from lack of sun, but seeds for every known species waited in the cool storage under every major city, to be planted when the Eyes bathed the Ert in glorious light again.

Sorreg examined her lichen samples. The species on which she was currently focusing her research grew in thick green colonies on smooth stone. Like everything on Ert, it could be hostile, secreting a toxin on its tiny leaves. When animals ate the lichen, it made them dizzy and disoriented; at high doses, it could be fatal. But it didn't affect humans, except to induce a short-lasting gastric upset.

It was her best hope, if she could figure out how to modify it to anesthetize humans.

"What do you think, Kratch? Are these ready?"

The Berunman turned his glowing eyes to the specimens under their glass domes. Each one looked slightly different, depending on the rock it grew on. He pulled three of the rocks forward on the bench.

"These three ready."

Sorreg steeled herself for what came next.

They both pulled their fume hoods off the small rack near the ventilation nook. Yet another of the amazing advances the Berunfolk had introduced to science, the hoods were the empty skin from the head of an underwater beast that dwelled in deep rivers flowing far beneath Ert's surface. One of the Berunfolk's staple foods, the creatures breathed through gill filters in the area where human and Berunfolk mouths would be, and peered through thick, clear eyelids. The Berunfolk skinned the heads, eyelids and gills intact, and Embalmers tanned the hides. Sorreg and Kratch pulled their hoods over their heads. She took a few shallow breaths, adjusting to the filtered, herb-scented air. She blinked under the sewn-shut eyelids and pulled the drawstring tight around her neck.

While Kratch's long robe and the hood hid most of his alien features, watching him work on the plants always made Sorreg uncomfortable. He talked like a man, sort of, but he had far more in common with the bug-faced specimens in the jars than he did with Sorreg and her kind.

Kratch tightened his hood and pushed up his sleeves, revealing clawed hands on thin, chitin-skinned arms. The hunched back under his robe writhed, and from the wide left sleeve protruded a dark gray tentacle. It shone with a veneer of slime, and a line of pulsing suckers ran up one side. The tentacle undulated beneath Kratch's left hand as he carried the first specimen over to the cut-out area in the back wall, where ventilation holes kept fresh air sweeping across the little workstation. It was safer to open questionable specimens there, as long as the wind was blowing any toxic fumes away.

Sorreg followed him, staying back as he placed the domed rock on the flat surface. He raised his tentacle to check the airflow and nodded. The dome rose from the lichen, gripped gently in his claws. Fresh slime welled up on the tip of his tentacle, and he allowed a drop to fall onto the lichen's surface before replacing the dome.

"How do you control that?" Sorreg asked, watching him repeat the process with the second specimen.

"Gentle with glass."

She frowned. "I don't mean the domes. How do you make the slime when you want to? Is it all the same slime, no matter what you're trying to do?"

He replaced the second dome and turned to her, blinking. "All slime different. Depends on need."

All humans agreed that Berunfolk weren't as intelligent as humans, but they could interact with almost every living thing on the planet in some way or another. Animals could be influenced to do what the Berunfolk wanted, within reason. A hungry predator would still eat them, but if the creature were not hunting, Berunfolk could encourage it to prowl in a different area. And most of the plant life was amenable to growing in ways that would benefit the Beneathers. Sorreg knew it was how they survived the long years of light, when the surface world's brightness blinded them and burned their hard skin plates. Most animals avoided bright light, and many could not survive it.

"So how do you control what you need here?"

He carried the second dome back to the workbench and paused. "Kratch think about what is needful."

"And what does that mean here?" Sorreg gestured at the lichen.

After a moment's thought, he replied, "Need to open. Need to be ready."

The answer didn't satisfy Sorreg, but she knew what he meant. Whatever this particular slime was, it made the plants he dripped it on more receptive to manipulation. Instead of taking generations of selective breeding to bring out a desired trait, a lichen or fungus could be made to reproduce with another species, or utilize a different food source. Sorreg had pages and pages of research detailing hundreds of combinations. Almost all of them had proved to be either useless or dangerous, but such was the way of science.

"And can all Berunfolk make the slimes like you can?"

He cocked his head to the side. "Can all humans make the science like Sorreg?"

Her back straightened. "Of course not. I'm highly trained and have a natural aptitude for research. It's why the Embalmers chose me as a child." *Wow, defensive, aren't we?* She softened her tone. "We're all good at different things."

Kratch gave his odd, tentacle-enhanced shrug. "Us too."

The final specimen was growing on the smooth, dark-stained stone with the mirror-slick top. Instead of the normal green, its little leaves were brown and mottled red in the center. Under the ventilation chamber, Kratch dripped the "ready slime" onto it.

When the plants had incubated, Sorreg would begin the exhaustive process of transferring the lichen onto new pieces of stone to make multiple samples. Some would be left alone as control specimens. Others would be fed various compounds, mostly derived from human tissue in hope of sensitizing the plant to produce a sedative that would work on humans.

"We can do this," she said to Kratch. "Next time Zarix comes down here to check on us, we'll have something amazing to show him. He won't regret my promotion."

Kratch turned away, but not before Sorreg noted the narrowing of his eyes, gone in an instant.

He doesn't like my boss. If she was honest, neither did she. When Zarix was around, Sorreg always felt...slimy. Like one of Kratch's stomach-turning tentacles was slowly sliding down her throat, wiggling its way across her tongue and into her stomach. But he was a genius, Somteh's Prime Embalmer. Her career depended on his goodwill.

No, she'd make him proud. No matter what it took.

— CHAPTER SIXTEEN —

The dyed gladiators fanned out along the back edge of the torchlit arena, keeping as much distance as possible between themselves and the three huge beasts in the center. Rayli stood next to Carrol, who trembled, staring wide-eyed at the skitters.

"Stay together. Don't get separated," came a call down the line, nearly drowned out by the cheering crowd.

The skitters stood still, eyes narrowed. They seemed confused, snorting nervously with heads lowered to reveal thick back plates with narrow joins between the armor of head, thorax, and tail. Their rear ends were clear chitin, guts glowing faintly blue inside. It was a tempting target, but the huge, tattooed gladiator hadn't said to go for the rump.

Rayli was a rancher. The skitters before her looked like huge, hairless versions of the ghotes she and Dolen had raised. When it was slaughter time, a ranch hand would straddle one of the small creatures, steadying it between their legs. One knife plunged straight into the neck between the chitin plates of head and thorax made an instant, clean kill. Rayli and the hands usually did most of the slaughter; it broke Dolen's heart to kill the ghotes they raised.

She breathed slowly now, blinking across the sand at the giant monsters.

The crowd's cheers quickly turned to boos and hisses when nothing happened. The skitters didn't move, and neither did the unwilling gladiators.

So the two huge guards that had accompanied the announcer onto the arena floor started throwing chunks of meat onto the sand. The first few landed near the skitters, which dashed for them, chomping the food down in fast gulps. Rayli couldn't see what kind of meat it was, but she had her suspicions.

The feeding frenzy energized the skitters. Two of them fought over the last chunk of meat, one bowling the other over in a tangle of legs. When the food was gone, they turned their eyes to the Risen cowering against the wall.

And more chunks of meat flew, this time from behind the ill-equipped fighters.

A half-rotted human leg plopped onto the sand just in front of Rayli, and Carrol screamed, leaping away.

Yep, thought so.

All three skitters rushed for the line of gladiators, who split down the middle to avoid being trampled. As soon as the meat was consumed, the skitters retreated to the middle of the arena, but their eyes glowed fiercely, sizing up the Risen.

One made a dash straight for Rayli's group.

She had no time to think, leaping and rolling out of its way. A sickening crunch made her cringe. *Please not Carrol. Please not Carrol.*

It wasn't. It was a middle-aged man died purple. The other two skitters raced over to join the feast, tearing the man's body in half.

Ata Lashka, we were not Raised for this.

Did a soul go to be with the Atamonen if it was consumed by a beast? Surely that was as good as fire.

Guess you'll find out very soon.

The largest skitter turned toward Rayli, who found herself alone in the middle of the arena. Dark blood covered its face, sharp mandibles, and front legs.

It took three steps toward her and crouched to pounce.

Think Rayli! Think!

She raised her knife, but the creature took no notice.

It wasn't afraid of weapons. They came from a dark tunnel, prodded out by...light.

Rayli was not a powerful Lightshaper. The strongest Lightshapers could weave a single candle's light into a huge flash, growing the flame inside them and releasing it into any shape. The best Rayli could usually manage was the transfer of a candle flame to her cookstove, or into a small beam that could cut through meat on the table.

But her innate gift took over.

As the skitter leaped toward her, she pulled all the light from the high torches ringing the arena, shaping it into one huge flash that radiated out from her body.

The skitter froze in the air, landing with a thud that flung sand onto Rayli's skin where it stuck to her sweat and the red dye dripping off her hair and face. The beast scrambled to its feet and raced away from her to the far side of the arena.

From above came the announcer's booming voice.

"Oh ho! Seems we have a Lightshaper in our midst! Hope you all bet on Red today!"

Rayli wiped sandy dye from her eyes and looked around the arena. The skitter she'd temporarily blinded had rushed over to its pack, where they were tearing up more Risen. How many were left? Eight had walked in. Three were gone already. She caught site of Carrol's orange dye on the far side. Rayli's former boss stood there with the blue kid and a tall man dyed yellow. Across the arena, a heavy woman dripping green stood rooted in place.

"Light! They're afraid of light!" Rayli yelled. Her magic wouldn't hold out long in big flashes like that. Already she felt fatigue in her limbs from its use.

She ran across the sand to where Carrol, Blue, and Yellow stood.

"Torches! The knives are useless. Get a torch!"

Thick, dark smoke poured from torches mounted in heavy brackets all around the smooth, high walls. The tall man couldn't reach high enough to grab one, so he grabbed Carrol and boosted her onto his shoulders. She wiggled a torch from a bracket and tossed it down to Rayli, who waved it before her.

All three skitters backed away.

The three gladiators sidled down to the next torch and repeated the boost. In moments, all four of them held a torch at arm's length. Embalming herbs made Risen very flammable, but flames were better than a beast's mandibles, if today was the day for the final death.

The skitters turned toward the lone woman in green.

A huge cheer went up from the crowd as they tore her to bits.

One of the skitters shoved another aside, grabbing for the last chunk of the unfortunate Risen. The second one lunged at the first, grabbing it with long legs and sharp claws. They rolled into an enraged tangle, leaving one beast alone.

Go for the neck. Now.

"Come with me!"

Rayli and the others dashed toward the lone skitter's glowing rump. It was scrounging in the sand for any last morsels of Green.

Rayli dropped her torch and pointed, and the tall man boosted her up as he'd lifted Carrol, shoving her onto the creature's back.

It whirled around, and she gripped for purchase on the smooth plates, latching onto one of the heavy spikes that lined the edges of the chitin. She pulled herself forward as her torch-wielding friends surrounded the creature, forcing it back to the wall.

The neck. Go for the neck.

Rayli pulled her knife from the strip of leather around her waist. She didn't trust the weapon alone. Channeling her Lightshaper gift, she pulled fire from the remaining torches behind her on the wall and edged the blade in hot, white flame.

Just like a ghote. Only bigger.

She plunged it down between the plates, straight into the soft skin below. Flesh parted before fire-honed force, and beneath her, the skitter quivered once.

As the beast jerked, Rayli yanked out her knife and released the light around the blade. Her right hand was singed, but she felt no pain, only smelling the slightly cooked flesh. She leaped from the monster's back as it crashed to the floor.

The crowd went wild.

"Red! Red! Red!"

Rayli dimly heard the announcer over the chant. "Ladies and gentlemen, have you ever seen such a thing?" He joined in the deafening chant. "Red! Red! Red!"

The dead skitter's legs curled in around its body with one final, jerking movement.

Across the arena, one of the others was down. It tried to rise, but the battle with its fellow monster had broken all three of its legs on one side. It managed to shove itself in a circle but couldn't get its belly off the ground.

Rayli's torch still burned, lying in the sand. When she picked it up, she saw that the skin of her right hand was black, and the smell made her stomach churn. Cooked Risen spiced with embalming herbs did not smell appetizing.

But cooked skitter surely would.

"Rip off the legs."

She and Carrol waved their torches, keeping the remaining mobile skitter at bay while Blue kid and Yellow man tore a leg off the dead beast and tossed it over to her. She lit it on fire and threw it as hard as she could across the arena.

The skitter watched it go. Nostrils flared as the appealing smell of cooking meat wafted across the space.

Food that didn't have weapons was a lot easier to eat. When the flame went out and left the leg smoking on the sand, the skitter dashed over to it, chomping it down in one gulp.

When Rayli turned around, she found her fellow fighters better armed. They had ditched their chitin knives, which had proven to shatter with one blow, and instead, Carrol and Blue kid each held one of the dead skitter's sharp mandibles. Yellow man waved a skitter claw dripping dark green ichor. He turned back to the dead skitter, but Rayli called him off.

"My knife is fine. Get ready to run."

She stuffed her torch in the space between the dead skitter's backplates, and the arena filled with the smell of cooking meat again.

Across the sand, their target smelled it.

"Run!"

They dashed away as the starving skitter scuttled across to its dead companion. It rolled the body over and ripped off the belly plate, plunging its head into the soft meat inside.

Rayli glanced over at the one with the broken legs. Its circle was widening, but it was still no threat. She needed to focus on the one that could move.

Kill this one and we might live through this.

Its back was turned, and she made the boost gesture to Yellow again. He flung her onto the creature's back and she scrambled for a grip. But the beast leapt to the side, and she slid away, rolling across the sand.

By the time she scrambled to her feet, the skitter had grabbed Blue in its mandibles. He pushed against the glowing eyes, screaming in terror, legs kicking.

Rayli let out a burst of light pulled from the torches, but the beast only took a single step back, vision shaded by Blue's form impaled in its sharp jaws.

Blue kicked out, his feet straddling the skitter's head as it chewed through his ribcage. He pushed with Risen strength against the wide thorax.

The head popped straight off the beast, dropping to the ground with Blue still in its mouth.

Rayli, Carrol, and Yellow rushed around to Blue and knelt next to him.

The sand was stained with dark blood. Blue's face was white, his gray eyes unfocused.

"Did I do it?"

Yellow nodded. "You did it."

They tried to pull the mandibles off, but they were embedded in his flesh, driven deeper when he fell back-first onto the ground with the head on top of him. His legs weren't moving, and his ribcage was crushed. Every breath was a bloody foam from between his ribs and out his mouth and nose.

"We have to finish this," Carrol said. "For all of them."

The broken-legged skitter still hauled itself in circles. From above, crowd noise blended into a background that Rayli's rage shut away.

Red, Orange, and Yellow advanced across the arena, torches and weapons bared—the colors of fire and light against a creature of shadow.

It whirled to face them. With half its legs broken, it listed to the left, belly dragging on the ground. But the jaws and claws could still be fatal.

The announcer's voice pierced Rayli's haze.

"We've never seen anything like this, folks! Could three survive today? Don't you wish you'd bet on Orange?"

Rayli sidled around behind the skitter, leaving Carrol and Yellow in front. The fight with the other one had left a large hole in the clear chitin that covered the creature's guts. Her torch guttered out, but it wouldn't matter.

She plunged it into the hole in the chitin and called on her last speck of Lightshaper power, pulling the torchlight from all around her into the protruding wood. It sputtered into a weak flame, and Rayli dropped to her knees, using every ounce of strength to shape the dwindling light.

The skitter screeched as its guts melted.

Rayli was dimly aware of Carrol and Yellow dragging her back by the shoulders, away from the dying creature flailing as it burned from the inside.

The last thing she heard before she blacked out was the announcer's voice, screaming along with the crowd.

"Congratulations to Clan Tornado's newest gladiators!"

— CHAPTER SEVENTEEN —

Dolen sat by the fire, back pressed against the low ridge of stone in the dwindling foothills. Marskateh lay miles behind him, and the land was flattening out. Snow still covered most of the path, but the river he followed ran clear, carrying chunks of ice from the mountains. Bare stone jutted out of the snow like the teeth of some ancient monster, providing a break from the cold wind that stole his heat and slowed his limbs.

He'd hoped he would make better time than this, but his Risen limbs, though strong and tireless, succumbed to the cold so easily. Arms and legs stiffened into useless logs. In the first days of travel, he'd pushed too long, nearly ending his quest before it began. With unbending fingers, he had struggled to scrape his flint, sparks dropping uselessly into the snow around the pathetic pile of scrubby branches he'd made. Finally one had caught, and Dolen crouched next to the tiny flame, sheltering it from the wind as fire crackled through the damp kindling. It took forever for his frozen body to loosen up, and he vowed not to go so long without a heat break again.

Now he pivoted, rotating his backside to the fire to warm himself through for the next leg of the walk.

In the near darkness of Nightfell, light was a beacon and a warning. Creatures who hid in the vast tunnels beneath the land came out to feast on abundant plant life; on each other; and on humans, dead and alive. Many of those creatures emitted their own glow from parts of their bodies in hypnotizing colors and patterns. Tails shone green. Strange, dangling lures glowed yellow, hanging in front of the mouths of small ambush predators, luring smaller, flying insects for a close look. Red eyes blinked from expressionless faces. These last sent shivers down Dolen's spine.

Even the plants glowed. Back at home, this had allowed Dolen and his hired help to find good patches of grazing for his flocks, searching for the diffuse colors lighting up the snow from underneath. Down here, the snow cover was thinner, even absent where winds swept it away. Lichen and mushrooms big and small lit Dolen's path.

But where there were plants, there were grazers. And where there were grazers, there were predators, emerging from their dark caverns to prowl the open land. Dolen thought about the ancient story of how the land was once gripped in darkness all the time. Once again he gave thanks to the Atamonen Eyes in the sky. Just a few more months and they would open. The nightmare of darkness would end for another ninety years.

And then what?

He'd never considered it before. He'd thought he had years of life ahead of him, a lifetime with Rayli and their baby to enjoy the sunlight of the Eyes, feeling their warmth on his face as they worked in the endless day, pulling shades on the windows at night, leaving cracks around the edges where the light leaked through.

I'll never see the Eyes again.

The idea hit him like a crushing stone.

The moment the Eyes opened, Risen fell. Whatever they were doing, they would crumple to the ground, voices stilled in mid-sentence, suddenly changing from Risen to corpse. Dolen had never seen it, but his great-grandfather had, and the old man had loved to terrify young Dolen with tales of the beasts of night, and the sounds the Risen bodies made as they hit the floor, lifeless for another century.

That would be him. In just a few short months, he would die again.

It wouldn't hurt. The Risen ranch hands had not been newly awakened. They'd said the time between falling and rising felt like an instant. Some of them had Risen with words on their lips, finishing a thought from almost a hundred years earlier, spoken to someone now long dead.

Dolen knew that was true. The blackout that took him from Rayli had seemed momentary. He hadn't even realized he'd died.

The thought made him pat his pockets. Naren'da's herbs were there in the little paper pouch. Dolen scooped up some snow and tipped a small amount of the ground substance into the cup. He held it over the fire on a stick, pulling it back when the stick caught, threatening to dump his embalming soup into the flames.

He sipped most of it, inhaling the faint scent straight into his lungs and dipped his fingers in the last dregs, smearing it over his face and hands. There was no way to bathe in it here, but the most important skin would be protected. The rest of him would have to stay embalmed from the inside. But he was heading to Somteh. There would be Embalmers there, the best on Ert, it was said. They would preserve him when he fell into death again.

An endless life of darkness, ten years at a time.

How long would he last? Two Nightfells? Ten? Eventually, even the best Embalmers would fail. Or he'd have some sort of accident that even replacement limbs wouldn't fix. Brains couldn't be replaced, and a paralyzed spine would never heal. Would it hurt if he were still Risen when they consigned him to the flames?

He regretted not asking more questions of the Risen that came to work on the ranch. Even thinking that he had a life ahead of him, he should have known it was his last chance to talk to those who had gone where all humans eventually went. But it hadn't seemed important.

The heating rocks were ready. Dolen left the fire going as he stuffed them into his pockets, trusting them to keep him warm for the next hours of walking. It would be warmer still in the desert plain below, but true heat wouldn't return to the land until Daybreak.

Rayli would be there in Somteh. She had to be. The firelight reminded him of their first night together as husband and wife on the ranch. They had dismissed the ranch hands out to their bunkhouse and built up the fire in the hearth. Snuggled together on a thick ghotewool rug, they'd planned for their future. A ranch full of children: golden-haired daughters like Rayli, and dark, strong boys like him. They would've raised them to be kind and strong, taught them everything they knew about herding and being stewards of the land. In time, they would've added to their lands and built homes for their children as they'd married and brought grandchildren into the loving arms of the family. When they became old and gray, the young ones would take care of them, and life would be golden and bright in the land of the Eyes. They would die together, hand in hand, as in love as on their wedding day.

It should have happened. They should have lived until just a few decades ago. Instead, they faced a different lifetime, growing weaker not with age but with the decay that herbs could only hold back for so long. And if he found Rayli in Somteh, he would never let her go again.

He looked up into the night sky. Ata Lashka was there, a dull red glow high in the sky. The Kisamonen moon was nearly set, evil white craters faint against the cloudless sky. Stars made patterns. The Lady. The Beneather with its streams of star tentacles. The Cottage. The Great Mushroom. Ancient humans used them as guides, sending wishes to the images sparkling in the blackness.

Dolen had only one wish.

He left the fire burning and headed off down the path toward Somteh and his love.

— CHAPTER EIGHTEEN —

Sorreg awoke to yelling in the hallway outside her room. She sat bolt upright in the darkness and fumbled for a flint on the table beside her narrow bed.

"Stay inside. Do not come out. Do not come out. Stay in your rooms."

Someone was running down the hall shouting those words.

Stay inside? Why?

Unlike the past few nights, there was no smell of smoke. Her room in the cliff's interior had no windows—those were reserved for people higher up in Somteh's elite than her. But unlike some, she had a door, and she scrambled out of bed, crossing the small space to make sure it was locked.

She waited, leaning against it, straining to hear anything in the hallway. Sound didn't travel well through the stone walls, but all the ventilation ducts connected, and faint noise drifted up through the windy shafts. No words, just sounds. Shouting, maybe. An intermittent banging from somewhere deep beneath her high, privileged space.

The truce has broken. The Beneathers have attacked.

Sorreg's heart pounded at the thought. What else could it be? All over Ert, the monsters from below held siege against the great cities of humans. Their hatred of civilization and culture were legendary, and Nightfell gave them dominion over the years of darkness. Somteh had been spared, thanks to Zarix's truce. Working with the Berunfolk from underground gave Sorreg and the other scientists access to knowledge they would never have found on their own. Kratch and the other research assistants had adapted so well to the peace. Everyone benefited.

But in their hearts, they hate us.

She shook off the treacherous thought. Kratch didn't hate her. Yes, he was different, and his anatomy made her skin crawl, but he had never shown the slightest aggression. Zarix said all the Beneathers wanted was food. That they starved during the century of light when they couldn't emerge onto the land, and even now they would do anything for a meal. He laughed about it. Called them the best bargain since the Risen, who worked for nothing at all.

The hallway quieted, and Sorreg paused, hand on the door. If there had been a battle, there could be wounded. She was a medical Embalmer. They would need her.

You're a research scientist. You haven't sewn up a wound since you were a Journeyman. But it would come back to her. And she could hardly hide up here if people were fighting below.

She unlocked the door and eased it open a crack, listening. Nothing.

Just a step out. Just to see.

None of the other doors were open, and no one was in the hallway.

If there was fighting, it would be out on the plain in front of the cliff. A thousand homes squatted in the shadow of Somteh, spreading out into the desert. If the Beneathers with their monsters were attacking, that's where they would come from.

She padded down the hallway, hugging the wall. At the top of the stairwell she paused, listening. Faint sounds filtered up from far below, shouting voices and the clang of chitin on stone.

Just one flight. Just enough to see out the window.

Torches on the wall cast flickering shadows down the stairs. The landing below her had a window that overlooked the plain. She crept down, hand on the stone wall, feeling each step before she descended.

At the window she stopped, peering out.

Far below her, the houses sprawled, small mud-brick dwellings with faint light shining from inside chimneys and behind closed shutters. No fires burned. No beasts prowled. No shadow creatures conjured by vengeful, starving creatures loomed over the homes.

Outside the cliff, the plain was at peace.

Whatever was happening was inside Somteh.

From below, a figure burst around the stairs.

"Get in your room and lock the door!"

She couldn't make out the speaker's features, but the voice was female.

"I'm an Embalmer. I can help," Sorreg began, but the woman cut her off.

"Not yet. Get inside and stay there until you hear an all-clear." She shooed Sorreg up the stairs, following behind her.

"Is it Beneathers? Did the truce break?"

The woman shook her head. "No. It's the Risen. But don't worry. It's contained."

That's why I'm being locked away in my room. Because it's so well contained.

Sorreg did as she was told, returning to her room and locking the door. She sagged against it as the lock clicked.

Not Beneathers. No tentacled monsters coming after her tonight. *I shouldn't have suspected Kratch and his people. They're honest.*

It was just a Risen riot. More and more of those lately. Such a waste of the gift of life-after-death.

She sighed, padding across to her small desk overflowing with paperwork. Embalmers kept the Risen fresh, saving them from the final death. They should be grateful. They used to be, working alongside the living, toiling for the greater good. Weren't they treated well? Ten years out of a century was not much to ask.

Will you think that when it's you?

She pushed the thought away. Her knowledge would still be useful. Her skills wouldn't desert her, even in death. When she eventually died, she would Rise again to find a whole new generation of scientists who had taken her work and moved it forward. What new discoveries would await her as the centuries passed? Why would the Risen fighting in Somteh want to throw that away?

She moved the candle over to the desk and sat down to work. Hours later, someone ran down the hallway calling the all-clear, and she stretched. Time for another day. A kitchen servant, one of the living, delivered breakfast as usual, and the ventilation shafts were quiet.

On the way to her laboratory she paused at the window where she had looked out over the peaceful plain. All the homes were intact, but movement below caught her eye. She stood on tiptoe to lean out, peering over the wall.

Far below, lines of people were pulling carts out beyond the homes. Sorreg watched, squinting in the dim light. A line of torches lit the way, and the carts all stopped in an open area to the south. They dumped the carts out, and the contents rolled into the sand.

Bodies. And parts of bodies.

Even from that distance, Sorreg could make out the bound shapes, wiggling on the ground.

One by one the bodies were beheaded, the bodies falling still.

The heads would still be alive. Risen didn't die until the Eyes opened, unless they were burned to ash, or their brains were destroyed. They didn't need bodies to live. Sorreg shivered, remembering the demonstration in her training. Without lungs they couldn't speak. But the heads survived, at least for a while.

This was the worst possible punishment. Left in the plains, the heads and lifeless bodies would slowly rot, if something didn't eat them first. Denied the flames that would return them to the Atamonen, the Risen souls trapped inside would be lost forever. The final death, with nothing beyond.

She watched in horror as some of the bodies were loaded back onto the carts. The ones in the best shape could be used for parts, arms and legs for those Risen who lost them in battle or accidents, or flesh to replace what rotted away despite the best the Embalmers could do.

How long would the heads last? How long would those eyes stare up at the night sky, blinking away the blowing sand?

They didn't feel pain, but surely the Risen knew fear.

Sorreg backed away from the window and wiped tears from her cheeks as she plodded down the smooth stone stairway.

— CHAPTER NINETEEN —

Dolen stared around him, a mountain man in the crush of the second largest city on Ert.

So many people. I could never have imagined.

Somteh sprawled across the cool desert night, tightly packed homes, shops, warehouses, and businesses clustered near the base of a cliff that rose straight up from the scrubby land. He had always read about the city as being carved into the rock, a pillar of stone in the hot, dry desert. When the Eyes were open, it surely would be hot, but the endless night wind blew cold across this plain. Ata Lashka's red disk glowed on the horizon with the treacherous Kisamon moon high above. Dolen had never seen so much horizon. It stretched off forever, his distant mountain home only a shadow at the far end of his vision.

He crept between the houses. Small and squat, they'd been built half-submerged in the sandy ground. The homes were farther apart out here, some still wet from construction, but every step he took toward the cliff brought them closer, more numerous. The nearer he got to the city center, the more people hurried around, rushing from building to building. There were no stone-paved paths, but well-worn cart tracks crossed between the buildings, and streams of people carrying baskets and packs scurried along ahead of him. No one paused to speak to the Risen man who stared at everything with clear gray eyes.

"Excuse me," he began, but no one stopped to listen.

Some of the people walked more slowly, taking their time. Dolen stopped to watch for a moment, sorting out the traffic flow. The slow walkers were all dressed in plain gray or brown, robes or pants. Most had hoods or hats, but on the few that didn't, he noticed numbers tattooed on their necks.

Marked like property.

Risen weren't really people anymore. In Marskateh, they were employed by everyone who could afford their labor. Dolen had treated his Risen like any other worker, though when food was scarce, it was helpful to have a staff that didn't need to eat. He'd even given them time off, unlike some of the folks he knew. His Risen had also been numbered, their employment leased through the Somteh brokers who traveled to the smaller villages. It had meant nothing to Dolen as an employer.

It meant everything to him as a Risen.

He pulled his own hood more tightly around his neck. If he walked quickly, like the live people did, no one would notice him. In the dim light, the gray pallor of his skin didn't show. He couldn't pull it off in brighter light, but what else could he do? He had to find Rayli, and that meant finding the hall of records here. She would have a number; she would have been sold to someone ten years ago when she first Rose. She might not be here in Somteh, but it was the only place for him to start.

Dolen strode along the cart path, dodging people with baskets hung on both hips and pack animals laden with goods. He'd expected to find a city under siege, crawling with Beneathers and monsters of the deep, but no one seemed concerned about attack. Everyone had somewhere to be.

He turned onto a wide path that aimed straight at the cliff. The constant noise of conversation rang in his ears. To his Risen hearing, everything had an echoing, distant quality, but he could pick out individual voices all around him.

"...said there were a hundred Risen that got..."

"...left them to rot..."

"...burned half of the Weaver Guild before they..."

No one sounded particularly worried. Just gossip. The same as everywhere, just so much more of it.

He shuffled along, dodging people and carts, and stepping over trash in the street. Even to his muffled sense of smell, the place stank. Too many people. Too many animals. And a faint stench of rotting meat from somewhere to the south.

The cliff loomed up before him. Towering over the plain, it was dotted with round holes unevenly spaced all along its smooth stone face. Lights flickered in most of the holes, and the silhouettes of people passed across them. Windows, as high as he could see. How many people lived here? How far back did it burrow into the hills behind it? And how deep below? The tunnels that snaked through his home mountain range were said to connect all the way down here, running under every inch of the world. What creatures slithered and shambled just beneath his feet?

He bumped into the person in front of him, not realizing the line of people had stopped.

"Sorry," he mumbled, but the person didn't even turn around.

A long line waited to enter the doors at the bottom of the cliff. As he inched closer, he peered over their heads to see his destination. He'd expected something grand. A huge opening, torchlit and sparkling, entry to the great city. But of course it wouldn't be huge. It had to be small enough to defend when the monsters came.

When is that, exactly?

No one appeared to be concerned.

Obviously not today.

Above the door, the words "Welcome to Somteh" were etched into the stone, partially worn away and illuminated by lanterns hung on each side of the door frame. Step by step, he followed the line of people up to the guards flanking the doorway. Some people were simply waved through, while others were questioned at the entry.

His heart pounded in his chest. It felt familiar, yet foreign. Risen hearts beat slower by nature, but not when faced with huge guards with weapons casually held at their sides.

"Business?"

The voice jerked Dolen from his reverie. It wasn't the guard who'd spoken, but another man standing just inside the doorway. He wore a red robe and looked bored.

"What's your business in Somteh?"

Dolen faltered. "Um, hall of records?"

"What guild?"

Dolen gave the man a blank stare.

The man sighed. "What guild owns you?"

Heat flashed up Dolen's neck. *Don't say anything stupid. Remember what you are now.* But what was he? He was still Dolen Roald, wasn't he? Yes. And also...no.

He didn't know what he should say, and he only knew one guild from the snippets of conversation outside.

"Weaver Guild."

The man sniffed. "You involved in the trouble?"

Dolen had no idea what the man meant, but the answer to that question had to be "No."

A nod from the man, and Dolen was through.

The cliff opened before him to reveal a long, wide corridor that led to a junction with wide, tall hallways leading down each side. Colorful awnings hung over shelves and carts full of goods Dolen had never imagined: cloth and jewelry; smoked meats and live creatures in cages stacked higher than Dolen's head; fungus so fresh it still glowed. The scent of powdered spices filled the air, almost drowning out the smell of humans, living and dead. And the noise—it echoed off the sheer stone walls, dizzying and sharp.

People pushed past him from every side, spinning him around as he stared. *There are a million people here. I'll never find her.*

He caught the eye of the man in the doorway, who was peering at him.

You don't belong here. He can tell.

The man opened his mouth, but before he could call out, Dolen backed away, disappearing into the manic throng.

— CHAPTER TWENTY —

S lowly and carefully. Be gentle with the scraping. Good job, students."

Sorreg nodded and corrected her way down the long bench. Teaching apprentice embalming students was one of her favorite parts of the promotion. These young people were the future of science. In a few more years when they became full Embalmers, they would take up places in all the sciences of Somteh. Medicine for the living, preserving the dead, field ecology...endless options awaited them. Some might take their knowledge to the other cities, carrying her teaching all over the world. And since the treaty, new opportunities under the surface would be available to them as well.

Now, she guided them through their lessons in botanical medicine, teaching them how to transplant the lichen onto various substrates.

"Record keeping is critical," she said, "and make sure to note the time of transfer. If we get very lucky and one of these looks promising, we need to know how to replicate it."

A student scraped brown lichen from the shiny, brown-stained stone onto a small spatula. He spread some onto three different stones, and one sample of smooth human bone, part of a skull.

Sorreg paused, watching him.

Did this skull come from one of the Risen left out to rot? It showed no burn marks, and the cut edges were clean. Blood, bone, and other specimens were critical in developing compounds that acted on humans. So few of Ert's plants were good for anything except eating until they were sensitized with Berunfolk slime and grown with some kind of human tissue. Before the treaty, her specialized field hadn't existed. Everything she and her mentor Zarix had discovered was thanks to Berunfolk help.

Once all the students finished and placed their specimens under glass, she sent one of them out to the hallway to let Kratch in. He couldn't be around unless the plants were under the ventilation alcove. The sedative would work on him just fine.

He paused in the doorway, testing the air with a tentacle, and Sorreg heard whispers down the row of students.

"...filthy Beneather..."

"...should just kill them..."

"...tentacle-lover."

That last was surely aimed at her.

"Would you like to repeat that for the whole class?" She fought to keep the anger from her voice, staring blades of fire into the student who had said it.

"Repeat what, Miss Sorreg?" The kid blinked at her with guileless brown eyes.

She took a deep breath. *Steady. You're his teacher. Act like it.* "Do any of you have any questions you'd like to ask Kratchenialz?"

"Hardly."

It was barely more than a whisper, but a glance showed her that Kratch had heard it, too.

"Mr. Grold, please stand up."

The brown-eyed boy hauled himself to his feet with a sigh.

"Mr. Grold, do you have an issue with the Berunfolk who are our partners in the pursuit of science?"

"Of course not, Miss Sorreg. We are forever in their debt."

Oh, you sarcastic little... Sorreg cleared her throat. "Indeed we are." She glanced back to the doorway that led to the animal room where the lab specimens were kept. Kratch stood in the opening, red eyes flashing. "Kratch, weren't you saying we were low on skeets?"

The palm-size arachnids made great test subjects. Nonvenomous and easy to maintain, they didn't breed in captivity and had to be collected from the wild.

Kratch nodded.

"Right," Sorreg said. "All right, class. Field trip."

All five students huddled around Sorreg.

At first they'd been ecstatic about the chance to leave the lab. Then she'd told them where they were going.

Skeets infested the upper chambers of Beneath, the dry tunnels near the surface. Underground rivers flowed through the deeper caverns, but even with Kratch along, those corridors weren't safe for humans. Without Kratch, even the upper levels would've been extremely dangerous.

They followed him down the back stairways of the Embalming Guild, passing levels of laboratories and classrooms, the hospital wing, and the applied sciences, which always smelled of smoke and chemicals. Down and down, through the halls of the dead and past the vast chambers of empty shelves where the Risen would sleep in death through the long years of Day, regularly bathed and wrapped in herbs to preserve them for another Nightfell of service. No one except Embalmers got near those halls. For most, it was too grim a reminder that by the time the Eyes closed again, they would likely lie on one of those shelves, awaiting their time to Rise.

At the base of the cliff, a single long tunnel descended into darkness.

"Do we need torches?" asked the smarmy kid, Grold.

Not so cocky now, are you, little punk? "Of course not," Sorreg replied. "The Berunfolk are well adapted to darkness. It would be extremely rude to take bright light into their home."

Each of them was close enough to touch her as they followed Kratch down, inching along as their eyes adjusted. Small veins of silvery fungus lit the way, growing along the rough-cut walls. It was just enough to see a few feet ahead, and Sorreg forced herself to breathe slowly.

This was your idea. Teach the kids a lesson.

She'd been down into Beneath with Kratch before, collecting specimens. As the tunnel switched back, going deeper under the mountain, she smiled, knowing what lay ahead.

The students behind her gasped.

The tunnel opened onto a wide chamber pulsing with prisms of dim light. Pink phosphorescent stalactites hung from the ceiling high above their heads. Deep blue fungus marbled the floor, glowing softly in all the cracks. Along the distant walls, purple dots winked on and off as glowbugs signaled for mates, skittering up and down the carved-out chamber.

"It's beautiful," one of the girls murmured, and Sorreg grinned.

"Yes, it is. Don't touch anything."

Shadows darted in the dim recesses, and the students stayed close to Sorreg, who stayed close behind Kratch. He led them across the chamber and into one of several tunnels leading off the main hall. They twisted and turned, pausing here and there for Sorreg to identify the wide variety of fungus that clung to the walls. There were so many she had no names for, and Kratch's people didn't use speech to name things. He'd tried to explain how his tentacles made scents that communicated not only with other Berunfolk, but also with the creatures of the dark. Sorreg couldn't recognize the difference. The Berun language was only partially verbal.

They crept down a long, dark hallway until Kratch paused at an intersection. A small group of Berunfolk stood there, blocking the way, crowding together as they glanced at Sorreg and her students.

One of them, a smaller female, wore the distinctive gold-edged robe of Zarix's lab. Sorreg gave the fingers-over-mouth salute.

"Greetings, Orch," she said, nudging her students. "I didn't expect to see you today."

The students stared at her. With an apologetic look at the Berunwoman in blue, she made the introduction.

"Orch, these are Embalming apprentices. Students, this is Orch, first assistant to Prime Embalmer Zarix." When that didn't spur their manners, she whispered, "She outranks all of us. Kindly salute."

She didn't miss the narrowing of Grold's eyes as he gave the respectful greeting.

Orch didn't speak to her, but instead communicated with Kratch in the halting, guttural speech of their people. Sorreg detected faint whiffs of a bitter smell but had no idea what it meant in Berun.

In the hallway behind the Prime's assistant, she could just make out several long, empty, wheeled carts.

"We go this way," Kratch said, and Sorreg repeated the salute as she and her students continued straight down the tunnel.

After a few more twists and intersections, Kratch halted. He sniffed the air and motioned for them to follow, turning away from a wide junction. His steps picked up and they trotted along in the semi-darkness until he finally slowed down.

"Why so fast?" Sorreg whispered, and Kratch shook his head.

"No word. Big. Hungry."

Sorreg knew he meant that humans had no name for whatever was down that hallway.

"Can't you control it?"

He shrugged. "Maybe."

Ah. Or maybe it would eat us all, Kratch included. He was gifted with plants, but after their recent conversation, she realized there must be others who were stronger at controlling animals.

Finally, Kratch stopped. "In here."

Sorreg instructed her students to take out the jars they each carried. "Open the lids and be ready. I want you each to catch a skeet. Kratch will slow them down, but they're still fast. They aren't venomous, but it still hurts if they bite you."

Kratch entered a small, low chamber off the main hallway. Dim green veins cast shadows in the crags, and a wide crack in the floor opened into black nothing.

"All right. Be cautious, and don't step in that crack."

One of the girls reached out to touch the green, glowing fungus. As her hand approached, it sparkled with tiny yellow bursts.

Kratch slapped her hand away. "No touch. You die."

Even in the dark, Sorreg could see the girl go ashen.

Kratch turned to Grold. "You touch, okay."

The kid looked to Sorreg, and she shook her head. Across the chamber, Kratch's red eye winked at her. "Don't touch it. Don't any of you touch it."

As her eyes adjusted to the pale green light, she could see that the walls were moving. Skeets covered the surface, scuttling all along the rocks. The green fungus sparkled yellow where their tiny feet raced over it.

"Remember, class, Kratch will slow them down. Each of you grab one and put it in your jar. Make sure the lid is on tight."

A faint floral scent permeated the room. The skittering arachnids slowed along the walls.

The students huddled in the center.

"Go! We don't leave until you each have one."

Tentatively they shuffled near the walls, lunging for the slow-moving forms, staying well away from the green fungus. Grold was the last to try catching one.

Kratch, be nice, she silently willed her partner.

When Grold had a skeet by the leg, the scent in the room changed ever so slightly. The eight-legged, fist-size creature in the student's grasp lurched, whirling around, and latching onto Grold's wrist. He screamed and dropped it, shaking his arm. "Get it off! It bit me!"

From all around the room, skeets converged on the kid. Sorreg and the others backed away as Grold's boots were covered in tiny legs and dark bodies.

"Get them off! Get them off!"

They swarmed up his legs, and Sorreg cleared her throat.

With a flash of his eyes, Kratch nodded.

The skeets fell from Grold's legs, and Kratch strode over, picking one up and depositing it in the kid's jar. Sorreg and her students all hustled out of the room and back down the long, twisting tunnels.

"And that's why we owe a tremendous debt of gratitude to Prime Embalmer Zarix, to Orch, and to all the Berunfolk who are our peaceful allies," Sorreg said to her terrified students. "For the first Nightfell ever, we are not at war with the Berunfolk here in Somteh. Every Nightfell in history has seen the creatures of these dark tunnels overrunning the land. Every Risen and every living human fought to keep the cities from falling, and usually failed. A century of learning lost in a decade, every single time."

They crossed the beautiful, luminescent chamber.

"This time is different. Our learning will continue, and with the help of our allies and their knowledge of the deep, the scientists of Somteh will change the world."

She smiled at her students, still shaking as they climbed the long tunnel toward the torchlight of the surface city.

"Make sure those lids are on tight, students. Skeets get very angry when they hit the light."

— CHAPTER TWENTY-ONE —

Hours after passing through the entry to Somteh, Dolen located the hall of records—except it wasn't called a "hall of records" here. The Employment Contract Office was staffed by three living humans in no hurry to complete anyone's business. The line snaked back and forth around the small lobby and out into the main corridor. Dolen shifted from foot to foot, ducking his head under his cloak when anyone official passed by.

He had no idea what "trouble" the entry guard had been referring to, but the looks he received from the living all around him ranged from suspicious to outright hostile.

After half a day's shuffling forward, he reached the counter. The woman behind it didn't look up from her paperwork when she addressed him.

"ID number?"

Dolen hesitated. "I'm with the Weaver's Guild and we're looking for records on a Risen brought here from..."

The woman cut him off. "ID number?"

Dolen tried again. "The Risen in question would have been..."

With a deep sigh, the woman looked up. As if speaking to a small child, she said, "What is your ID number, Risen? All queries are logged by ID number. I cannot begin the paperwork without your ID number, and without paperwork, no queries are answered. What is your ID number?"

He made a guess. "Three-four-seven-eight."

Her eyes narrowed. "You're far too fresh for such a low number. Show me your tattoo."

Oh boy. The neck tattoos he'd seen on Risen plodding through the city were far more important than he'd imagined. And he didn't have one.

"I don't..."

The woman nodded. "No ID number. You're new to Somteh? Just died somewhere else and showed up on your own?" She pushed away the binder she'd been poised to write in and dragged another over from the pile of papers on her desk.

"Yes," Dolen said, relieved. Sort of. "I'm looking for my..."

She ignored him, gesturing to some living men behind her. Dolen hadn't even noticed them, but he took a step back as they marched around the counter to stand on either side of him.

"Name?" she asked, eyes back on her desk.

"Dolen Roald."

"Date of birth and death?"

He told her, along with his hometown.

Now we're getting somewhere. "I'm looking for my wife, who would have..."

The woman rattled off a six-digit number, copying it onto her ledger, and onto another small sheet of paper.

"Skills?"

Dolen thought for a moment. "I'm a rancher. I raise and..."

"Animal care," the woman said, making notes on both the ledger and the small paper. She eyed him up and down. "Condition: excellent."

Inside Dolen, frustration warred with stupid pride at the strange compliment. Yes, he was in excellent condition, but she'd said it like she would have appraised a ghote he was considering as breeding stock. *Because that's all I am now. A commodity. A thing.*

She handed the small paper to one of the men flanking Dolen.

"Come on, Corpse," the man said. "Let's go."

"But..." Dolen's protest was cut off as the men each took him by an arm, hustling him out of line.

Dolen knew he was stronger than this pair. He could hurt them, pull away, and try to disappear into the throng of people. But as they ushered him bodily out of the office and down the main corridor, he realized fighting would be futile. The whole place teemed with official-looking living humans. He might've been stronger and able to ignore pain, but he was woefully outnumbered.

Wait. Let them do their thing. Get the ID number and whatever job they want to give you. Then find Rayli once they stop watching you.

The guards chatted as they gripped his arms.

"What's the point of this?" one of them asked. "There's only a couple weeks of dark left. Send this one down to the fighting pit and be done with it."

The second one laughed. "Why, Halden, are you suggesting that the great and lawful city of Somteh has an underground corpse-fighting entertainment enterprise? The very thought of such a thing..."

Corpse-fighting? Oh, Dolen, you could be in trouble here.

"Yeah," the first one said. "There's no such thing. But seriously, did you see the last one? The Tornado girl they call Red? Killed three skitters on her own and almost took out the announcer. Tornado just went way up in the ranking."

A laugh from the second guard. "Didn't see it, but I heard about it. I've got a hundred scarabs on Duststorm this season. Should be an interesting match."

They led Dolen through endless hallways lit by gas flames that came from tubes running high along the walls. He lost count of the turns they made, working their way ever deeper into the warren of stone. The air got thicker as they walked, and the guards' grips got looser as they realized their quarry was not going to run.

Now. You should run now.

But where would he go? He was lost, a country rube in the big city with no friends and no idea where to look for help. Better to bide his time and learn what he could. A better opportunity would arise.

And if it doesn't?

It would. He was sure of it.

He and his guards entered a small chamber and stood in line behind three similar groups. When it was Dolen's turn, he obediently lay down on a low bench. A grizzled man leaned over him with a short, sharp blade and a pot of ink.

It was not true that Risen didn't feel pain. Dolen felt every slice of the blade as it carved the numbers into the skin of his neck. He felt the man's fingers grinding ink into the new cuts and the tight wrap of a clean bandage over the tattoo. His dark blood tickled, trailing down his shoulder. But the pain *meant* nothing. He could ignore it, as if it were happening to someone else. Just shut it off and think of other things. Like finding Rayli.

They locked him in a holding cell with eight other Risen men and gave them each a few strips of dried meat and a small handful of mushroom flakes to help them heal.

Soon they would sell his labor for the rest of this Nightfell.

Risen didn't sleep, but Dolen sat on the floor of the cell and closed his eyes to wait.

— CHAPTER TWENTY-TWO —

Rayli reclined on a padded chair in her solitary locked cell and rubbed her temples. As a Risen who ignored pain, she was only distantly aware of the headache, but old habits died hard, even for a dead woman.

I am a gladiator. This is how I serve Ata Lashka's wish. This is how they make me use her gift. Not to protect the living from monsters. Not to help them in their daily lives as a faithful friend and honored servant. But as a gladiator in an illegal, underground fighting ring, killing, being maimed, and likely dying the Final Death. All for the amusement of a living population that had nothing to fear from the ancient enemies her gift was intended to combat.

When she, along with Carrol and the man in yellow whose name was Flint, stood on the sand after improbably winning their first battle, the crowd had gone wild. The gladiators of Clan Tornado who had bought them all flooded out onto the arena floor, hoisting the victors onto their shoulders, and parading them around to the chants of "Red! Red! Red!" from the ecstatic audience.

Red. That was Rayli's name now.

She was officially already dead, expunged from the records of Somteh. Rayli Roald had suffered the Final Death, and Red was born that night. Carrol was no longer officially Carrol but called "Creech" after a little bug that lived in the deep forest and flew to safety at the slightest threat. Flint's name stayed the same because

Flint was a fine name for a gladiator. He was from a nomadic tribe in the northern hills and didn't seem as incensed about the change in his fortune as Rayli and Carrol were. But his life had been hard, and the first years of his Risen service even harder, working for a merchant who regularly sent him with wares on the dangerous, overland journey from Somteh through the Beneather's siege on Kamteh. He'd watched scores of his fellow Risen torn apart by the same sorts of monsters they now fought as gladiators.

Rayli touched the new tattoo on her cheek, the thick, black swirls of the whirlwind, symbol of Clan Tornado. As a full gladiator, she was being fed now, so the scabby skin would heal, along with the burn on her hand from the skitter fight and the three long, parallel lacerations down her left side, acquired in last night's fight against a swarm of brrrts. She had fought alongside five others of her clan in a battle against Duststorm, with their dotted cheek tattoos. The clan with the most kills at the end won the fight, and tonight they feasted on the victor's spoils of the salty brrrt meat.

Each day brought three hours of rest, required for the healing of wounds. Risen could work or fight without respite, but food and rest helped injuries mend faster.

Rayli hated those hours.

The rest of the days were spent training, practicing in a small, sandy training room, learning how to fight from the more experienced clan gladiators. Rock and Grappler, the two who had slipped her the dagger on her first fight night, were willing teachers.

"We win or lose together," Rock would say, throwing her to the ground without a scratch as she struggled with her training knife or staff.

She wasn't a fighter. She was a rancher, a weak Lightshaper, and a very lucky "bait corpse." A Last Man Standing exhibition battle like her first one was not supposed to end with any living Risen. The crowd placed bets on who would be the last one destroyed by the skitters, sacrificing Risen who could serve centuries into the future for gambling and entertainment. No one was expected to win. But win they had, which instantly made them celebrities among the depraved crowd. And because Red had delivered the killing blows, her new name was on everyone's lips.

Only two and a half months left.

She reclined on the chair, staring at the gray stone ceiling. If she could somehow survive the remaining months of this Nightfell, she'd return to the sleep of the dead until the next one. Assuming her body was stored with those who were doing more honorable work this time. Surely when this Nightfell ended and she fell back into death, her body would be treated with the respect due a Risen. Surely by next time, things would be different. Perhaps by then, people would remember to respect the Risen as they should. Perhaps these debasing games would be over, the clans dissolved over a century. Or at least the name Red might be forgotten, and next time she'd be sold to someone else.

Someone like Carrol.

Her former employer had the cell next to Rayli's. Sometimes they used their rest hours to talk, telling stories of their lives or remembering good times they'd had once Rayli was brought to Somteh. But Carrol had been injured in last night's fight, her right leg torn off at the hip. She'd managed to crawl to the edge of the arena and survive until the last brrrt was killed and the victory awarded to Tornado. The Embalmers took her from the sand and attached a replacement leg from some unfortunate who would not Rise again. Carrol was lucky in that the leg was nearly the same length as the one she lost, so once it healed, she wouldn't limp too badly. It was nowhere near the same skin color, but that hardly mattered. Many of the gladiators had limbs that hadn't originally belonged to them. It was only a matter of time. Risen could survive losing all four limbs. They would even live for a while without a body at all.

Rayli had learned this the night of her first victory. After the cheering crowds collected their winnings and the arena torches were extinguished, the other gladiators took her to the clan's quarters for a celebratory meal of the butchered skitters she'd just killed. The hallway that led from the arena to their private cells was bare stone with a high shelf running down each side, the whole length of the corridor. On that shelf were heads. Most of them bore cheek tattoos, the grisly remains of gladiators from other clans, destroyed in battles that Tornado won. The spoils of victory were more than just monster meat. Some heads were from unmarked, "bait corpses" less lucky than she had been. The freshest had been added as they paraded by: the head of Blue, whose body was maimed beyond repair in the fight. Limbs could be replaced, but for some reason a whole torso could not. Rock said the Embalmers were working on it, with an eyeroll that clearly stated *not working very hard*. Risen were replaceable.

Blue had stared down at her with wild eyes rolling in his head, all that was left of him. They placed him at the end of the shelf and gave him a little salute. Heads couldn't talk—they didn't possess lungs to push air through their throats—but they clung to life, sometimes for months. No one really understood how Ata Lashka's gift worked, but eventually with no heart, Risen just stopped functioning, eyes fixed forward, lips unmoving. They were presumed dead for good...but were they? Rayli shuddered to think they might still be in there, locked inside a motionless shell, haunted by terror and maddened by the inability to move. When Day broke in a few months, they would sleep and be burned, returned to Ata Runi. Until then, they were a horrifying reminder of the fate that would befall Rayli if she failed in a battle she'd never asked to fight.

All Risen were prepared to be destroyed in defense of a city full of living. That was the bargain. But this was grotesque.

Despair washed over her in these hours of rest.

Oh, Dolen. I'm so glad you aren't here to see what I've become.

He had surely returned to find her dead and raised their son, living to a frail old age. He wouldn't Rise. Wouldn't serve or fight. Wouldn't end up a head on a shelf, going slowly insane, unblinking in a dark tunnel.

Thank you, Atamonen, she prayed silently. *Thank you for sparing Dolen this shameful city's degradation.*

Risen didn't make tears. Just another of the complexities of their return to life. But she shook with grief. She would never want her husband to see her now, but she ached at the knowledge that she would never see him again.

— CHAPTER TWENTY-THREE —

The lab animal room was a mess. Sorreg had fired four Risen animal care workers in the past weeks, and her sullen students were having to fill in the labor. They hated being used as common servants, and it showed in their work.

She stomped out of the lab and glared at Kratch. "We need a worker. That room is filthy."

Kratch just nodded, long used to Sorreg's moods.

"And where are the Risen? We were supposed to have ten test subjects today. They're late."

A shrug from Kratch.

The tests had gone well so far. Of all the lichen they had transferred, the specimens planted on human bone were growing the best. Lichen on the smooth, flat mirrorstone was also growing well, and both domes quickly filled with spores as they grew. Those spores were soft brown on the bone and a brighter red color from the stone. When the lab animals were exposed to the spores, nothing happened, which told Sorreg that something had changed in their chemical structure. In its original form, the lichen gave off a powerful sedative to protect itself from predation. These new samples had no effect on several species of Ert life they tested; from the small, skittering skeets to the larger insect species nor the shaggy, furred creatures brought down from the mountains.

When bubbled through the water of a bowl containing small green fish, it was similarly ineffective.

It's as safe for the planet as we can make it. Now let's hope it works on us.

There was nothing else on Ert that was anything like humans. No creature brought from the depths of Beneath; or from the deserts; towering mushroom forests; or high, cold peaks seemed to have anything in common biologically with humans. Religion taught that humans were the children of the Atamonen in the sky, created to love and worship them, and to care for the lands and waters of Ert. Science seemed to agree with that. The astronomers grumbled in their high observatories, peering into the night sky in vain to see the gods whose eyes closed, leaving their children to the mercies of the beasts of darkness, but it made sense to Sorreg. *We are different. We are alone.*

She wondered how medicine progressed during the years of light when no Risen were available to test new drugs and medical procedures. Violent prisoners were the first living test subjects, but they were in high demand by every department of Medical Embalming. Sorreg felt lucky to have a few more months of Nightfell with plenty of Risen available. It wasn't the same, of course. They couldn't die if the drug were truly dangerous. But Sorreg knew the signs when something went wrong. A flicker of the eye. A mottled, dark ripple across the skin as their cells died and were almost instantly reanimated in waves. The Risen had tried to describe what it felt like: moments of confusion and detachment, a shimmer of vision and hearing. Anything that caused a reaction like that was immediately shelved. Another failure. Another experiment ended.

"Dead people ready."

Kratch's voice startled her out of her thoughts.

"All right, then. Let's hope we get some sleepy Risen today."

Kratch had already prepared the thin glass jars, filling them with spores from the two promising lichen samples. She followed him down the hall to the testing room, where ten Risen were already seated on benches around the edge. The plain, oblong stone chamber's ventilation holes were already stuffed with thick cloth, blocking the airflow. Sorreg entered through the short, narrow doorway corridor. Its main door was one of the most expensive things in Somteh: solid, clear chitin that made an airtight seal. It was protected from the Risen's reach by a thick, barred barricade an arm's length inside the hall. She would be able to stand behind it and observe the spore's effects, making notes of any telltale signs. If nothing happened, the Risen would unblock the airflow to vent the room before stopping to bathe in buckets of water, washing off any residue on their hair or clothing.

"Thank you for coming," she began, as if they'd been given a choice. "The spore we're testing today is something brand new, so I need you to be very aware of anything you feel when it's released. It cannot harm you, as you're already dead, but if you feel anything at all, I need to know so I can extrapolate it to how this might affect the living."

"What if we don't want to be your lab skeets?"

Sorreg glanced at the Risen woman who'd spoken. "It's your duty to protect the living, just as we protect your bodies. You're perfectly safe."

The woman snorted. "Then you're going to be sitting in here with us?"

Sorreg ignored her. "Remember, please say anything you're feeling when we release the spore. Breathe deeply. Thank you for your service today."

She backed out and pulled the barricade shut. Another two steps back and she pushed the outer door closed standing just behind it, and pulled on her fume hood, just in case.

"Ready?"

Kratch sealed his own hood, his glowing red eyes blinking behind the clear eye caps, looking even more alien than ever. He nodded and held up the jars containing the red spores to be tested today.

A long, thin hole connected the inner chamber to the outer hallway. A hollowed out blackslug tentacle lined the tube, sealed on the test subject's end. Kratch lined the jars of red spores up inside the tube and sealed his end with twine, rolling it over to prevent leakage. Using a long stick, he shoved the tube forward, pushing the glass jars out to crash onto the floor in the test chamber. The air shimmered with the pale red dust.

Sorreg held her notepad, peering from face to face.

Nothing seemed to happen.

Patience.

The spores coated everything in the room, and the Risen dusted it from their faces with slow movements.

"How do you feel?" Sorreg called through door.

One man said, "Kind of tired."

"Tired like overworked, or tired like you need sleep?"

He laughed, red dust snorting out his nose. "I don't remember sleep much. But...yeah. Maybe more like I need sleep."

A happy shiver ran down Sorreg's back. *Maybe we're onto something.*

The Risen's movements slowed further, their eyelids fluttering.

Yes! This is it!

But after a few long moments, they shook their heads and wiped their eyes.

The man who had spoken said, "Kind of...wearing off now. I felt like I might actually fall asleep there for a second, but now I feel normal."

It's a start.

She left them in there for an hour, but nothing else happened. Finally, she ended the experiment.

"Okay. Please remove the cloth plugs from the ventilation shafts. You'll find buckets of water on the floor. Once the air is clear, please wash down the walls and floors, and wash your bodies and hair. Remove the clothing you're wearing, and when you come out, put on the robes I'll leave here in the hallway. We'll be waiting outside."

The Risen emerged in record time, faces glowing from the scrubbing. Sorreg led them down the hall to a small debriefing room and stood before them with her notes.

"So it made you feel sleepy? All of you?"

Nods all around.

An older woman with thinning hair said, "I almost felt like I might fall asleep for a few seconds, but it passed too quickly. Maybe a bigger dose would let me sleep? I miss sleeping."

Sorreg made a note and smiled. "I know. I can't imagine how that must be, and it's the purpose of this research." One of them, anyway. But Sorreg's excitement mounted. If it made Risen a bit sleepy, it might act as the sedative she was looking for, the primary focus of this experiment.

"Why do you want us to sleep? So you can drag us out and stake us down to rot?"

The Risen man's tone stopped Sorreg cold. "Of course not. We want you to be able to sleep because it might make you happier. Less restless."

"Less combative, you mean." He scowled. "Happy little zombies who do what we're told."

Sorreg rubbed her temples. "Not at all. I mean, happy, yes. I do want you to be happy."

The man's shoulders dropped, and his face relaxed into a small smile.

"All right."

And he really did look happy.

"Good," Sorreg said. "Because that's what I want."

The man scratched a hand over his face. "I'm happy. I'm not, but I am. I'm angry to be used like this, but I'm happy." He stood up and took a step toward Sorreg, who backed away.

"Please sit down."

He hustled back to his seat.

Odd.

"I didn't want to do that," the man said. "I'm still so..." He scowled, brows knitting even as his lips kept smiling. "So angry inside, but also happy. What did you do? You messed up my mind." He struggled for a moment, pushing his hands against the wall behind his seat. "You messed me up. I'm going to—"

"Bite your tongue," Sorreg snapped. "Just be quiet until I..." She paused. The man's jaws clenched, and dark blood spilled out from between his lips. After a long, horrifying moment, he spat out a small, pink blob of flesh onto the floor. The Risen around him jumped back.

Sorreg peered at the blob. Bloody and still twitching, it was the front three inches of the man's tongue. Her stomach turned at the grisly sight.

Swallowing hard, she forced out a low whisper. "What did you just do?"

His eyes were wide. Words bubbled out in streams of blood, thick and garbled. "You say... Bi....bi...bigh gug."

Bite tongue. She told him to bite his tongue, and he did.

She addressed the whole room.

"Everyone stand."

They did.

"Everyone sit."

They did.

Every command was obeyed instantly. Stand. Hop on one foot. Do a handstand. They all tried their best, with varying degrees of success.

She made them all sit down and took notes with shaking hands.

"Did you want to do those things?"

Heads shook no.

The older woman spoke up. "I can't do a handstand, but as soon as you told me to, I had to try. It felt like there was nothing else I could possibly do."

Sorreg turned to Kratch. "Please send a message to Prime Embalmer Zarix. Let's get this room cleaned up and transfer all the lichen we have to new bone samples." She glanced at the Risen man, blood still trickling down his chin. "And let's get this man to a surgeon to get his tongue sewn back on."

— CHAPTER TWENTY-FOUR —

Rayli stood in the arena, shoulder to shoulder with Rock, Grappler, and another female gladiator called Scar. Carrol was still out of commission, and Flint, the yellow-dyed Risen who had survived the first fight with them, had been destroyed the night before in a battle with Clan Star against a Corpse Eater. He wasn't completely consumed by the monsters they were fighting, and Rayli's heart broke to think of his head on their trophy shelf. If she could get to him, she could burn him and set him free, but the clan's quarters were separate, and she was locked into her cell when not training or fighting.

Risen were stronger than live humans. If they all attacked together, she knew they could overpower their living guards, even unarmed. But weeks ago when she was brought here, it was through multiple locking gates that clanged shut and locked behind her. They could kill the living humans that held them here, but there would still be no escape.

So they fought.

The announcer's voice boomed over the crowd, who quieted to listen.

"Tonight we bring you a timed event. The fierce warriors of Clan Tornado versus...well, you'll just have to see, won't you?" He paused for laughter. "Place your bets now. Will the blessed of Ata

Lashka survive thirty minutes in the arena? Or will the monsters of Beneath cut them down?"

Nope. No chance.

"What do you think it is?" Rayli muttered. She pushed hair out of her face, sticky with dye. The clan leaders insisted she still be dyed red for every fight, though now they painted it on in streaks through her blonde hair and stripes down her face, arms, and torso.

"Who knows?" Scar said. True to her name, her shadow-dark face was bisected by a thick, cruel scar that ran from one temple to the opposite jawline. Her left eye was missing where the scar cut across it, and where it passed her lips, they were healed into a permanent sneer. She looked fierce but was actually a very sweet person. In life, she had worked for the service wing of the Embalming Guild in Kamteh, watching over the orphans in their care.

Grappler didn't talk much, and Rock was her primary trainer. He was friendly enough and seemed to want to get to know Rayli a lot better. This confused and repelled her. Though her husband had been lost to her years before, she couldn't begin to think about being attracted to another man. And if she was? Certain systems weren't operable in Risen, though no one knew why. They couldn't cry tears. They could breathe, but they didn't have to. And the reproductive system was nonfunctional. She shuddered at the thought. What if it wasn't? Could she have a Risen baby? What a horror that would be, for a baby to be born into this life. She rubbed at the old scar on her lower belly, thinking of the child she had died to deliver. Perhaps he lived. *Please, let him have lived.*

"And now, let's meet our gladiators!"

The announcer introduced them one by one, and they stepped forward, waving at the crowd. When he called out "Here's Red!" she raised both hands to thunderous applause and cheers. It was the strangest kind of celebrity. Did they hope she would survive, or were they here to see her torn apart by a beast? It probably depended on how they had bet.

Thirty minutes. Survive thirty minutes to win.

"All right, let's bring on the monster!"

Singular, Rayli thought. *It's gonna be tough.*

At least they had better weapons this time: sharpened pikes and long, hardened swords. The torches lighting the arena had been moved up higher after their stunt using them as weapons, but Rayli was a Lightshaper. Their fire was still within her reach, even if her power was weak. She'd been training that, too, struggling to pull more light from dimmer sources, shaping it into what she wanted.

The four gladiators raised their swords as the heavy door across the arena cranked open. The chamber on the far side was pitch black. Rayli squinted to see what was revealed as the torchlight hit it, but the monster inside seemed to suck up the light.

It stepped forward into the arena.

Huge. Horrible. Words could barely form in Rayli's head as she stared at the thing. Her eyes refused to focus. It stood almost twenty feet high, striding forward on two legs. Hunched shoulders led to four thick arms, each of which ended in a hand with six-inch claws. Its head was round, with a gaping mouth in the center and no eyes or ears. Neither furred nor scaled, the creature was just smooth, and the torches didn't reflect off its night-sky surface. It was like a shadow made real.

Unlike the other beasts of Beneath, this one didn't shy from the light.

Behind it, the doorway closed partway, stopping about five feet off the ground.

"Behold," cried the announcer, "The Shadow Nightmare!"

Rayli barely heard the crowd's roar of approval.

The monster lumbered into the middle of the arena.

"Strategy?" Rayli called to Rock.

He shot her a blank stare. "Don't die?"

They split into two groups. Rayli stayed with Rock while Grappler and Scar ran across the sand to the other side of the arena. The monster stopped moving, crouching low in the center.

"What's it doing?"

Rock shook his head. "No idea. Never faced anything like this."

"Has anyone?"

"If they did, they didn't come back to tell us about it."

Reassuring.

The beast swung left, toward Scar and Grappler.

"Now!" Rock yelled, and they rushed forward.

They split, racing for the beast through the deep sand. It was focused on its prey, who stood their ground. Rayli pulled light from the torches and set fire to her blade and Rock's. In unison they struck, slicing clean blows through the creature's legs, just above the knees where the hamstring tendons should've been.

It roared and whirled around, backhanding Rayli across the arena.

She rolled, catching herself on the edge of the half-open doorway through which the Shadow Nightmare had entered. For a moment she faced away from it, into the darkness of the room beyond. Six red lights bounced in pairs for a second before winking out.

Rayli turned back to the arena and leapt to her feet.

The Nightmare was crumpled in the middle, but as it shoved itself up with its arms, Rayli watched in horror as the gashes on its legs sealed up without a trace.

It heals. We're dead.

"Run!" she yelled, but she knew her friends wouldn't hear her over the screaming, stomping crowd. She rushed back to Rock and hauled him to his feet. His head bled from where the Nightmare must have knocked him senseless. He took deep breaths, leaning on her shoulder and wiping his forehead.

Across the arena, the Nightmare advanced on Grappler and Scar. It swung out with a claw at Grappler, knocking Scar out of the way with the other three arms. Rayli barely had time to flame Grappler's sword as he whirled it toward the creature's hand, severing three of the claws. The other two impaled him right through the stomach, and he dropped his sword as the creature raised him high.

"Now!" Rock yelled again, and Rayli dropped her eyes from the gruesome sight. They raced to the beast once more, hacking at its legs. This time it kicked them away.

The crowd went berserk, cheering madly at the sight of Grappler dripping blood down the Nightmare's arm. With a ground-shaking roar, it raised its other arms and ripped Grappler in half, throwing each part across the arena.

Rayli screamed with rage, light flaring from her sword.

And for a tiny moment, the Shadow Nightmare flickered.

"Did you see that?" Rock said at her shoulder.

"I think so."

But they had no time to talk further as the creature advanced on them. They split up, each circling one side of the arena. The Nightmare followed Rock. Rayli ran to where Scar was standing. Three new gashes bled on her left arm, but she didn't bother to wipe the blood away. "Now I look like you, Red." Her eye sparked with crazed terror.

"Split and run. Just stay away from it. You can't hurt it."

As Rayli ran past the dark room, she glanced inside. The six glowing spots were back. One of the pairs blinked.

Something is in there. Something with luminous red eyes. *Another beast? Why hadn't it come out?*

They ran and doubled back, jumping out of the way of the nightmare's grasp. How long had it been? Five minutes? Ten? Rayli jumped over the upper half of Grappler's body. He was still alive, trying to pull with his arms to get out of the way, but he was done for. Legs could be reattached, but Grappler ended just below the ribcage, guts dragging behind him. A new lower half would never work.

She pulled light from the torches and flashed a bright white burst at the Nightmare's head, illuminating the arena for an instant. It didn't flinch. Once again, it shimmered, appearing to wink away for a split second.

Light doesn't scare it, but light makes it waver. And it heals like...like nothing.

Rayli was a Lightshaper. She could shape light into fire on the end of a sword, bending it to her will. Could she create a shape like this out of light? Her mind flashed to the glowing eyes in the dark chamber. *If I'm a Lightshaper, could there also be...Shadowshapers?*

She'd never heard of such a thing, but the Beneath held secrets she couldn't have imagined.

She bolted toward the open door. The glowing eyes were huddled in the back. Hands raised, she made a small, bright ball of white fire, hurling it straight at the red glow.

Berunfolk. Three of them flinched away from her light, which splashed out against the back wall, harming nothing.

But she knew their secret.

She whirled around in time to see the Shadow Nightmare flicker, becoming pale gray and translucent as the Berunfolk casting it recovered from her light attack.

"Here!" she yelled to her friends. "To me!"

Rock and Scar ran across the sand. Scar limped badly, and Rock bled from wounds all over his body.

When they reached Rayli, she pointed into the dark room. "It's them! They're making it! Kill them!"

The Shadow Nightmare roared.

Rayli pulled light from the torches, dimming the arena. Her power was fading, and even as Scar and Rock pushed past her, she knew she couldn't hold out for long. Gritting her teeth, she faced the Nightmare, casting light behind her into the room where the Shadowshapers hid.

Pulse the light. Blind them. Distract them.

The Nightmare advanced on her, claws raised and bloody.

From behind, she heard a grunt and a thud.

Ahead, the Nightmare shimmered and shrank.

Ten feet away, it crouched to lunge.

Rayli's Lightshaper magic expired.

As the beast leaped toward her, she backed into the dark chamber beyond.

A huge, clawed arm swung into the room and passed right through Rayli's body. She looked down, feeling nothing, and watched as the translucent shadow shimmered away into the air.

Rock and Scar dragged the three dead Berunfolk out into the arena and threw them down. The Shadow Nightmare was gone.

And the crowd went wild.

— CHAPTER TWENTY-FIVE —

You been bought. Stand up, Risen."
Dolen jumped at the guard's voice. He'd been confined to a small cell since they'd brought him here and tattooed a number on his neck. They'd provided one meal, and since then, nothing. No contact with anyone besides the other Risen in the cells on each side of his.

Prisoners. They treat us like prisoners.

And his only crime had been dying.

The Risen on his left had shared a bit of knowledge, and Dolen's head was still spinning. There was no war with the Beneathers here; instead, the living fought the dead. Or vice versa. Tensions were high, and Dolen paced the length of the cell, back and forth, for hours, three strides and turn. Three strides and turn.

Bought. The guard said he'd been *bought.*

He didn't mind the idea of working for the living. That's what he was brought back to do. But some of the stories...he shuddered. Somteh was sick. And Rayli had been brought here alone.

Under his robe, his necklace was cold against his skin. Etched with the Eye of the Atamonen, the smooth disk hung from a strip of leather. He pressed it to his chest now, muttering a quick prayer to Ata Lashka.

The door clanged open, and he followed the guard down the corridor.

"Hope you like Beneathers."

Two glowing red eyes peered out of a hood on a short figure at the end of the hallway. The guard stopped and gave Dolen a little push. "There you go. Your new boss. Do good, or it'll eat you." The guard spun on his heel and left Dolen staring at the creature.

A Beneather. An actual Beneather, just standing there, staring at him.

"You take care animals?"

The thing's voice was clipped and short, a low, scratchy croak.

Dolen took a step back. His childhood was filled with stories of these monsters, the intelligent life that ate human flesh. The great armies who would emerge at Nightfell and destroy the cities of humans. Controllers of beasts, filled with fury and rage.

This was just a small figure in a brown cloak.

"You take care animals?" it asked again.

"I'm..." Dolen hesitated. "I was a rancher. Raised ghotes in the mountains."

The thing cocked its head to the side. "Ghote? What ghote?"

"Um...long fur, six legs. Meat and wool for clothing."

The creature spat. "Ghote. Stupid name. You come."

It turned and headed down the corridor, obviously expecting Dolen to follow. After a few steps it stopped and turned with a sigh.

"You new?"

Dolen nodded. "Please don't eat me. I have a wife. I'm trying to find..."

It spat again. "No eat. You work. Big man make small paper. Says no eating. You work, I work, all work."

Small paper? "You mean the truce? Is that for real? You don't attack us, and we give you food?"

The red eyes narrowed. "You *give* food. Yes. We so happy. Dance all day in happy for food. No eating dead or live."

With the creature's strange syntax it was hard to tell, but Dolen thought he heard sarcasm. He looked behind him, but the gate back to the cells was shut. Might as well follow.

He kept a distance behind the Beneather, who led him out of the holding area and into a wide hallway. People gave the Beneather a wide berth, and Dolen noted the looks on the faces of the living and the few Risen they passed. Sneers. Disgust. Hostility. Truce there might be, but the people of Somteh were not fond of the creatures in the cloaks.

"Where are we going? Who bought my labor?"

They turned down a small corridor and Dolen caught up with the Beneather.

"Sorreg."

He hurried to keep up. "Is that a Guild?"

The creature stopped and turned to face Dolen. Its red eyes glowed beneath the hood, and Dolen peered under. Thick chitinous plates covered its face. Its hands were long and thin, tipped with sharp-looking claws. Its back was hunched, but the hunch was moving. *Tentacles*, he remembered. They had tentacles that grew out of their backs. Full of poison, according to some of the stories.

"Sorreg is doctor. Makes medicines. Animals for testing. You clean and feed. You work."

It spoke slowly and clearly, as if talking to a child—which, Dolen reasoned, wasn't inaccurate. He'd never left the mountains in his life. Here in this huge city, he was like a child.

"I can do that," he said. "I'm happy to take care of animals. It's a laboratory? Is Sorreg an Embalmer?"

The hunch wiggled. "Doctor. Waiting."

It turned and headed down the tunnel.

Dolen followed it, asking more questions and getting terse answers. No, they wouldn't be stopping to look at the records to find Dolen's wife. No, it didn't know Dolen's wife. The corridors were empty and narrow, and Dolen had the feeling that humans didn't use these tunnels much. The air was thick and close, and the only light was from smears of phosphorescent fungus on the walls. They climbed dark staircases, twisting through the heart of the cliff.

The creature ducked out of the small tunnel into a much taller and brighter corridor clearly meant for humans. They twisted and turned through more hallways, some marked with signs. It was the Embalmer's Guild, and Dolen sighed with relief. He would be preserved here when his service was done. And Embalmers were the most favored by the Atamonen. It was an honor to serve the greatest Guild in the city.

"What's your name?" he asked the creature leading him.

It stopped and turned again, sizing him up.

"Kratchenialz. Sorreg just say Kratch."

"Should I call you Kratch?"

Somehow its hard face softened for a moment. "Kratch," it agreed.

Finally, they arrived at a closed door. Kratch opened it to reveal a long, narrow room full of glass terrariums and cages. Creatures large and small scuttled within their housings. The place smelled, and Dolen snorted.

"How long since someone has cleaned in here?"

Kratch shrugged. "Last human gone a week."

The Beneather strode toward the front of the room but stopped in the doorway and shrank back, listening. Beyond, Dolen could see a bright, large room with long worktables along each side. A man and woman were talking, and when Dolen approached, Kratch motioned for him to stop.

"Big man," the Beneather whispered. "Sorreg talk to big man."

From the tone of its voice, Dolen knew Kratch was not a fan of whoever the "Big Man" was. Dolen crept into the shadow on the other side of the doorway and peeked out. A tall, thin, red-haired woman in a plain robe was talking to a very tall, olive-skinned man. He wore a long black beard and mustache and was mostly bald on top. His robe was similar to the woman's, but embroidered with gold sigils and runes down the front that identified him as a person of rank. Dolen listened from the shadow.

"You say they just do what they're told? Anything you tell them?" the man said.

"Yes, Prime Embalmer," the woman answered. "It seems to last hours. They say they can't help it. As soon as they're told to do something, they're just compelled. Almost like their bodies are acting on their own."

Silence for a moment. Then the man said, "Sorreg, this could be an amazing discovery. Have you tested it on the living yet?"

Dolen peered around and saw the woman shake her head. "Not yet, sir. The spore was meant as an anesthetic, and I still have hope that it may work on the living as I intended."

The man's face creased in thought. "Perhaps, perhaps." He straightened. "I will require a demonstration tomorrow morning. I'll supply both living and dead. If this works as you say, my dear, you may have changed the world forever. The names of Zarix and Sorreg will live on long after we are gone."

Dolen met the red eyes of the Beneather. He'd only known the creature a few minutes, but was already beginning to read its expressions.

Kratch didn't like the "Big Man" one bit.

— CHAPTER TWENTY-SIX —

D olen cleaned.

The animal room attached to the science lab was a mess, but Risen never tired. After the Prime Embalmer left the lab, Dolen's boss introduced herself.

"I'm Sorreg," the tall, thin woman said. "Sorry it's such a disaster. Never enough hours in the day, are there?"

She left it to Kratch to show Dolen around. The Beneather gave him a quick rundown of all the species, including which were venonous.

"Doesn't hurt dead. You safe."

The creature wasn't unfriendly, exactly. The more Dolen got used to its strange syntax, he realized it was just the way of Beneathers—or Berunfolk, as Sorreg corrected. And Kratch was a he, not an it. Sorreg looked tenuous about that last part, but Kratch didn't contradict her.

"Anyway," she finished, "just let me or Kratch know what you need. Glad to have you aboard."

Dolen took his chance.

"Actually, there's one thing I would ask," he said. "When I've got the animal room in shape, is there someone who can direct me back to the hall of records—er, the Employment Office? My wife is also Risen and was brought here years ago. If she's still here, I have to find her."

Sorreg nodded. "Sure. Tomorrow's going to be busy, but I can run you down when the demonstration is finished."

So Dolen cleaned.

Students arrived a few hours after he started. Dolen listened to Sorreg's lecture as he worked. She mentioned some herbs he knew of from the mountains, but most of it made little sense to him. He liked the way she interacted with her students, though. *I got lucky here.*

Kratch scuttled in and out of the room, checking on him and gathering supplies for whatever he was working on. Dolen's initial shock was replaced by admiration. The Berunman was strong and fearless, and Dolen got the impression from watching the creature interact with Sorreg that Kratch was a lot smarter than anyone outside Somteh would believe.

Berunfolk were supposed to be monsters. Eaters of children. Destroyers of cities. Kratch just seemed to be a strange looking person.

Dolen was asked to dispatch several of the small creatures called skeets and take one out to each student. He used a small, sharp blade, plunging it where the head met the thorax to kill the palm-sized insects quickly, and delivered them to the wide-eyed young people at the lab bench. One of the boys shuddered when he accepted the dead thing, and Dolen caught a muffled chuckle from Kratch. At least, he was pretty sure it was a chuckle. By the time the day was over, the students had dissected the creatures down to their tiny hearts, and Dolen collected the remains for incineration.

Sorreg and Kratch left for the night, but Dolen worked on, needing no sleep. A robed figure arrived sometime later, bearing a meal that Dolen happily accepted, strength surging through his muscles as his disused gut devoured the fermented fungus. He was almost out of the herbs Naren'da had given him a lifetime ago up on the mountain, but he was an Embalmer's Guild Risen now. When his skin started to lose its freshness, they'd supply more.

Dolen had always thought Embalmers just...embalmed. But the Guild here seemed to encompass all the sciences, and, to hear some of Sorreg's comments, most of the government as well. There was power within these stone halls. And ambition.

When Sorreg returned the next day, she paused in the doorway, sniffing.

"Dolen? Are you still here? The place smells great."

He smiled. "We don't sleep. Got all the cages clean, and everyone's fed and happy."

Her face clouded. "I know you don't sleep, and I think it's part of the problem. We'll need you to carry samples for the demonstration today, so...I hope I can help you. Or at least set the stage for someone else to help you next Nightfell." She paused for a moment. "To help us both, I suppose. I'll be Risen by then myself."

And it will seem like no time at all has passed.

They gathered up jars of the red dust Kratch had been working on and loaded them onto a wheeled cart. Dolen followed Kratch and Sorreg out of the lab and down to another room. The Big Man from yesterday was waiting.

"Ah, Sorreg. I was beginning to think you'd forgotten."

"I'm sorry, Prime Embalmer," she stuttered, eyes wide. "I thought this was our meeting time."

He gave a predatory smile. "No matter. We're here now, and I see you've brought another Risen for the demonstration. Excellent."

The Prime Embalmer turned to Dolen and gave him a little shove. "Right in there. We'll be with you shortly."

Sorreg started to protest, but the Prime ignored her. Dolen looked from her to Kratch, who gave a strange little shrug.

Demonstration? He didn't like the sound of that one bit. And the Big Man's tone grated on Dolen. Sorreg's whole body language was different in front of this guy, her easy confidence gone. It got Dolen's back up, but in the short time he'd been Risen, he'd already learned there was no point in protesting.

I thought I was taking care of the lab animals. Looks like I am one as well.

The Big Man scowled at Dolen. "In there," he repeated, then turned to Sorreg. "They gave you a genius, didn't they? Looks fresh, though."

I'll show you fresh. But Dolen shuffled down the thin tunnel as directed.

In the next room he found five other Risen. They all looked pretty fresh as well, though two of them had scorch marks on their skin, and one was missing an arm. Dolen took his seat beside them on one of the long benches against the walls.

Kratch closed the barred door and lowered a transparent membrane seal around the opening. The Prime Embalmer took his place just past the seal and made a gesture to Kratch.

Through a small hole in the wall that Dolen hadn't noticed came six jars of red dust. They were shoved through so that they fell and shattered on the floor. Dust filled the air.

A wave of dizziness washed over Dolen, followed by a moment of nausea. Pounding filled his head, and his lungs felt heavy as he coughed out the dust. Pressing his hand against his chest, he muttered a quick prayer to Ata Lashka, comforted by the feel of his rune necklace.

"Stand and raise your right hand."

All the Risen jumped up from the benches and held up their right hands. Dolen hurried to comply.

"Raise your left hand."

Everyone did, except Dolen and the man who didn't have one.

He felt the Prime Embalmer's eyes on him. "I said, raise your left hand."

This is stupid. But Dolen did it, and the Prime Embalmer nodded.

"Stand on one foot."

Seriously? They brought us here for a child's game? All the other Risen did as directed instantly, as if they were just waiting for the command. With a sigh, Dolen lifted a foot.

Across the seal, the Prime made another gesture, and two more jars of dust crashed into the room. Again Dolen felt the wave of dizziness, then nothing.

To the first Risen woman in line, the Prime said, "Tear off the first finger of your left hand."

As Dolen watched in shock, the Risen did it. Dark blood pooled on the floor, and the woman stared at the finger in her grip, mouth wide.

"How did that feel?"

She gaped through the barred door. "I... why did I do that? Why did you make me do that?"

A chill gripped Dolen's stomach. *Not why. How? How did he make her do that?*

"Did you want to do that?" The Prime Embalmer didn't sound remotely surprised.

"No! Of course not. But I had to."

A nod from the Prime Embalmer. To the next man in line, he said, "Rip all the hair from your head," and the man rushed to comply. Long gray hairs fluttered around the room as the man frantically pulled it from his scalp.

"Excellent," the Prime muttered. "Everyone jump up and down until I tell you to stop."

Why are they doing this? After a moment's hesitation, Dolen decided to do what he was told. He didn't want the man's eyes on him, didn't want to stand out. Whatever the dust was, it apparently affected every Risen in the room except him. He felt no compulsion to obey this man, but he'd spent the day before watching Sorreg's students dissecting skeets. He had no doubt that if he were found to be an outlier here, the bearded man in the doorway wouldn't hesitate to examine his organs one by one to find out what made him different. Dolen didn't need a stomach, but without a brain, he'd be truly dead forever. So he jumped.

"Stop."

Dolen did, an instant behind everyone else.

Air rushed into the chamber, and the Prime Embalmer disappeared from the doorway. Inside, the Risen stared down at the blood and hair on the floor.

"How do they do that?"

The man who'd pulled out his hair shook his bald, patchy head. "I don't know. I didn't want to do it, but it was like my hands moved on their own. I couldn't stop. Like I was stuck behind a wall, and something else was controlling me."

Dolen knelt to examine the dust on the floor. "It's this stuff. We made it in the lab. Some kind of spore or something. It makes us do what we're told." He looked up at the bald man. "Raise your right hand."

The man did.

Dolen nodded. "So it doesn't matter who tells us to do it. We just have to."

The barred door creaked open, and a living man stumbled inside. His arms were tied behind his back, and his ankles bound so he had to shuffle along, inch by inch. He fell to his knees, and Dolen helped him up. The living man wrenched his shoulder away from Dolen's grasp.

"Don't touch me, Rotten."

He heaved himself back onto his feet and took tiny steps over to the wall, as far away from the group of Risen as possible.

In the doorway behind the seal, a figure appeared. Its head was covered in a translucent hood through which Dolen could barely make out the long beard and mustache of the Prime Embalmer. More jars of the red spore crashed into the room, and for a long while, no one spoke.

Finally the Prime asked, "Prisoner, how do you feel?"

The living man scowled. "Feel like I'm stuck in a tomb with a bunch of dead people."

"Not tired?"

"Tired of being here."

"Prisoner, raise your right hand."

The man spat on floor. "Embalmer, go screw a Beneather."

So it didn't work on the living.

They waited another hour, with the Prime Embalmer issuing orders through the sealed door, and the Risen instantly complying. Finally the Prime addressed Dolen.

"Kill the prisoner."

Oh, Ata, no. Thoughts raced through Dolen's mind. *You have to do it, or he'll know the stuff doesn't work on you.* He walked over to the man, who was backed up against the far wall. *But you can't kill a man just because you're told to.* He reached for the man's neck. *It's a prisoner. A criminal. Probably sentenced to death for a crime. It's just. And you have to do it. It's him or you.*

Dolen grabbed the man around the throat.

Don't think. Just do it.

As the man struggled under his Risen-strong grasp, Dolen had a moment to contemplate. He could stop this right now. Smash through the bars and that transparent shield and kill the Prime Embalmer instead. *Run. Escape.*

But Rayli might still be here. The next batch of Risen in this room might include his wife. Would she be immune as he was? Or would she do whatever horrible thing that man told her to do?

Do what you have to. Find Rayli and get out of here.

He shut his eyes tight and squeezed with shaking hands until the man stopped struggling.

And a few minutes later, the man Rose, breathed in the red spore, and became an obedient slave to the Prime Embalmer behind the clear doorway shield.

— CHAPTER TWENTY-SEVEN —

Sorreg watched the horror unfold in the little test chamber. Her stomach flipped when the Risen woman ripped off her own finger without a thought. She knew they didn't feel pain, but there was so much blood. And the man pulling out all his hair was almost worse because it took so much longer—handful after handful. He plucked himself like a gillt for the stewpot, gray strands floating around the room and landing on the red-dusted floor.

The Red Spore. Her creation.

I never meant for it to do that.

But Prime Embalmer Zarix was thrilled.

"Astounding! Sorreg, your little lichen will change the Risen forever. We'll end the riots and clean up the city. All of Somteh will chant our names."

She stared past him through the thick, clear panel. "I can't believe it," she murmured.

"Believe it," he said. "As long as this dust does not affect the living, the world is about to change."

This can't be happening.

He sent for a living subject: a convicted murderer, his life forfeit to science. Sorreg shrank back as guards pushed him into the chamber. When Kratch shoved in more Red Spore jars, she silently prayed that the man would die or at least become violently ill. Something to stop this madness.

The man didn't die—not until Zarix ordered Sorreg's new Risen animal care tech to kill him.

It's not his fault. He can't help it.

She saw the horror on Dolen's face as he choked the life out of the prisoner.

Compelled. He has no choice. Did he see his hands moving like they belonged to someone else? Was he screaming inside, unable to stop himself from committing the ultimate sin against Ata Lashka? The Red Spore could make a Risen into a killer.

But that's not what it's for. It's to make them stop killing.

She caught herself echoing Zarix's thoughts. No, it wasn't to make them stop killing. She'd never meant it to control them. A sedative. It was supposed to be a sedative. Too late now. The skeets were out of the box, never to be returned. If only Zarix had never seen it...but he had. He knew.

And he was determined to make them famous.

The murdered criminal Rose, still bound. Zarix gave commands, and the man joined the others, hopping around the room. He couldn't disobey. For a brief moment, Sorreg was glad of that. He was already a prisoner, guilty of some heinous crime. With the strength of the Risen, he would have been a true danger. Now... now he was just a puppet. A strong, tireless, obedient puppet.

They filed out when the door was opened and Dolen shuffled behind Kratch, who waited in the shadows.

"Show me the lichen," Zarix demanded, and Sorreg did.

He examined it closely under the glass dome, pulling off his hood. "It grows on stone?"

She nodded. "Mirrorstone. Kratch's chemicals allow the lichen to adapt."

"And how long does the effect last?"

"A few hours. At least, that's how long it lasted for the last subjects."

Zarix squatted in front of the cart containing the specimens. "We'll need to find a way to deliver it continuously. A few hours isn't enough."

Hope flared up in Sorreg's heart. "Of course not. Maybe for a particularly difficult job, but it won't change them forever. Its uses are limited."

"Perhaps..." Zarix straightened up and addressed Kratch. "Bring this trolley to my laboratory." He turned to Sorreg. "I'll take it from here. Congratulations on your success so far." With a swirl of his gilt-edged robes, he strode out of the room.

In the shadows of the corner, Kratch and the Risen man waited.

"I'm so sorry," Sorreg said to Dolen. "I had no idea he would make you do that."

He said nothing, just staring at his hands.

"Dead weapons," Kratch said, red eyes downcast.

They truly would be. Dangerous weapons, ready to attack and kill at the whim of whoever commanded them.

"It wears off fast." She forced false brightness into her voice. "And we don't know if it's as effective in future uses. Risen might develop a tolerance to it. So many things could change. Most new medications fail at some point in their development." *Hoping your own discovery is a failure.* The scientist in her was appalled, but the human stood firm. "It won't see widespread use."

With a dragging shuffle of his feet, Kratch moved to the wheeled cart containing the lichen samples. "Take to Big Man. Change world." He squeaked away, leaving Sorreg alone with Dolen.

"I'm sorry," she repeated, but he waved her off.

"If you don't mind, I'd rather not talk about it."

She stepped back. "Of course." *The poor man must be in mental agony. And still feeling the effects of the spore.* He'd do whatever she said, so she chose her words carefully.

"Didn't you say you were looking for your wife?" *He had a life before your lab. He was a real person.* Of course she'd always known Risen were real people. She'd just never thought about their lives before. Not like this.

His head snapped up. "Yes. She was brought here from our village when we both died."

"This was just a few days ago?" Her footsteps echoed in the narrow corridor as she exited the testing area.

"No. We died at the end of last Nightfell. I just arrived here, but she would have been here the whole time." His steps behind her were quieter.

The hallway ended in a wider tunnel, well-lit with gas lanterns. Sorreg stopped and considered.

"Do you want to go down to Employment and see if we can find her?" It was the least she could do, considering how shamefully little consideration she'd given him before this moment. And she didn't want to return to her lab. Not yet.

"Please, ma'am, I would like that very much. She has to be here. She just has to be."

Sorreg turned left into the main hallway and led Dolen through the winding maze of Somteh. When they finally arrived at the Employment Contracts office, she skirted the line and approached a side desk set apart from the rest for ranking Guild members. A young man smiled at her, setting his ledgers aside.

"How can I help you, Embalmer?"

Sorreg turned to Dolen. "Who are we looking for, and when did she arrive?"

The Risen man gave a date from a hundred years ago, and Sorreg marveled again at the gift of Ata Lashka. In a hundred years, she would be just like him, reborn to continue her work. Usually the thought made her smile, or at worst, worry that science might progress so far as to make her skills useless by the time next Nightfell came. This time she wondered if her work might be best left unfinished. *If someone perfects it, makes it last...that will be me. Killing at someone else's whim. Doing whatever they tell me to do.*

The man disappeared into the back office for a while, returning with a thick book, which he laid on the table and opened. Sorreg and Dolen bent over the page he turned to.

Names were entered under the date they arrived, with later notations as to the disposition of the Risen in question as their labor was contracted. Older dates would have long entries, as Risen woke time after time—at least the lucky ones who didn't die the Final Death in the jaws of some attacking beast. That didn't happen in Somteh this time, though. *Zarix's triumph,* she reminded herself. *He's a good man.* Saved countless lives and Risen with the truce. And got her Kratch as an assistant, something no scientists before them had ever known. But—her mind shied away from the memory of his expression as the Risen woman had ripped off her own finger.

"Here we go," the man said, finger tracing down the list. "Rayli Roald."

The entry showed her being sold as a personal assistant over nine years ago to someone in the Accounting Guild. There had been no change in status until a few weeks ago, when her entry was updated to read "Out of Service."

"What does that mean?" Sorreg asked the man, dread sinking in her chest.

"Means Final Death. This one's gone."

Dolen's voice was a whisper. "How?"

The man shrugged. "Doesn't say. Might mean she burned in the riots. Maybe she messed up something bad enough that whoever owned her had her staked out to rot. Lots of reasons." He pulled the book away from Dolen's shaking hands. "Anything else I can help you with, Embalmer?"

Sorreg shook her head.

Beside her, Dolen's gray face was truly corpselike, pale and sunken.

"I'm so sorry, Dolen. We're a few weeks too late."

— CHAPTER TWENTY-EIGHT —

Dolen followed his boss through the passageways of his stone prison.

Out of Service.

That was the entry for the end of Rayli's life.

Because that's all we are. Servants. Slaves to the living, compelled to do their bidding, no matter how depraved.

And he'd only missed her by a few weeks. What had happened? Someone in the Accounting Guild had owned her for nine years, and then one day, Out of Service. Just like that. He knew Rayli. She wouldn't have done anything to get herself punished with Final Death. Whispers of Risen riots here had reached his holding cell, but she wouldn't have been part of that.

Would she?

Dolen had been Risen for a few weeks. His rebirth had happened right around the time of Rayli's Final Death. And he hated it. What should have been a joyful service, giving his body to the defense of the living as his gods commanded, had become a desolate slavery. What he had been in life didn't matter—only what he could give in death.

But that was unfair, wasn't it? Sorreg had been a fine employer so far. She'd chosen him because he'd been a rancher and he understood animals. *And she created the dust that makes us into obedient zombies.* It was clear from her reaction that hadn't been her intention. All the same, she was responsible. The Prime Embalmer was right—it would change the world forever if they figured out how to make the effect last.

As he thought about it, a tiny part of him was relieved that Rayli was gone. That she would never have to endure the red dust, to feel her control taken by someone else. She'd never have to watch her hands do something horrible and be powerless to stop it. Rayli had done her service and gone on to Ata Lashka. She wouldn't know what Dolen had done this morning. She would never be a pawn of the living, dancing for someone's whim. It would have to be enough.

But I know.

His thoughts churned as he climbed the stairs behind Sorreg, who had mercifully stopped apologizing. Dolen was a murderer. It didn't matter that the man he killed was a criminal. Didn't matter that he'd had no choice but to comply as if the dust worked on him the way it worked on everyone else. He'd done it to avoid dissection or worse. *And if you'd known then that Rayli was gone?* He pushed the thought away. Nothing mattered now.

Sorreg stopped at the top of the stairwell that led to the floor with her laboratory. The landing gave a clear view up and down, and no one else was in earshot.

"Listen, Dolen, I know you're still feeling the effects of the Red Spore. But I want you to know that I intend to stop this from going any further. I don't have a plan yet, but Prime Embalmer Zarix has the lichen in his laboratory. I don't have access to get in and destroy it, but I'll find a way. This is my fault, and I have to fix it. Will you help me?"

"Of course," Dolen answered immediately, but Sorreg shook her head.

"No, I said that wrong. You had to say yes." She took a deep breath. "Do you want, of your own accord, to help me?"

She thinks it's the spore. "Yes. I do want to help you. This spore is—an abomination."

With a relieved sigh, Sorreg pushed through the door from the stairwell. Halfway down, they ran into Kratch, who blinked at Dolen.

"Big Man ask for dead man. This one dead. Go to lab now."

Sorreg frowned. "The Prime Embalmer wants Dolen? Why?"

Kratch gave his strange, wiggly shrug. "No one tells Kratch."

The Prime Embalmer's lab. Where the Red Spore had been taken, or at least Dolen hoped so. "Someone tell me how to get there, and I'll see what's going on." He gave Sorreg a pointed look, which she appeared to understand.

As he climbed the stairs to the next level where the Prime Embalmer's labs were housed, Dolen considered the timing. How long had it been since the spore test that morning? Should he still be obedient? He decided to err on the side of caution and pretend it was still working.

The Prime Embalmer's labs were huge. Taking up five times the space of Sorreg's lab one floor below, the place was a hive of activity. Dolen stopped in the open doorway, checking out the lock. He knew nothing about lock picking, but the door itself would surely give way to the strength of a Risen. He could break in if he wanted to, but the damage would be obvious. If Sorreg wanted stealth to destroy the spore, they might need help.

"You dead from morning?"

Dolen looked into the face of another Berunfolk. At first glance he thought it was Kratch, but the voice was slightly higher, and the structure of the jaw wasn't quite the same. This one wore the same kind of hooded robe as Kratch, but the sigil on the shoulder was embroidered in gold and bore the Atamonen Eye symbol. Clearly a higher rank of Beneather.

"I don't understand what you're asking."

The creature sighed. "You from Sorreg?"

"Yes."

A nod, and Dolen was escorted through the busy front room. They passed long tables full of glassware and specimens Dolen didn't recognize, with robed scientists bent over charts. Groups of two and three huddled together, pointing at plants and dead animals, and, in one alarming case, a live creature suspended by hooks from the ceiling, twitching as its belly was slit open. It made no sound, but its mouth gaped open, soft skin rippling. A yellow light dangled from a hornlike appendage on its forehead, and as Dolen stared, the light grew dimmer and dimmer, and finally winked out.

"Here. Go."

Dolen followed the Berunfolk's direction, walking down a long hallway from the back of the lab. Windows opened into other rooms, and Dolen looked inside each one as he plodded on. Some were dark, but most contained more scientists crowded around tables or pointing at writing Dolen couldn't make out. The last three windows showed the feet and legs of a human lying face-down on a table, with two scientists leaning over the torso and head.

He rounded a corner and stopped behind two other Risen who waited outside a closed door. No one spoke, and Dolen asked no questions.

One by one, the people in front of him were allowed through the door.

Dolen's heart raced, pulse throbbing in his temples. *They know. They're going to cut me apart to find out why I'm different.*

The door opened, and a Berunfolk motioned him inside.

Another corridor. Another door.

Dolen entered one of the rooms he had passed in the other hallway. A window looked out where he had peered in as he passed. Two robed doctors waited next to a table.

"Lie down on your stomach."

Dolen hesitated, staring at a tray of instruments next to the table. Sharp tools. Suture and needles.

One of the doctors frowned and opened a small jar, wafting Red Spore right into Dolen's face.

"Strip to the waist and lie down on your stomach."

They didn't know he was immune. Was that better or worse?

He removed his shirt and Ata Lashka amulet, folding them on the side bench, and lay down on the table. The dizzy feeling increased. It seemed like a wide, dark curtain enfolded his brain from the outside, smothering him until he stood in a tiny corner, buffered from the world by hazy blackness.

"Lie still and stop breathing."

He did it without thinking.

Dolen felt tiny stings from the razor that shaved a spot on the back of his head. He felt the slice of the blade that opened that shorn skin. He felt the drill that ate a round hole in the back of his skull. But they had told him to lie still, so he did.

Oh, sweet gods. Whatever they're doing is working. I'm not immune. I'm one of them.

"Careful. Not too much," one of the doctors said. "Just enough to live in the bone."

Something slimy was wiped into Dolen's skull, and a needle bit his skin, suturing over the hole.

"It's brilliant," the other doctor said as she stitched. "The lichen lives on bone. It's a constant supply of the spore straight into their brains. Truly, we are blessed to have Prime Embalmer Zarix. He's a genius."

They implanted the lichen right into my skull. They'll do it for every Risen they Embalm. Dolen had to admit, it truly was genius. Evil, horrible, terrifying genius. And Sorreg would weep when he told her.

"Sit up. You may breathe."

Dolen did as asked, his limbs moving automatically. The slight vertigo of the spore waved through his brain, clouding him behind the wall of obedience.

"Raise your right hand."

He watched it lift.

The doctors nodded. "You may dress and return to your work."

Despair weighed Dolen's shoulders as he stood up. *There is no Dolen now. I'm a living tool. I'm in here, but I'm nothing. Just a body that does what it's told.*

He wasn't sure of the spore's limits. They had told him to return to his work, and the compulsion moved his hands. Would that command last forever? Could he do anything else? Inside the shimmering dark cloud, Dolen screamed for fire, for a blazing pyre to throw himself onto, burning this contaminated body and releasing him to his gods, where Rayli must surely wait for him. But no one had told him to burn himself. He knew without trying that he would walk right past such a pyre unless ordered to throw himself in.

His shirt scraped over the new sutures on his scalp as he pulled it over his head, and he dropped the long leather thong with the wide, smooth disk bearing the Eye of Ata Lashka around his neck. He tucked it under his shirt, its mirrored surface laying cool on his skin.

Back to work. He had to get back to the lab.

He left the horrible room and retraced his steps, feeling the need to return to Sorreg's lab as a deep hunger inside him.

At the large hallway junction, he tried to turn left, away from the lab, instead of right, but his feet felt like they belonged to someone else, and marched him steadily down the corridor. *You're theirs now. You'll do anything they say.* He shook with rage, but continued. *Back to work. Back to work.* He could do nothing else.

The shadow of the compulsion hung over him like a thick fog. With every step he took, he fought it, struggling against the dust's power.

Walk slower.

He shuffled his feet against the stone floor, a tiny rebellion against the command. With a spark of joy, he realized it was working. *Slower.* With all his will, he made himself stop, standing in the middle of the hallway, hands clenched into fists. Like a man walking through a thick swamp, he turned around, forcing his legs to take a few steps back down the hall.

I don't have to go back to work. I can fight it.

He gritted his teeth, taking deep breaths. With every passing moment, the effect drifted away like smoke pulled up a chimney until he felt in control again.

Finally the dark fog lifted from his brain. He was aware of the lichen still living in his skull, felt it pulsing with the shimmer of obedience.

His shoulders sagged with relief.

I am immune. It was harder with the lichen inside him, but whatever power he had over the spore had reasserted itself. The need to return to work as he'd been commanded was gone. He had no idea why the spore didn't work on him, and he considered the thought as he plodded down the hall past a line of Risen who had no idea what awaited them when it was their turn in the operating room. What was different about him, compared to all the others here?

He'd been frozen for almost a century. Had that changed his brain? It didn't feel different. Since he'd gotten used to the strange hollowness of his senses, he'd felt like the same old Dolen as he'd always been. *But how would you know if you felt different?* He wasn't sure. Could it be Naren'da's herbs? A spike of fear drove into his stomach at that thought. He was almost out of them. Working for the Embalmer's Guild, he hadn't been worried about it—they would see to his preservation. Despite everything he'd witnessed and been subjected to, he still assumed they would take care of his body. Can't let your obedient, living zombies rot away. Did they use the same herbs here? People seemed to marvel at how good he looked, and he could tell his skin was softer and more lifelike than most of the other Risen he'd seen. Until this moment, he had assumed it was because they were longer dead than he was, but perhaps Naren'da had something special? Something that made him immune?

And when he finally ran out, would he succumb to the Red Spore like everyone else?

— CHAPTER TWENTY-NINE —

R ayli rushed at Scar and grabbed her right arm. Dropping
to her knees in front of her sparring partner, Rayli shoved
with her shoulder and pulled on Scar's arm, knocking her
opponent's feet out from under her and flipping her over the top
of her back. She landed and tried to roll away, but Rayli kept the
hold on her arm and threw her leg over Scar's torso, wrenching her
shoulder around behind her.

"Great job," Rock said. "When it's for real, keep pulling to the
side. If it's somebody little, you might be able to wrench the arm
right off, especially if it's a replacement. If not, at least you can hold
them down while one of us gets to you."

She hopped off Scar, and they both got to their feet.

Heart pumping, she brushed the sand from her knees. Clan
Tornado had a small practice room, and all around her the other
gladiators rolled and flipped, honing their skills. She smiled,
watching Carrol duck under a heavy punch thrown by one of the
bigger men. Rayli's former boss had been slower to adapt to their
new circumstances, but they were both trying to see the bright
side of death. They were stronger than they'd ever been in life.
Rayli could swear she got stronger every day. Faster, too, and more
coordinated. Maybe that was just the training. The skills they were
learning would keep them around through this Nightfell, Ata
willing, and hopefully serve them well the next time they Rose,

when the world might be a different, less bloodthirsty place. So much could change in a century. Surely next time they wouldn't be made to fight for the entertainment of others. Risen fought the monsters of Nightfell. Next time she'd be ready.

A high-pitched whistle split the air, and everyone stopped, heads swiveling toward the entrance.

Blubberlips stood in the doorway. He had a name, but Rayli hadn't bothered to remember it.

"Gladiators, listen." He smiled and stepped aside to reveal a man in Embalmer robes behind him. "It's time for your renewal treatment."

Rayli looked down at her hands, permanently stained red from the dye she wore in combat, her trademark. The herbal cream she rubbed on her skin every day worked well. While nothing could take away the gray cast of death, she wasn't flaky or squishy. No rot inside, either, thanks to the foul-tasting brew she drank once a week. It wasn't time for a full renewal, the monthly soak in a steaming tub of chemicals, was it? Had it been a whole month?

They lined up and followed Blubberlips and the Embalmer down the dim corridor, past the grisly, anguished heads lining the shelves, and queued up outside the medical chamber. Carrol stood behind her, and Rayli smiled at the older woman.

"You looked really good doing that heel hook. If you got your legs locked, I bet you could flip a skitter with that move."

Carrol grinned back. "It feels great to take somebody down like that, I have to admit." She straightened up with the praise. "Every new move I learn makes me feel more confident."

Torchlight threw long shadows as they waited, inching forward. Whatever treatment they were getting today, it didn't seem to take very long.

A new guy stood in front of Rayli, rubbing a tear in the skin of his forearm. He turned back to the women with a timid glance, holding out his arm. "Do you think they'll fix this for me?"

He was young, barely in his teens, and Rayli's heart broke for the kid. Death wasn't forever, but this was as old as he'd ever get.

"Of course," she said, examining the wound. "They make a fortune off us. Gotta keep us in top fighting shape."

They certainly were fed well, two meals a day of either meat from an arena kill or a thick, tasty stew with leathery mushrooms.

The kid leaned in and whispered, "Who's 'they'?" He didn't even have his Tornado tattoo yet.

Rayli caught a slight whiff of decay in his breath and reassessed him. He'd died young, but this kid had been dead a long time. He was probably older than her, if you counted Risen time. "I'm honestly not sure," she said as they moved a few steps closer to the medical room. "But the crowds we draw are huge. Somebody's making a fortune." And she'd become a draw, a crowd favorite. They chanted for her when she entered the arena. "Red" had quickly risen through the Clan Tornado hierarchy, such as it was. The thought gave her hope. *I'm worth a lot.* That had to count for something.

"What's your name?" she asked the kid.

"Tod."

"Next!" came the call from inside, and Tod ducked into the room, leaving Carrol and Rayli in the hall.

Carrol leaned against the cool, smooth stone wall. "Are you fighting tonight?"

Rayli shrugged. She never knew when the call would come, but she'd been idle for three nights now as other clans took the arena. The sounds of battle, of screaming crowds and roaring beasts echoed down every corridor. "Probably, but who knows? Not like I have a day planner." That had been one of her many jobs when she'd worked for Carrol: keeping track of the accountant's schedule.

An odd smell came from the room. New herbs? It didn't smell bad, whatever it was.

After a few minutes, Tod walked out. His torn arm hadn't been stitched.

"Oh, they didn't fix it?"

He turned to her with a glazed look on his face, then glanced down at his arm. "No. But I'm fine. I'm satisfied." It was an odd thing to say. He walked down the hall past the women, and Rayli entered the room when "Next" was called.

When it was over, she couldn't have said how long it took. They gave her a jar to sniff, and she inhaled sweet-scented red dust that tickled her throat. A cloud descended around her mind, and she blinked. They told her to lie face down on the table, and she couldn't comply fast enough. She held still while they parted her red-stained hair and drilled into the back of her skull, smearing something inside the bone. It felt cool and somehow carried that same sweet smell, as if she could tell its scent right through her brain. The pain meant nothing. The sutures in her skin over the new wound also meant nothing.

"Stand up, Red."

She leapt to her feet.

"You may return to the training room." Her feet flew down the hall, not pausing when Carrol called her name as she raced by.

From inside her own head, Rayli trembled, fighting the dark fog that enveloped her. She could feel her legs obeying, trotting to the sandy practice arena. *Of course I want to go train more. I love training.* But this didn't feel right. Shadows pooled in her mind.

"Line up along the wall, and do not speak." Blubberlips pointed to a spot next to Tod, and she hurried over next to the kid.

She wanted to ask him if he was all right and why they hadn't stitched his arm, but Blubberlips had said not to talk.

What's happening to me? Just ask him.

Her lips didn't move. She stood there, back to the wall.

Oh, sweet gods. Why can't I talk? Panic swelled inside her, battering against the shadow, but her legs were stone, rooted to the floor. *He's controlling me somehow. From inside my head.*

She waited there until the rest of her clan was assembled and the Embalmer returned.

"Go ahead, see for yourself," he said to Blubberlips, whose eyes turned to Rayli.

"Red, step forward."

Her feet moved on their own. Inside, Rayli cursed.

"Tod, step forward."

Blubberlips glanced around. "Rock, hand Red a knife."

Her hand reached out to take the blade. No tremble showed the raging fire inside her as her fingers closed around the handle. Blubberlips smiled. "Tod, stand still. Red, cut Tod's head off." The kid just stood there. No panic filled his eyes, but as Rayli watched her hand raise the blade, she knew he must be screaming inside, silent in his terror.

Her hands moved on their own, obeying the command. Rayli was helpless to stop her body from doing what she was told. The shadows in her mind made her grip the blade tighter and raise it to Tod's neck.

She sliced his neck and blood fountained up from the wound, pouring down over his chest. He stood rock-still as she sawed at the muscles and tendons with the dull blade.

Sweet, Ata, no. Please, please no.

But the shadows flowed around her, trapping her inside as she hacked away the spine until Tod's body flopped on the ground and she held his dripping head by the hair.

"Excellent work, Red. You may drop the knife and the head."

She did, and Tod's face rolled in the sand, coming to rest against her foot. Inside she fought down the mental urge to vomit, though her body felt no nausea. *No one told me to throw up.*

Blubberlips turned to the Embalmer. "I wouldn't have believed it. You spoke true, sir. How long does the effect last?"

A tiny speck of hope clawed at the shadows. *Not forever. Not forever.*

"We don't know yet," the Embalmer said with a small shrug. "That's part of what this larger group is intended to help us determine. The lichen should grow on the bone of the skull and become a permanent supply of the spore straight to the brain. The Risen should be obedient as long as the lichen lives. At least, that's the hope."

Hope.

Rayli looked at the head of the kid she'd just met, the severed thing that would slowly rot on a shelf, delivered by her obedient hands.

Clan Tornado had purchased her labor and used it for entertainment. Now her bloody hands truly belonged to them. She'd be obedient as long as the lichen lived.

Inside she screamed and screamed as her body stood quietly, hands sticky with blood.

— CHAPTER THIRTY —

Sorreg sat at the head table, at the right hand of Prime Embalmer Zarix. This conclave had been hastily called. Every discipline of science was represented. All the Senior Embalmers filled the private dining room, chairs turned to face their leader, and Sorreg's face flushed under their gazes. Supportive smiles came from some of her colleagues...and envious scowls from others.

I don't want to be here any more than you do, she silently told the polite audience. Any hope she'd had of keeping the Red Dust quiet had evaporated when Zarix called the conclave. In moments, every scientist in Somteh would know the horror she'd unleashed on the Risen.

Zarix stood, and the room fell silent.

"My dear, esteemed colleagues, thank you for coming on such short notice."

As if anyone had a choice.

"I'm thrilled to share exciting news, a scientific breakthrough that will change the world as we know it." He aimed a full-toothed smile at Sorreg. "Senior Embalmer Sorreg from Medical Research has made an astounding discovery, and I have taken her preliminary work to another level of genius."

Excellent. Please, take all the credit. I don't want my name on this atrocity. She glanced to the back of the room where Risen servants stood at attention. *I'm so sorry. I never intended this for you.*

Every eye in the room was fixed on Zarix as he spoke, candles on the long table beneath him casting strange shadows upward on his angular face.

"The Risen in our fine city have gone unchecked for far too long. Their strength gives them courage, and they riot in the corridors. They destroy our livelihoods, terrorize our citizens, and even kill to add to their numbers." His eyes narrowed. "But no more."

Around the room, no one moved. Zarix held them all in his powerful hands.

"Senior Embalmer Sorreg developed a lichen that emits a spore which, when inhaled by a Risen, makes them compliant and obedient to commands. I witnessed this astounding phenomenon and immediately set to work. By implanting the lichen directly into the skulls of the Risen, they receive a constant, permanent supply of the compound. Instead of a hoard of thugs, we shall have the obedient workforce that Ata Lashka always intended. Those of you in the Preservation sciences will immediately amend your rituals to include this procedure, in the name of the Atamonen who have guided us to this magnificent accomplishment."

Sorreg held her breath, scanning the faces of the crowd. She had no close friends among the Seniors, but the few she was closest to blinked in confusion, looking from Zarix to her. She couldn't meet their eyes. *I know. It's horrible. I never, ever meant this.* But many of the faces shared Zarix's elation.

She wanted to stand up and scream, "Don't you understand this is wrong? They are dead, but they're still human! And if you don't care a skeet's bottom for them, think of yourselves. Next Nightfell, you'll be among them, complacent zombies bent to your master's will!" But she held her tongue. No one spoke in a conclave unless recognized by Zarix. And even if she had screamed it, they wouldn't have understood. They hadn't seen the spore in action.

They would.

"The lichen grows quickly on its preferred substrate," Zarix continued, "and our stock increases by the hour. Tomorrow morning, samples will be sent to Kamteh and all the other major cities on the continent, with instructions for the addition to the embalming ritual. And cultures of the lichen will be installed inside the very walls of our fine city, growing on their own to deliver the spore to every Risen in Somteh. This will ensure peace and safety for all until every Risen can be imbued with the actual growth." He glanced down at Sorreg next to him, and she kept her face still as stone.

Oh, sweet Atamonen. Tomorrow morning. Her dinner churned in her stomach. Until this meeting, she'd held out hope that this horror might be confined to Somteh, and maybe even be lost by the time another ninety years passed. But Zarix thought of everything. Growing it in the ventilation system so every Risen in the city would breathe it in without knowing. *And that's why he's Prime.*

He held up his hands as a murmuring zipped through the scientists. "I know you must be worried, though, about all those who perish and Rise outside our walls. Those who will lack our ministrations, forced to endure the indignity of substandard embalming, or rot from its lack. How will they receive this new blessing?"

She held back a shudder, hardly believing how it kept getting worse.

"Along with the samples heading out to the cities, we will also send forces to spread the lichen to all corners of the natural world. It's hardy and grows on stone as well as human bone. Once it takes hold, the winds of Ert will carry it everywhere. No matter where one dies, the Red Spore will be there to calm the mind and pacify the soul as soon as the dead Rise again."

"Oh, Atamon..." Sorreg murmured, freezing into silence as Zarix's head whipped around to stare at her.

He smiled again, the predatory grin. "Atamonen, indeed, my dear." He chuckled, and the room chuckled with him, though they certainly had no idea what was funny. "I can see that you're overwhelmed, and who could blame you? Your little discovery in my hands has become so much more than you ever dreamed. Truly, you and I are the saviors of humanity." He turned back to the group. "No more fighting. No more looking over your shoulder as you slink through the hallways, hoping a gray-faced terrorist isn't following your steps. No more huddling in fear in your rooms as the fires burn and the Risen, who should be our protectors, loot our city. The ancient contract given to us by Ata Lashka is restored. The dead serve the living, and the living preserve the dead. So it has always been, and so shall it ever be."

The room erupted in applause.

Zarix sat and leaned over to Sorreg. "Look at them," he murmured. "They love you. You've saved us all, my dear Sorreg. And no one will ever forget it."

— CHAPTER THIRTY-ONE —

Dolen heard the lab's outer door open over the quiet scratching of the lab animals in their cages. He stood just inside the doorway to the animal room, peering around the frame. No one should've been in there at that hour.

"Dolen, are you here?" Sorreg's quiet voice echoed across the lab. He stepped out of the shadows. "I'm here."

She scuttled in, pushing the door closed behind her and glancing all around. "Are you alone?"

No, I'm hosting a dead person dinner party back here.

"Just me and the animals."

Her shoulders relaxed, but tension still cramped her features. "Good. Dolen," she began, "I know you got the lichen today. I'm so very sorry. You have to know I never ever meant to create something so horrible. I should have known better than to share it with anyone. Should have burned it the moment I realized it wasn't what I intended."

Dolen hadn't yet told her he was immune. She seemed sincerely regretful, but she was a scientist. As soon as he let on that he was special, she wouldn't have any choice. The regret for making it, if that were sincere, would force her to do whatever she had to do in order to figure out what made Dolen different. Cut him open. Drain his blood. Who knew what she might do in her need to find out what kept the slimy growth from working on him?

"It's disgusting," she continued. "It was never supposed to make you into slaves. All of you." Her eyes unfocused for a second. "All of us."

Ah, there it was. *Us.* Sorreg had seen the future. Her future as a Risen the next time it came around. He could hardly blame her. The moments of control he'd felt when the dark shadow had enveloped his mind until his system overcame its dreadful power...no one would want it. She had no idea.

"I understand. You couldn't have known." *You still don't.*

She sagged onto one of the stools. "And it's so much worse than I thought. Zarix has it. He's growing it and sending it out to the other cities tomorrow. He's going to make it part of the embalming ritual so all the Risen get it forever. His students have already started seeding it into our ventilation and releasing it to grow all over the world. Risen will never be free again."

For a brief moment, Dolen thanked the Atamonen that Rayli was truly dead. The thought of her in the grip of that control made his gray heart skip in his chest. Better she rest in the arms of the Atamonen.

"We have to destroy it."

Dolen's ears perked up.

"It's in Prime Zarix's lab somewhere. We have to do it tonight, and we need to destroy it all. He doesn't know how I made it." She paused. "Honestly, I'm not sure, either. Kratch made the change. Opened it to affect the Risen. I'm not even sure he knows for sure how it happened." Her eyes looked down the row of tables. "It grew first on the mirrorstone, but then..." She shook herself. "It doesn't matter. We're going to destroy it, and I'll make sure that it's never made again."

Dolen nodded. "We have to destroy it tonight."

The stool squeaked as Sorreg stood. "I knew you would understand. The lab should be empty this time of night, but there's still risk, more to my career than to you, but..." She peered at him. "Oh, Ata. Look what I just did. Of course you agree. Of course you'll go. You've got the rotting spore in your head. You can't possibly decline."

For a moment, he considered telling her the truth.

"Dolen," she said, "please look at me."

He met her stare.

"I want you to think about what you actually want. Ignore that I told you what to do. I want you to think about what you truly want, if you truly wish to help me with this tonight. Can you do that?"

She thinks I'm stupid. He nodded.

"Okay," she said, shoulders tense again. "Dolen, tell me the truth. Do you want to enter Zarix's lab and destroy the spore?"

He nodded again.

"Excellent." She relaxed. "From now on, I want you to think on your own. Treat everything I say as an option to consider. Not a command. Can you do that?"

"I can do that. The spore doesn't affect my thinking, just my actions."

Her face twisted for a moment, realizing the horror of the statement. "I'm sorry," she repeated.

Dolen turned and re-entered the animal room. He grabbed a large shovel and a small tool kit Kratch had showed him. "I hope I won't need the shovel, but we might need the tools. Are we bashing down the door or just destroying the lock?"

She blinked at him. "I... I hadn't thought about it." The gaslights on the wall were dim, but Dolen could see tears glittering in her eyes. "I have no idea. We'll need a cart, maybe. To bring it all back here."

"No." Dolen nodded toward the back of the animal room. "There's a chute straight down from here to the incinerators in the lowest level. Waste disposal. There's bound to be one in his lab, too. We just have to find it and dump all the samples straight down. They'll be cooked before we leave the lab."

He remembered Kratch pointing it out during his orientation. "Fire below. Don't fall in." The chute wasn't nearly big enough for

Dolen to fit inside, and with a start, he'd realized the Beneather was making a joke. "Should we get Kratch, too?"

Sorreg shook her head. "If this goes south, I don't want him involved."

This gave Dolen a moment's pause. Sorreg honestly seemed concerned for the Beneather. They crept out of the lab and down the hall. Dolen remembered the way he'd come earlier in the day, sutures in his head scratching when he moved his neck. Up the stairs. They peered around every corner, but the gaslights were dimmed, and no one roamed the halls. At the entrance to the Big Man's lab, they stopped. A sign on the closed door read, "Prime Embalmer." Nothing indicated the sinister contents that lay behind it.

Sorreg kept watch while Dolen peered at the lock.

"I don't know how to pick locks so you can't tell it was done."

She shrugged. "Doesn't matter. He'll know someone was in here when he sees all the cultures gone. As long as he doesn't know it was me, it won't matter."

"You don't think he'll know?"

Her jaw clenched. "He announced it to forty other scientists tonight. Any one of them could think my 'wonderful discovery' is something the world doesn't need."

The lock looked simple enough, just a bolt thrown from the door into the frame.

Time for some Risen strength.

The lock groaned as Dolen leaned into the door, planting his boots on the floor and throwing his shoulder into the wood. After three tries, the bolt broke free and the door flew open, spilling him into the dimly lit room.

Sorreg followed, shooting past him after closing the door. It didn't latch and swung right back open. Dolen grabbed a bench stool and set it in front of the door to keep it closed.

"All right," Sorreg said. "Let's find the spore, destroy it, and get out of here."

She headed for the back of the huge room where specimens sat under glass domes, just like in her own lab. They wouldn't all be the Red Spore lichen, but its brown growth was distinctive. "Find the disposal chute," she said to Dolen. "I'll start lining up the right ones."

He searched along the back wall. A long line of leathery, oblong eggs lay on one of the benches. Each was as long as his forearm, pale green in color, and very slightly translucent. Small tags identified each with a date and words Dolen didn't recognize. They gave off a faint odor—sour, like some of the animals he cared for.

The disposal chute was helpfully labeled.

"Found it," he called to Sorreg. "Did you find the lichen?"

She hurried over with the first domed specimen in hand. "There are so many. We need to be quick."

With a hiss of gas, the lights in the room brightened to full force, and the voice of Zarix boomed across the lab.

"Not quick enough, my dear. Not quick enough."

— CHAPTER THIRTY-TWO —

Rayli stood in the middle of the arena, arm held high with its grisly burden, weeping inside.

All around her, the crowd chanted, "Red! Red! Red!"

Please, Ata Lashka. Just let me die.

But she was already dead, inside now as well as outside.

It was supposed to be a "Two-Limb" fight. When clans of gladiators fought each other before their screaming fans, a fighter was defeated when two of their limbs were removed. Left to bleed while the battle finished, they would wait for one clan to triumph, and be carted off to get replacement arms or legs attached. No gladiator would desecrate another further than this: a downed warrior was out of the fight.

Everything changed with the surgery.

They hadn't even closed her cell door after the horrifying demonstration of its power. Whatever they had put in her skull made her a slave. Her body instantly obeyed any command. They told her to stay in her cell, so that's what she did. Inside she raged, willing her legs to carry her through the open door, but no thoughts reached her muscles. She could bash her fists into the stone walls and scream until she was hoarse, but she could not pass through the doorway.

And when they told her to kill, she knew Clan Tornado and its star fighter, Red, were lost forever.

Blubberlips had called the fighters together before the battle. Rayli, Scar, Rock, and another man called Backhand obediently stood before their owner.

"You're fighting Clan Star tonight," he said, looking over his property. "They're brutes. Big and tough, but slow." He shrugged. "Whatever happens, I win. I bet on them, so if you lose, I'm a bit richer. And if you don't lose, I don't have to get new fighters. It's good to be me."

The grinding of her teeth was loud in Rayli's ears. *I'll kill him myself.* But of course she wouldn't. She'd do whatever he told her to do. And he knew it.

He paused before her and adjusted the leather straps that served as her only clothing. His hands were soft and sweaty, and his fingers lingered where they shouldn't have. A delighted grin lit his features. "I do hope you survive, though. I surely do."

Kill him. Kill him now. She stood stock-still, seething.

"Aw, smile for me, Red. You're my little warrior, aren't you?"

Her lips turned up, and she felt her eyes crinkle. Inside, she pictured her hands around his neck, squeezing and squeezing with Risen strength.

Blubberlips stepped back and nodded at his fighters. "Here's the thing: the rules have changed. Tonight you give no quarter. You fight until they are all destroyed. Decapitate them or crush their heads. Blade through the eye. Whatever works. It's Final Death for any defeated gladiator. You may discuss your strategy as needed to succeed and help each other in the arena. Do you understand? Say yes if you understand."

They all answered.

"Kill them all, or die trying," he said. "What are you going to do?"

As one, they repeated, "Kill them all, or die trying."

And they did.

They walked out into the arena, Rayli's red dye sticky on her body. Blubberlips had applied it himself, gleefully finger painting on her skin.

She couldn't even die on purpose. She would fight with every ounce of skill she'd learned because that's what she'd been told to do.

Clan Star was, indeed, a group of big brutes. When they entered the arena, she eyed them across the sand. Three men and one woman, all as big as Rock. They wore leather, like Tornado, and collars studded with chitin spikes. Every inch of their exposed flesh was tattooed with stars. Weapons lay all around the space, and Rock had whispered to her not to take them for granted.

"Some of them will be good and sharp," he said, "and others will snap as soon as they touch skin."

The crowds would love that.

She lined up between Rock and Backhand, with Scar right behind them. A whistle signaled the start of the battle. Bodies blurred as everyone raced for a weapon. Rayli grabbed a short sword, holding it by the handle and testing the blade. It broke clean off in her hand, leaving her with a useless grip and a sharp blade without a hilt; it would slice her fingers off if she gripped it tight enough to use.

Movement to her left jerked her gaze around. One of the huge, tattooed Star men raced toward her, knife over his head.

She reacted automatically, dropping the broken weapon and leaping to the right. As he swung the knife toward her, she grabbed his wrist with one hand and his collar with the other. She charged into him with her shoulders to break his balance, then quickly turned, and as she slid to her knees in front of him, she tripped him with her body and used his momentum to flip him over her shoulder. He landed in the sand with a whoosh of breath, and the crowd went wild.

They're big. But we're fast. And skilled.

She jumped on top of him, crouching across his neck and wrapping his shoulder up against her body, wrenching his shoulder back to rip the tendons, but the man was a beast and knocked her sprawling. He lunged at her on his knees, still gripping the knife. Rayli ducked its swing, stepped on his leading thigh, and launched herself over the back of his arm, driving a knee into his throat as she tumbled across his shoulder. She hit the sand and rolled away, leaping to her feet as he collapsed onto his back. Blood flowed from gashes in her knee where his collar had ripped her skin. The throat blow would have killed a living man, but Risen didn't need to breathe. In a second he was up again, eyes full of rage.

You're not my enemy, she wanted to scream. *We don't have to do this.*

But of course they did. The slimy stuff in their skulls commanded them.

He came for her again.

Time for the tornado.

Rayli and Rock had worked on the clan's signature move for weeks. She had mastered a half rotation, but this guy wouldn't go down with a half. Time to go for it.

She launched herself at the Star brute's chest, using her arm against his shoulder to whip her legs up, wrapping them around his neck. She locked her ankles together as her momentum spun her around a full turn, until she dropped her hip. The spin flipped the man underneath her into a front roll as her feet touched down on the sand, and he flopped onto his back, her thighs still locked around his neck. The spikes on his collar shredded her skin, breaking off and embedding into the muscle, and she pushed the pain away from her thoughts. *Kill, or die trying.*

Risen didn't need to breathe. And they could survive for a while without blood flow to their brains. But a solid choke would eventually rob them of enough strength to move.

Rayli squeezed her thighs together as she held down her opponent's arm with her body, the two of them lying perpendicular on the ground, locked in struggle. The man bucked and fought, pressing up with his legs, beating at her with an arm over his head. He grabbed her ankles and pulled, trying to break her shins. Agony flared up to her hips, but she ignored it in the way of the Risen. Slowly his grip weakened. She pulled back on his arm pinned underneath her, trying to break the elbow, but the joint wouldn't give. He had shoved them halfway across the sand, and she was dimly aware of fighting all around her, but at this moment, nothing mattered except the throat between her legs.

A knife lay just within reach. She grabbed it and released her hold, swinging her body around before the man regained his strength.

The blade bit into his throat, blood boiling onto the golden surface below.

Just cut. You've done it before. As if she could have done anything else.

Kill, or die trying.

The blade broke before his head was completely severed, so she had to rip the vertebrae apart to finish the job. When it gave way, she flung it across the arena.

One down.

But when she looked up, three were down.

Scar staggered away from her opponent's lifeless body with a huge, gaping wound from her shoulder through her torso. She held it closed so her guts didn't spill onto the ground.

Backhand lay in a tangle of limbs with one of the Clan Star men. A leg and an arm twitched, but neither of them were getting up on their own.

And across the arena, Rock was locked in combat with the Star woman.

Rayli raced over to Scar, still holding the broken blade she'd used to decapitate her opponent. When she reached her dazed friend, she took a deep breath.

"Hold still. This is going to hurt."

She pulled the skin and muscle of Scar's belly away from the writhing guts inside and plunged the knife through both sides of the wound, pinning it closed with the blade. Pink, wriggling tubes still bulged around the sides, but nothing was spilling out.

"Check Backhand, and finish the other guy if you need to," Rayli told her. "I'm going to help Rock."

The woman had him pinned down and whaled on his face with her fists. Rayli slammed into her from the side, knocking her off, and they rolled across the ground. The woman was quicker than she looked and was on Rayli in a flash.

All the weapons were out of reach.

But a Lightshaper didn't need one.

She summoned the power of Ata Runi, grasping for the light of the distant torches she could shape into fire.

Nothing.

The woman wrapped her star-tattooed hands around Rayli's neck.

Rayli had never been a powerful Lightshaper, but the power had been there since before she could remember. The darkness around her mind that made her an obedient slave closed in around her when she reached for the place inside her soul where the light lived.

Nothing.

Gods, they took that, too.

She wanted to lie quietly. Just let the woman with the star on her battered face squeeze until there was no more shadow in her brain. No more obedience. No more sand and screaming crowds, and no more leering men. No more Rayli—forever.

But she had been told to fight.

She slammed her fingers straight into the woman's eyes, digging as hard as she could.

Most of a Risen's body had the strength of the dead, but eyeballs resisted the embalming herbs, and this woman wasn't as fresh as Rayli. In a gush of rancid, clear fluid, they popped.

Rayli pushed harder until her fingers dug into the squishy softness of her opponent's brain.

The woman's hands lost strength, and she collapsed in a sticky heap on top of Rayli.

Rock helped Rayli to her feet, not even wincing at the foul liquid running down her wrists.

She glanced to the barred entrance where Blubberlips beamed. He made a gesture, and as Rayli understood his meaning, she felt her body begin to obey. *He doesn't even need to talk.* Powerless to resist, she strode over to the head of the man she'd killed first and wound her sticky fingers in his hair.

To the roar of her name from the maddened crowd, she held it aloft in devastating triumph, sobbing inside for what they had made her.

— CHAPTER THIRTY-THREE —

Dolen's eyes were getting used to the dark. Three days in the tunnels beneath Ert's surface and the faint light of the phosphorescent algae, or whatever it was that clung to the walls, was starting to feel normal. He still regularly bashed his head on rocks and the sharp stalactites that hung from some of the ceilings, but at least he wasn't walking into the walls anymore. Mostly the ground was blue and the stalactites pink, and small, purple dots blinked on and off all over the sides. It was that blinking that kept messing up his vision, fouling up his depth perception.

"Move faster." The Berunfolk who prodded Dolen in the back wasn't Kratch, but they still all looked alike to him.

This was his punishment. The Prime Embalmer hadn't called it that, but Dolen wasn't stupid. When the man had caught him and Sorreg in his lab, he'd taken her into "protective custody," muttering about her needing to understand the bigger picture and not being so sentimental about things that didn't matter.

Things like Dolen.

The Big Man's face had showed his contempt for Dolen, nothing but a dead man walking and talking. Dolen had still played the obedient corpse and didn't dare let on that the lichen Sorreg created didn't affect him. He still had pause that she made such an evil thing, but her dismay couldn't have been faked. Sorreg hated the stuff almost as much as Dolen did. *And when she dies and Rises to feel the effect for herself, she'll really understand, far too late.*

He stumbled along through the dim passageway with three other Risen and five Berunfolk. The Risen took turns pulling a cart that was almost full of large, leathery eggs, the same as the ones he'd seen in Zarix's laboratory the night they were caught in the break-in. The Big Man had ordered him into the tunnel, and he might have refused, maybe even attacked the man, but a group of Zarix's Risen had entered the lab right behind him, bound to his will. There had been no escape for Dolen or Sorreg.

He hoped she was okay.

Now Dolen worked for the Big Man as well. He trudged along on this subterranean mission, hunting for clutches of the eggs they found stuck to the walls of the lower tunnels where stagnant water dripped into pools from tiny cracks in the ceilings above. The blobby, slow creatures that laid them were easy to kill, sometimes spewing out more eggs when cut open, pouring a rancid stench through the deep tunnels. The smell clung to all of them now as they pressed on for one more find to fill the cart.

Dolen shuddered, remembering the first day he'd been down here. The Berunfolk had told him to wait in a small, low chamber down a long hallway off what seemed to be a main passage, alive with Berunfolk hurrying back and forth. After what felt like hours, three live humans were shoved in with him, and the chamber closed with some kind of thick, clear membrane sealed around the edges with slime from one of the Berunfolk's tentacles.

One of the people was holding an egg.

"Break egg." The command was directed at him, and he had a split second to consider refusing. But the hard, expressionless faces with the glowing eyes held no sympathy. He broke the egg.

Instead of the blob embryo he expected, when the thin skin gave way, only gas came out. Faintly green, it swirled in the dim light. Dolen held his breath as the gas stung his eyes.

The humans also held theirs, blinking, tears pouring down their faces until they could hold it no more and took gulping gasps.

In seconds they went down, clutching their throats. Blood poured from their noses and mouths. They hacked up sticky chunks of pink flesh, and Dolen watched with horror as they writhed, choking on blood and their own dissolving lungs. He could hold his breath almost forever, and pinched his nose, backing away from the drowning, suffocating people.

It was over in a couple of minutes. The dead people finally stilled, lying on the ground in their own gore.

"Dead man breathe."

Dolen stared at the Beneather through the clear membrane. Could he pretend somehow? Why bother?

He inhaled a big lungful.

It burned and he coughed. No blood came up and he waited.

"Breathe more."

He breathed again. Not pleasant, and the gas still stung his eyes, but no blood came up. No bits of his lungs. After a few more hesitant gasps, he breathed normally. Whatever it was didn't affect him. He said a silent prayer of thanks to Ata Lashka.

The Beneather in the doorway looked angry. Another one came up behind him and they conferred for a moment in their language. After a while, they turned and left him.

Dolen stepped over the bodies to poke at the membrane. Far tougher than he imagined, it held under his prodding. He worked his fingers around an edge through the slime and pulled down, ripping it away from the entrance. A tap on his shoulder from behind made him whirl around.

The dead had Risen and stood there blinking at him, blood drying on their chins and hands.

"I'm sorry," Dolen said. "I wouldn't have broken the egg if I'd known."

The dead man in front of him opened his mouth, but nothing came out. He frowned, flapping his lips silently.

"Oh, rot, I'm really sorry now." Dolen glanced at the popped egg on the ground. "That stuff ate your lungs. You can't talk without air." At the panicked looks from the three new Risen, he added,

"It's okay. You're Risen now. You don't actually need to breathe. You'll be fine. You just won't be able to talk."

The man clearly mouthed, "Ever?"

Dolen nodded. "I think not ever. We heal pretty well, especially if they feed us. But stuff that's gone doesn't actually grow back." He paused for a moment. "But maybe the Embalmers can sew in new lungs from somebody that...I don't know...gets their head cut off by accident, or something. I know they can't fix it if your head comes off, but maybe they can get you new lungs. It doesn't seem to matter if they're not yours. If we lose an arm, they just sew on a new one and it works after a while." He tried to smile at the horror-stricken people. "I work for an Embalmer who's all right. When we get back to the surface, I'll ask her. Don't worry. It's not that bad being dead."

Not that bad for you.

But these new Risen didn't seem to be affected by the familiar Red Spores the Berunfolk brought back.

Of course they aren't. They can't breathe them in.

When the Berunfolk had that sorted, six more of the creatures entered and ordered Dolen to help them hold the new Risen down as they drilled holes in their skulls and wiped in the slimy lichen. They didn't bother sewing the skin over it, just smeared their tentacle slime over the wounds and the skin stuck together. Dolen watched as the shadow descended over the Risen's minds. Obedient, but still shocked and terrified, they all followed the Berunfolk down the hallway.

"Stop. Quiet."

A quick command from the Berunman in charge of this egg-collecting mission brought Dolen back from the horrible memory of the start of this trip. He and the other Risen stopped, pressing their backs into the shadows of the rough corridor.

"Go. Kill. Get."

Dolen unsheathed the short sword hanging from his belt. Neither he nor the other Risen had any skill with their blades, but it didn't take skill to kill the blobs. They'd been killing blobs and harvesting their eggs for days. At first Dolen had handled the eggs with care, expecting them to break and release more of the eye-burning gas, but these eggs were much tougher. Zarix must be doing something to the eggs in the lab, changing their contents somehow. But why would the Prime Embalmer be making a poison to kill humans? Maybe it wasn't supposed to kill them. Maybe the horror in the chamber was a failed experiment. *Time to find a new formula before you kill the whole city, Big Man.*

The Risen crept around the corner. A huge shadow hulked in a shallow pool.

Dolen raised his sword and strode toward the creature.

It unfolded on thick legs and bellowed a roar that echoed across the dripping stones. Six red eyes opened, and a wide mouth rimmed with teeth reflected the dim light. The creature lunged forward, raking razor claws across the Risen next to Dolen. The man splattered into the wall in pieces as shouts of alarm carried in from the Berunfolk behind them. Not a blob. Dolen had no name for this clicking, angry nightmare.

Slipping on fresh blood, he turned and raced into the darkness.

— CHAPTER THIRTY-FOUR —

P lease tell me exactly what the Prime Embalmer ordered you to do."

Sorreg stood in the open doorway to Prime Zarix's sumptuous apartment. Hulking Risen guards stood on each side of the quiet hall facing her. Zarix had the only apartment on this highest level of the rock-hewn cliff city, and in the three days Sorreg had been confined here, no one had traversed the hallways except the Risen who brought them gourmet meals twice a day, and Zarix himself. These two guards never slept. When she tried to walk past them, they gently pushed her back inside. Only one of them ever spoke, and Sorreg wondered if the second one had been devocalized in some way. If someone had told him to cut out his own tongue, he'd have done it. She hadn't the stomach to look.

"He ordered us to not let you leave. To guard this doorway and keep you inside, and not to harm you in any way."

"Right." Sorreg sighed. "Before that."

"He ordered us to not respond to any commands except his. Nothing anyone else directs is to be obeyed."

The scientist inside her frowned. Only a week since they'd learned what the Red Spore did, and already Zarix had found a way to skirt around their inability to disobey a command.

"What if there's a fire?"

She watched the guards consider this.

"We would guard the doorway and keep you inside." The man shook his head. "Look, we've heard you. Don't you think we'd love to let you out? Stop whatever this stuff is he put in our brains from going everywhere? Do you honestly think you could possibly hate this more than we do?" The two guards shared looks of helpless anger. "You made this rotting slime, but I believe you when you say you didn't mean it to do this. I may be dead, but I'm not stupid."

Sorreg leaned her head against the open doorway. "Let's try this." She cleared her throat. "Prime Embalmer Zarix has ordered me to command you to let me out."

The man shrugged. "I *can't*. I honestly can't." He scowled. "Can't you find some kind of cure? You made this. You did this. Can't you undo it?"

Under her forehead, the stone was cool and smooth. "Maybe, but not from in here. This isn't a lab, it's a rotting luxury apartment. If you let me out, maybe I can find a cure." She sighed again. "Can you just...close your eyes for a few minutes? Face the wall and close your eyes?"

"We'd hear you. And... no. He was very clear."

Sorreg rubbed her temples, feeling the oncoming headache. "I'm sorry. For all of us." She backed into the apartment and closed the door.

The place was immense. A wall of windows overlooked the vast plain in front of the cliff, with torchlit homes and shops dotting the near field, which gave way to empty land and snow-topped mountains in the distance. Stars shone overhead, alongside the small red ball of Ata Lashka keeping her watch over the Kisamon crescent moon. Of course she knew that Ata Lashka was just a tiny, dim sun, as were the other Atamonen Eyes overhead, dark now. She could only see it because the bright Eyes were closed, a phenomenon even their most learned astronomers could not explain. Since Nightfell began, they had watched the stars moving through the heavens in their predictable paths. The moon moved as well, and even Ata Lashka traveled across the sky, but the Eyes were always overhead, still and reliable. In just a few weeks they would open, bathing the land in light again. The Berun of the city would once again be relegated to indoors or underground, only venturing out in thick hoods to protect their chitinous skin from the suns. Without the covering they burned in hours, blistering in painful welts, as did so many of Ert's creatures.

Why are we different? Humans had no thick hair to cover their soft skin. Why did the Eyes burn only the Berunfolk? She knew the old myths, but Sorreg dealt in science, not religion. Nothing she had read ever explained why the Eyes closed, why they opened again so predictably, and why their light was so deadly to the beasts of Beneath.

She mulled it over, peering out over the dim land, seeing her own face reflected in the glass.

Nothing she had read.

An idea struck her, and she spun around, looking over the room, a wide, comfortable living space with soft chairs and a long couch facing the window. An immense table sat back from the window, where Zarix claimed to have made decisions and deals with the highest authorities from all over the continent. Sorreg took her meals with him at that table, pretending to listen as he droned on about the good her lichen was doing and how the Risen were being pacified all over the city. He seemed to honestly want her buy-in. He could have imprisoned her when he'd caught her and Dolen in his lab, but instead he'd brought her here.

You're a brilliant scientist. You proved your worth and made him a hero for the ages with the lichen. He won't give that up without a fight. He thinks he can use you.

She wondered what had happened to Dolen. But he was Risen, and obedient. Zarix wouldn't harm him. The Prime Embalmer wasn't wasteful, and a compliant slave was valuable, if only for another month.

Reading. Focus.

There was nothing to write on in the living space, and she had already searched her own bedroom for anything she might use, envisioning herself wielding a weapon and fighting her way past the guards, as laughable as the idea was.

She tried the door of Zarix's private office. He wouldn't be back for hours, not until dinnertime. The door opened, and she entered the small room. Shelves of books lined the walls, and she spent a few moments distracted by the titles, scientific tomes she longed to peruse.

Focus.

He had commanded the guards outside to only answer to him. She circled the desk and plopped down behind it, pulling open drawers. Could the guards read? If so, would they recognize his handwriting? Even if they didn't, there would surely be some documents in here that had his signature on them. She could cobble together something, cutting words from his writings to spell out something simple like "Let her go" and attaching his signature. The Prime Embalmer commanding them through writing? They would know it wasn't real, but maybe it would allow them to obey their order to only respond to his commands, and still let her out of here. It was worth a try.

She grabbed a thick book from the bottom drawer and opened it on the desk, flipping through pages for the words she wanted. A heading caught her eye. It was dated just a few days ago.

Experiment 1368 continues apace. The compound dissolves coobla embryos easily within the eggs, leaving the shell intact but fragile.

Sorreg remembered seeing the blob-creature eggs on the bench in his lab. What was he doing with them? Forgetting her goal in the face of Zarix's private scientific observations, she read on.

The Beneathers continue to prove themselves both valuable and incredibly stupid. They believe we are searching for a new formula that will change the effect of the Eyes on their chitin, allowing them to walk freely when the light shines bright. And it's true that the liquid they helped me create might do that with some more tinkering, but my knowledge of their systems puts theirs to shame. My personal experiments are promising. Though their lungs are primitive, they are lined with the same kind of cells that cover their chitin. I have been able to reverse the process, and experiments on lower animals shows tremendous effect. The gas dissolves their primitive respiratory systems within minutes, killing every species I have tried it on. Risen are unaffected, as are the living human prisoners exposed to it. Within a few days, I will have perfected the compound. The stupid Berunfolk will carry the eggs into their filthy underground homes and breathe it in, expecting immunity from the Eyes. Instead, they will find agonizing death. Once we have rid the tunnels beneath Somteh of their scourge, we will ship the eggs all over the continent. Never again will Beneathers rise from the ground at Nightfell to kill humans. Between Sorreg's lichen that controls our dead and the decimation of the only other intelligent species on the planet, we will finally be safe for eternity.

Sorreg read the passage three more times.

He means to kill every Berunfolk on the planet.

The human part of her recoiled. Wipe out an intelligent species. Kill Kratch, and every other Berunfolk. *They trusted us. Signed the treaty.* And they were unwittingly helping Zarix create a poison that would destroy them all.

The scientist part of Sorreg was also revolted. Zarix was out of control, ignoring every safety protocol. How many species had he tried this on? How many humans and Risen had been put at risk to prove it safe? He was power-mad to even think of releasing something like this in the tunnels beneath the city. There could be long term consequences, not only to wiping out a whole species and, from the sound of it, most of the other creatures who shared evolutionary lineage with Berunfolk, but even for humans, living and dead. How could he know what the gas might do in a week? A month? A year? A lifetime?

You selfish ghote. Worrying about what this could do to humans when he's very clear what it will do to other life on Ert.

She had to get out of here. Clearly this book was one he used too often. She couldn't cut it up without him seeing. She shoved it back in the drawer and opened another.

From outside, voices drifted in.

Out of time for today. Prime Embalmer Zarix was home.

— CHAPTER THIRTY-FIVE —

B y the time Zarix entered, Sorreg had scuttled back to her own guest room. She strolled out, willing her hands to stop shaking.

"Ah, Sorreg," Zarix said. "I hope you had a relaxing day."

She walked over to the huge windows that looked out over the dark plain. "I did, Prime Embalmer. I've had a lot of time to think these past few days." Far below, firelight flickered from homes, and lined the streets between them. From up here, Somteh's spill over city was beautiful and serene.

In the reflection of the glass, his shape loomed up behind hers. "It's a lovely view, isn't it?"

She nodded. "I keep looking over to where they used to stake out the Risen to rot." She turned halfway back and looked up at Zarix. "There haven't been any since the spore."

A huge smile split his face. "No, my dear, there surely haven't. You have saved them that horrible fate."

Inside, Sorreg fumed. *Is what they have better than that? Endless years of servitude to anyone with a voice?* But she forced herself to relax. *Tell him what he wants to hear. Get out and figure out how to save Kratch and his kin.* "How is it progressing?"

Zarix moved away from her, back into the living room. "It's a truly miraculous thing." He took off his outer robe of office, revealing a loose shirt and pants beneath. He laid the robe over the back of the chair and stretched. "Supplies of the spore are on the way to Kamteh, and should arrive long before the end of Nightfell. The capital will be able to see the results immediately, just as we have. It's been installed throughout our ventilation system, and patrols of Berunfolk have already been dispatched to seed it across the land itself." He pulled a glass bottle from a closed cabinet and chose two glasses, pouring without asking Sorreg if she wanted to join him. "We aren't sure how well it will grow in the colder regions, or the driest desert, but..." He stopped and grinned straight at her, holding out one of the full glasses.

Sorreg took the drink and sniffed it. Somteh's wine came from fermenting fruits that grew in the higher tunnels beneath the city. High in alcohol, the drink was an acquired taste, but she sipped politely, managing to keep her features serene.

"I haven't told you, have I?" Zarix motioned for her to join him on the long sofa facing the window. Sorreg sat on the far side, peering over her glass at him. "The spore is truly amazing," Zarix continued. "We've been drilling into the Risen skulls and inserting the lichen directly, but it turns out the potency of the spore means that step isn't necessary. It appears to be quite capable of forming its own colony in the high bones of the Risen sinus within a few days of being inhaled." He took a long drink and chuckled. "While I certainly like the ritual of inserting it ourselves, the ability of the spore to grow in them on its own ensures that even those who Rise without proper embalming will be subject to it as long as they're somewhere the spore grows. Which will soon be everywhere on Ert."

Sorreg's stomach fell. Too late. The spore she created was already out there in the world, and no Risen would be spared.

A knock on the door saved her from having to respond. She sprang up to answer it and admitted three Risen bearing trays of food. They set out the meal on Zarix's long table and left without speaking. *This is what we all have to look forward to.*

Sorreg joined him for dinner. Half of the dishes were foods she'd never seen before, and the wine warmed her. *Be careful. Stay on track.*

"So truly, we are safe from Risen uprisings, and they are safe from their own base instincts. Your discovery will go down in history as the spore that restored us to the Atamonen's intent."

The food was presented on fine, smooth pottery, glazed in muted colors. Sorreg scraped her fork across a puddle of sauce, pulling it out into a spiral pattern. She was dying to talk to him about what she'd read in his private notes, but only one thing truly mattered: getting out. As his prisoner in luxury, she could do nothing. Kratch and his people had to be warned and the toxin stopped if possible. And if she could manage that, she might have a bit of time left this Nightfell to work on a cure for the Red Spore, some kind of antidote that would stop its effect. Once Nightfell ended, the Risen would return to death, and she would have no chance to test any compound she might create. By the time the Eyes closed again, she would be long dead. Perhaps some other scientist would find a cure. If they wanted to. If not, she would Rise as a slave.

Get out. Get back to work.

She peeked over at Zarix, looking up through her eyelashes as she'd seen other women do when trying to manipulate men. "Prime Embalmer, I know it's a miracle. I couldn't believe it at first, but...now I have to make a confession."

He stopped chewing and put down his fork. "Of course. I'm here to listen, my dear."

"I'm frightened," she said in a small voice. "Next Nightfell...it will be me. I'll be long dead, embalmed by the greatest Embalmers of Somteh. And when I Rise, I'll be like them. Anyone will be able to command me." She blinked at him. "Who knows who will be in charge of our city by then? How could it possibly be someone with vision like yours?" She dropped her eyes, focusing on the plate before her. "I'm afraid to become like them."

Zarix rose and strode around behind her, placing his hands on her shoulders. "Oh, my dear, sweet Sorreg."

She forced herself to not flinch away from his touch.

"I have already foreseen this and made plans to compensate. Of course you're frightened, and I should have told you." He kneaded her shoulders as he spoke. "I have had a vision, a message directly from the Atamonen themselves."

I just bet you have.

"They have shown me that leaders like us are called directly to their care," Zarix continued. "They have decreed that all Senior Embalmers from all divisions shall not be subject to the Rising. Upon our deaths, we shall be fed immediately to the flames, sending our souls directly to the Atamonen who will welcome us into their ranks. We will not Rise to serve the living, but ascend to guide them from the sky, joining the very Eyes themselves to watch over the living and the Risen from above."

Sorreg sighed, looking across the room and out the windows. *Play along.* "They have shown you this? Are you certain it will be done?"

"It shall be as I say." He gave a final, hard squeeze on her shoulders and withdrew to return to his place at the head of the table. "You needn't worry. The Atamonen await us when our work here is through."

The warmth of the wine spread over her with shame. She'd come up with the ploy to manipulate him, convince him that the only reason she tried to destroy the spore was fear for her own Rising. But it was true. The horror her work had inflicted on others terrified her. If she couldn't find a cure in the days left to her, she would at least be spared the degradation of becoming a Risen slave after her death. Thousands of others in the city would not be so fortunate.

She beamed a smile at him, only half faked. "Truly the Atamonen are wise. I'm fortunate to share their wisdom through you."

He blinked at her. "Indeed you are."

"Prime Embalmer, I've had a lot of time to think up here." She gestured out the huge window. "I look out over the lights of the city, and I see peace. Your peace. I admit that the Red Spore scares me. I thought it was too much control, too powerful for us. But when I think about the other cities out there, fighting monsters from Beneath, and here we sit sipping wine..." She batted her eyelashes at him. "Well, the Red Spore might be too much power for most men, but in the hands of someone with vision, it's a gift. One that I'm so happy to have been a small part of." It was all she could do not to vomit. Surely he'd see right through her. Zarix wasn't stupid. Flattery like this couldn't possibly work.

But it worked. With a promise to return for dinner the following night, Sorreg went home to her own apartment. She had no idea how to reach Kratch at this hour, but Zarix's notes had indicated a few more days before his poison would be ready. Head full of wine, she lay awake staring at her own ceiling, burning in shame for the world she had made.

— CHAPTER THIRTY-SIX —

A ll sense of time was gone. In the twisting tunnels of Beneath, Dolen crept on alone, peering around corners, clutching the sword in front of him like a talisman. Risen didn't need to eat. Risen didn't need to sleep. So he walked, bereft of direction, certain he was going in circles.

From his limited conversations with Kratch in the lab, he knew these tunnels connected all the great cities of the world, burrowing through the mountains and under the plains. When he was brought down here on the mission to collect blob eggs, they had descended at every turn. Led by Berunfolk, Dolen had paid little attention to the path they'd taken. But they had gone down, so now, when faced with a choice of tunnels, he chose the one leading up.

He quickly realized it didn't much matter where he emerged. Nothing bound him to Somteh except loyalty to Sorreg. She hadn't intended the results of the spore; he believed her about that. But Nightfell was nearly over, and his contract would end when the Eyes opened. How long was that? Weeks? Days? The urgency of not knowing, and the creeping dread of what might be following him in the darkness, pushed him on.

The tunnels were a mix of beauty and despair. Their luminescent glow stunned him in places where pools of water reflected hanging pink stalactites or glittering blue motes on the walls. A few of the caverns had shown him tantalizing peeks of the outside world, only slightly brighter than the cave interior with moonlight streaming in. How he longed to see the bright beams of the Eyes. But those days were done for him forever. When the Eyes opened, he would fall dead. And if he were alone in these tunnels, his body would rot as the embalming herbs gave way to decay. By next Nightfell, nothing would remain of Dolen but his bones. His robe was tattered now, hanging open at the chest, but the interior pocket still held the last remnants of Naren'da's gift. He could brew one more pot of herb tea, drinking the brew and inhaling the steam to preserve his insides. If he had a pot. And water. And fire. And it wouldn't matter anyway. The effects wouldn't last ninety years. If he didn't find his way to Embalmers before the end of Nightfell, his flesh wouldn't be around to Rise again.

He rounded a corner into one of the larger corridors, wondering at the three very different kinds of tunnels down here. Some were obviously natural, craggy shafts of varying height and width, full of the glowing algae and other slimy things. These were the most dangerous, as they often ended in impassible shafts or sheer drop offs to black depths. The widest tunnels were perfectly circular and smooth, as if bored out by some kind of giant worm that chewed through the stone. These had no hard turns, but gentle curves heading up or down, with Y junctions instead of Ts. And in the middle were connectors and shafts that bore recent tool marks, hacked out to Berunfolk-height and cart-width. Some of these felt very recent with little growth of fungus or lichen to light Dolen's way.

The tunnel he walked through now was one of the round, smooth variety. Dolen searched his memory for stories of worms that might have bored them out but came up blank. He listened at every turn, hoping to hear something to guide him, though any noise would present a difficult choice. The Berunfolk of Somteh were allies of humans, but the rest of the world had no such treaty. If he came upon any who were not friendly, he wouldn't stand a chance. And all sorts of beasts prowled the darkness. Dolen was safe alone, until the Eyes opened. Then he was done for.

A tunnel opened off to his right, Berunfolk-made but old. Brighter light beckoned from beyond, and he left the smooth corridor, creeping along with his shoulders hunched to avoid the low ceiling. It bent and wound, branching until he lost track of the turns he had made. Here and there, cracks in the ceiling let in starlight, and he pressed forward, knowing he was within a few human-heights of the surface above.

He stopped at the entrance to a room. Enough light shone through for him to see it was not a tunnel, but a confined space, rare in this endless warren. It was packed with shapes, hard corners reflecting the dim glow from above.

Dust covered everything. He held his breath, brushing off the nearest surface.

Metal.

This place held a fortune in metal.

His whole life, Dolen had only seen metal in tiny quantities. Mined from rocks, it was incredibly rare, and worth its weight in scarabs. But this room was full of it. Large boxes were made entirely of metal. Others were banded with metal, made of some other hard substance he had no name for. Dolen circled the pile of boxes in the little space, wiping ages-old dust from every surface. Some were labeled with words that meant nothing to him in a language he didn't understand. A few of the letters were familiar, but most were odd scratchings. He continued around until a small box on top of one of the stacks caught his eye.

Ata Lashka.

The rune on the box's surface matched the one on the carved, mirror-bright stone that hung around his neck. Dolen offered a quick prayer and picked up the box.

It fit easily into his palm, and he turned it over, looking for hinges or a lock and finding none. Smooth all around, it had no obvious opening. A small slot on one side was clogged with dust, and he blew it out, motes sparkling into his eyes.

The box spoke, though the language of Ata Lashka was far above his ability to comprehend and he did not understand a single word.

"...indigenous popula...casualty..."

Dolen almost dropped the box in shock. *The goddess's voice is trapped in the box.* He dared not open it, in case her words were lost, but he stared at it in wonder as she spoke in gentle, flowing syllables. *Sweet Ata, speak. I hear you.* Dolen closed his eyes, listening to the halting, broken words of his god, and dropping to his knees in the dust.

"...light-averse...mining in jeopar...satellite cool down interval... bionanotechnology unreliab...reprogram to revive only during..."

Ata Lashka spoke from the magic box, and Dolen listened. The final words were, "Live well, in service and hope. Lashka Brommen. Atamonen Mining Corporation." The distorted message repeated from the beginning, and Dolen mouthed the unfamiliar language along with the god, trying to commit the nonsense syllables to memory. This was Ata Lashka's message to her people. Her final words, confined here in this metal box beneath the ground. Was this the very tunnel where Kisamon betrayed her? Perhaps this was her anguished confession before she emerged to chase her enemy through the sky forever. Lashka Brommen. Ata Lashka's full name, or a title? Dolen didn't know, but he had always prayed to just Ata Lashka. It was good enough for him.

A distant roar cut through Dolen's prayer. He leapt to his feet, peering into the darkness outside Ata Lashka's underground temple.

He waited, not breathing.

A second roar echoed down the tunnel. Louder. Closer.

If a beast tracked him here, he would be trapped. Worse, the beast would defile this temple, perhaps destroying these holy relics.

Dolen tucked the box into his tattered shirt pocket and raced from the room. He headed away from the roar, running with his head ducked, twisting and turning as the tunnel led upward. The roar sounded again, and he risked a look back over his shoulder.

Something chased him. The light was too dim to name the creature, but it loped along, chest high to Dolen, closing ground with each stride. Where it passed beneath cracks in the roof, the light of the moon reflected off smooth, chitinous plates.

Dolen ran, sliding around corners and bouncing off slick walls. He glanced behind again and ran straight into a dead end.

Behind him, the creature advanced. From above, a small hole let starlight in. Dolen scrambled for purchase on the slick walls, lunging for the edges of the hole above. The beast leapt, and Dolen swung his legs up away from grasping claws. He hauled himself up, kicking against the ceiling, bracing his back inside the hole. Cold breath wafted up from the beast's open mouth, snapping jaws at Dolen's feet. The sharp edges scraped his back as he shoved himself upward through the narrow chimney.

With one final pull, he hauled himself up, flopping out onto hard ground. He rolled over on his tattered back, looking up into a cloudless night sky. The dim red Eye of Ata Lashka looked down on him from the edge of the flat horizon.

Thank you, sweet Ata, he prayed. *I've brought your words to the world. Live well.*

He reached into his pocket to touch the holy box and let the words of the god sing into the open air, but his hands found only torn cloth.

The magical box was gone.

— CHAPTER THIRTY-SEVEN —

Rayli lay back in the washtub, breathing the thick, herbal steam.

This would likely be her last embalming bath before the end of Nightfell. The slick water filled the pores of her skin, sealing the tiny holes where rot could start, preserving her flesh for the final weeks of darkness. She inhaled, coating her throat and lungs with potent fumes, protecting them from decay for a bit longer. The water tasted bitter, but she sipped it down from cupped hands, feeling the hot liquid pour down her throat, preventing decay from the inside. It would find its way all through her system, into veins and through her heart, up into her brain.

Maybe it would kill the slime that festered in the hole at the back of her scalp. She doubted it. As she submerged her head under the bath's surface, the darkness followed her, cutting her off from her Lightshaper power. Making her a slave.

They'd do a more thorough job of preserving her once Nightfell ended and she died again. This time she'd probably keep all of her organs, but they would cut her open and pack the lining of her belly with embalming herbs. They would stuff her throat with more, forcing the little grains down her throat and into her lungs, filling her mouth and nose. Her eyes would be smeared with jelly and sewn shut to protect them, and thick, wet bandages would enshroud her. Over the long years of Daylight when the Atamonen watched over the living, Embalmers would continue to anoint her bandages with more herbs, preserving her flesh inside so that in ninety years when the Eyes closed again, others would unwrap her to Rise again.

What will the world be then?

If she had a prayer left in her, it would be for the disgrace of the arena to be long lost to history. For her next Rising to go as Ata Lashka intended, serving a grateful living humanity, or fighting to protect them from the dangers of the dark. Not this. Never this. But Rayli was all out of prayers. Every time she marched past the shelves of Risen heads, staring helplessly, silent but for the blinking of eyes and the flapping of decaying lips, her prayers drained away until nothing was left inside her. The Atamonen were gone. Never would she see their light on the mountains again, and in this dark place of misery, they had abandoned her.

"You done in there?"

Scar's voice brought Rayli up from beneath the water. She breathed in steam one more time, then stood up in the small tub, dripping fragrant drops. She had washed the prior night's dye from her hair, but the left side of her blonde locks were permanently stained pink now, along with that side of her face, neck, torso, and arm. Clan Tornado didn't fight every night, but the stain never had time to fully fade away.

Rayli stepped from the tub, standing to the side as Scar approached and stepped into the water.

"You should have let me go first," Scar said, cupping a handful. "The water's pink."

Rayli smiled. "I'm sure it still works fine. Make you look more lifelike."

The huge wound in her friend's belly was neatly stitched but not yet healed. Extra rations would help her heal more quickly, and the embalming bathwater would probably seep into the scab, which could only make it better.

"Does it still hurt?"

Scar glanced down at the stitches. "Yep. Pain is still weird, though, isn't it?"

The chill of the underground wrapped around Rayli's wet skin. "Yeah. Hurts just as much, but you don't have to care. Weird."

She let the water dry on her skin before pulling on her scratchy pants and shirt. Behind her, Scar blew bubbles from under the bathwater, and Rayli chuckled as she left the bathing room. Clan Tornado had the night off, and the roar of the crowd echoed through the walls as some other clan battled for the entertainment of the bloodthirsty living.

Eyes in heads on shelves followed her down the hall. In the early days, she had talked to them as she passed, hoping to ease their horrified anguish with words, stories, or anything to distract what was left of them in the long nightmare of decay. But she had no stories tonight. The heads at the far end were the oldest, stinking of rot. Most of them were motionless, eyes melted to jelly. Embalming eventually failed, and surely these souls were long gone, released to the arms of the Atamonen. She trudged along as the heads got fresher, ending with the eyeless face of the Star woman Rayli had terminated in their battle. Her thumbs had penetrated the woman's brain and sent her to the Final Death. Rayli paused, staring at the stars tattooed all over the cheeks and forehead. Her hand stroked her own cheek where the Tornado mark was long healed, a black swirl in her skin. Star's gladiators were tattooed everywhere. She peered closer. The stars looked old, fading slightly to blue around the edges. This woman had been a fighter long before Rayli.

I got lucky when I beat her. It could have been Rayli's head adorning Clan Star's trophy shelf.

Or unlucky. She could have been released to the Final Death.

A long table stretched down the dining room. Rayli dipped out a ladle of thick, chunky stew into a bowl and found a seat between Carrol and Rock. When she had first arrived here, this little room had been full of chatter at mealtimes, sometimes strained as battered warriors talked away the stress of their last fight, other times honestly lighthearted, with Risen recounting the stories of their lives. None had Risen before this Nightfell. Only the freshest were worthy of gladiator status. If the arena survived another century, Rayli hoped that would still be true. She could stand a bit of decay if it meant she was spared this fate again.

She chewed a bite of meat, looking down the table. Carrol was a mess. Both of her arms had been replaced, and the left one was not yet functional, twitching at her side as the nerves found the signals from their new body. Her face had a new line of stitches crossing her nose, but the small woman was proving harder to kill than anyone imagined.

"Eat up," Rayli said. "Gotta stay strong. Just a few more weeks."

Carrol smiled with the side of her lips that still worked. "Ata Lashka, make that true."

Rayli's spoon scraped the bottom of the bowl as she scooped up the last chunk of meat. She glanced down, mouth open for the final bite, and froze in horror, staring at the gray, cooked flesh.

The edges were fading to blue, and only half of it was visible in the ragged square on the trembling spoon.

But there was no mistaking the tattoo of Clan Star.

— CHAPTER THIRTY-EIGHT —

The next morning, Sorreg told Kratch.

When she entered her lab after being gone for days, she found everything tidy and clean. A slight smell from the adjacent lab animal room told her that Dolen had not yet returned from whatever punishment mission Zarix had sent him on, but the lab itself was spotless. Kratch hadn't been involved in the break-in, and either Zarix had decided not to include the Berunman in the retribution, or he couldn't tell one Berunfolk from another and didn't bother to find out which of the many robed figures in the embalming sciences was Sorreg's lab assistant. Either way, he'd kept the place neat while she was gone.

She spared a few moments worrying about Dolen. Based on the notes in Zarix's private office, she knew he'd need a lot more of the eggs he was using to make his poison than she'd seen in his lab. Maybe he had another supply of them ready to go, but she'd bet good scarabs that Dolen was somewhere in the tunnels beneath the city, gathering more.

Kratch poked his head around the doorway to the animal room. "Not prison? Not dead?" His eyes flashed with the tease.

Sorreg wrinkled her nose at the Berunman. "No, I'm free and very much alive. Thank you for your concern."

The little snort that passed for a laugh was all she'd get from Kratch. She strode past the long benches and gestured for him to move back into the animal room. The smell was stronger back here, but that space was farther from prying eyes and ears. She bent down to whisper into his hood, counting on the screeches and grunts from the caged creatures around her to muffle her words. No one else was in the lab, but she couldn't shake the feeling that somehow Zarix could be listening in.

"Kratch, you have to listen to me. Zarix is planning to betray you."

The hooded figure stood still, red eyes narrowing.

"He's telling his people that he's making some kind of treatment for you, something to make you resistant to the light. It would be amazing if it were true." Sorreg paused and glanced back toward the door. No one there. "But it's a lie, Kratch. He's making a poison, and when you open the eggs, you'll die. You have to warn the others." She paused. "Kratch, I think you have to get everyone out of the city. All your people. You have to leave before he betrays and kills you all."

She stepped back, watching his expression. The stiff face didn't allow for much movement, and he'd once told her that among themselves, Berunfolk communicated as much through scents made by their tentacles as by spoken words. She expected a whiff of something bitter or sour, but the slight scent she detected from inside his sleeves was sweet, like pollens in a fresh stream.

He blinked at her.

"How Sorreg know this?"

She chuckled. "I've been locked up in Zarix's apartment for days. I read his private notes."

Another blink. "Maybe Zarix lie? Know Sorreg look? Test?"

Sorreg straightened up, staring at her assistant. She hadn't even considered that. Would Zarix do such a thing? Plant false information, expecting her to snoop? Watching to see what she'd do to test her loyalty to the Prime Embalmer?

"I... I don't know. I guess it's possible." She deflated. She'd been so sure. But Prime Embalmer Zarix had made the treaty with the

Berunfolk. He knew their value. Why would he want to kill them now, especially when their work was so critical?

Kratch nodded. "Kratch find out. Kratch ask Orch."

A chill wrapped around Sorreg's shoulders. "She's Zarix's personal assistant. If you ask her and it's not true, she'll report it to Zarix. She'll know I looked."

The blankest look Sorreg had ever seen took over Kratch's stiff face. "Is risk. Maybe Berunfolk all die. Maybe Sorreg get trouble." He waved an arm toward her lab. "Sorreg choose. Risk Berunfolk, or risk job?"

She hated that she had to consider it. If Kratch didn't find out the truth in time and the notes she had read were real, thousands of his people could die in agony. If the notes were a lie meant to entrap her, she would certainly lose her position. Science was her life. Embalmers did not marry. She had no secret lover, no hidden children whisked away in the night for adoption by someone who was allowed to have them. Close friendships among Embalmers were rare, as fierce professional competition kept them secretive and jealous of their work. In truth, Sorreg could call only one person in all of Somteh "friend," and she was staring at him right now.

"Go ask Orch."

The sweet scent intensified for a moment, and Kratch turned to leave through the small passage at the back of the room.

"Oh, and Kratch," Sorreg added, "can you try and find out what's happened to Dolen? I'm worried that he's not back yet."

Kratch paused. "Dead man sent to tunnels with Berunfolk. All attacked. One Berunman return. No dead man."

Oh, Dolen, I'm so sorry.

Sorreg nodded and turned away. Tears welled in her eyes as she stepped back into her lab. The Risen had been a good man. All he'd wanted was to find his wife. When they'd learned she was lost, he'd died again inside. But he'd helped her, of his own free will. At least, she thought so. For that kindness, he was killed in the tunnels. If nothing else, he was with his wife now, safe in the arms of the Atamonen. Without the release of fire, he'd have had to find his own way through the night sky, but Dolen could do it. He would find the gods and his wife, and the peace he deserved. Assuming the Embalmer Priests were right. Never before had Sorreg so hoped for that to be true.

She wiped her cheeks on the collar of her robe and looked over her specimens, lined up on the lab bench. Only one culture of the Red Spore remained, the original growth on the very first mirror-stone with the dark brown stain under a glass dome. Her distorted reflection frowned, remembering when the lichen had first begun to grow. Kratch had used his tentacle slime on lots of cultures of the same lichen. Only this one grew the Red Spore that affected the Risen so dramatically. Why this culture alone?

She removed the glass dome. The spores were already seeded everywhere in the city and beyond. It was far too late to confine it now. Within a few years the whole continent would be suffused with it, and no Risen would ever be free again. She owed it to Dolen's memory to find a cure.

The brown stain tickled her memory. What was it? She searched for the image of the first time she touched the stone and remembered the smell of smoke. The Risen were fighting the living, revolting against their status. The man who had delivered the batch of substrate stones had reeked of it. He'd been burned.

He'd cut himself and bled on the stone.

Risen blood stained its silvery surface, leeching into the tiny pores. The lichen grew on Risen blood and this stone from the very beginning. Kratch's slime made it potent. What she hoped might become a sedative for the living turned into slavery for the dead.

She set the dome aside and pulled the stone toward her.

If she made it, she could unmake it.

Time to find the cure.

— CHAPTER THIRTY-NINE —

Dolen peered across the open plain, trying to determine his position. Howls of rage came from the crack beneath him, but the beast couldn't possibly wedge itself through, and eventually the noise abated. Dolen was certainly safer out in the open, but how far had he come through those twisting tunnels? And how would he ever find this place again, this hallowed ground where Ata Lashka's holy relics lay below? The Embalmer Priests would venerate the site if only Dolen could tell them where it was. He'd held the box in his hands. Heard the sacred words. And somewhere in his flight, he'd dropped it.

Another failure. This time, you failed the gods themselves.

The wide, flat plain onto which he'd emerged looked like the land around Somteh. Mountains rose behind him, and far in the distance, another range might be the mountains of his former home. How long had it been since he'd come down, newly Risen, confused and in anguish, dreaming of finding his Rayli? He shook his head. So naive. He'd imagined their reunion. She'd greet him with tears, and together they would travel to Kamteh, where their baby son had been taken when Rayli died giving birth to him. The boy would be grown up, grown old and died, but might be found as Risen like them. They would meet their son, their grandchildren, and great-grandchildren, and enjoy their stolen time in the world until the Eyes opened and they slept for what would seem like an instant before Rising again.

Fool.

Rayli was gone, and he couldn't even cry about it because Risen made no tears.

But their son might still be Risen. Maybe somewhere in this dark world there walked a man with Rayli's eyes. It was all Dolen had.

He considered Sorreg, his boss for a brief time. The Prime Embalmer had sent Dolen away on the egg retrieval mission while Sorreg watched, helpless. Had the Big Man imprisoned her for the break in? Killed her? If Dolen returned to Somteh, could he help her in some way?

Moonlight shone on the wide plain as he debated. A glow from across the nearby cliffs had to be Somteh. And somewhere, perhaps a few weeks' walk, his descendants might be in distant Kamteh. He looked at the sky, tracing the patterns of stars. The Great Fork constellation was high overhead, and the Shepherd's Crook barely visible in the east. Nightfell was nearly over. At best, a week remained before he fell. Not enough time to get to Kamteh. Dolen turned toward the glow of the cliff city, but paused at a sound in the distance.

He squinted at a bright haze approaching from the southeast. No beast shone with orange light like that. No beast clomped along making that much noise. Dolen folded his arms and waited as the marching feet neared.

A loose group of men and women wearing helmets and bristling with weapons and torches strode toward him. Dolen counted at least fifty, maybe a hundred. One of them carried a tattered flag with the emblem of Kamteh on it, and the number 103 inside a shield.

"Ho, traveler. Identify yourself."

Dolen waited for the man who had spoken to approach. As the soldiers surrounded him, Dolen eyed their uniforms. Chitin shoulder plates and helmets, metal-tipped arrows, metal-edged swords. Clearly these were more than average soldiers. Or maybe all Kamteh regiments were like this? Dolen had never seen any, but these were well-equipped fighters.

The leader thrust a torch at Dolen, and he flinched away.

"Oh, you're Risen?" the man said, pulling the torch back. "Who are you, and how close are we to Somteh?"

Dolen nodded. "I'm Dolen Roald, employed by the Embalming Guild of Somteh. Risen. We're probably a few hours' march away."

The man handed his torch to another soldier. "What are you doing out here alone?"

Dolen sighed. "I was on a supply mission. We were attacked by a beast in the tunnels. As far as I know, I'm the only survivor."

"Right. You better stay with us, then," the man said. "Beasts aren't just in the tunnels." He shouted to his soldiers, "One hundred third, move out!"

The regiment set off at a moderate clip toward the glow of Somteh. Dolen fell back from the leader and found himself between a couple of young men.

"So you guys are from Kamteh?"

The man on the left nodded. "Hundred and third elite legion. We're on the way to save your city."

This got a laugh from the other man. "Maybe from you."

Dolen cocked his head. "What do you mean?"

"We got orders a couple of weeks ago that your Risen were revolting. And even though Kamteh was running low on soldiers, we fought our way through the monsters at our gates and across all this land to put down the uprising. Nothing personal."

A chilly wind whipped across the plain, and Dolen wrapped his torn cloak around himself. "I think you're too late. One of our scientists found a new plant. Or made it. I don't know. It makes Risen obedient to commands. The uprising is over. Every dead person in Somteh does exactly what they're told now."

The man on Dolen's left stopped in his tracks. "Does it...does it feel like a dark cloud around your brain?"

In the moonlight, Dolen hadn't noticed. But a closer look revealed gray eyes, and a slight smell of decay. "Sure does. You're Risen?"

A nod. "I'm Borl. Got killed in a fight with some Beneathers on the way. Still part of the regiment, but I'm Corpseguard now. Stronger than the rest. But I could sure use some embalming. Even *I* can smell me."

Corpseguard. Dolen had never heard the term, but he didn't know any Risen soldiers.

The dead man, Borl, started marching again, and Dolen kept pace. "For the first few hours, I felt...I don't know. Distant."

It was a good description. Pain was distant. Sounds and vision were distant. Real and true, but far away and not always important.

"Then I started feeling the cloud," Borl continued. "Really sudden, and I didn't think too much about it. Figured it was just part of being Corpseguard. But then I was walking with my buddy who's still alive, and he told me to back off and stay away from him because I was starting to stink."

Even in the pale moonlight, Dolen could see the hurt on the man's face.

"And I couldn't get away from him fast enough." He looked across the marching regiment. "He's right over there, and I can't make my legs walk that way. I literally can't get near him." The gray eyes darkened. "Is it forever? How does it work?"

Dolen told him what he knew about the Red Spore, leaving out that he worked for the scientist who'd developed it.

Twelve of the seventy-three soldiers were Corpseguard, having died in the fighting between Kamteh and here. A few were missing limbs, and others were held together with quick field stitches. All were anxious to get to Somteh before the end of Nightfell so they could be properly embalmed, and all of them had apparently inhaled enough of the spore on the way to feel its effects. But soldiers followed orders anyway. Though they'd felt the dark clouding of their minds, none had fully understood the compulsion they were under until now.

It's already out here. It's everywhere.

When they called a halt a few hours later, Dolen reached into his pocket. Not much of Naren'da's herbs remained, but these soldiers needed it more than he did. A pang jolted through his heart as he pulled the pouch from his pocket. This was his last connection to his father. He'd snuck away from Naren'da's camp without saying goodbye. Maybe after he escorted this legion to Somteh, he'd return to the mountains and try to find them. Without Rayli, there was no reason to stay in the city. The herbs would keep him fresher for the journey, but these soldiers needed them now. He procured a pot and brewed one last batch of Naren'da's embalming brew. He and his new friend Borl and the other Risen passed it around, inhaling the steam to coat their lungs, sipping to perfuse their insides, and rubbing the dregs on their skin.

"That's all until we reach the city," Dolen said, "but there's no fighting between here and there. The Berun are peaceful in Somteh, so as long as we don't run into monsters out here, we should be fine. They'll get you all set up. Won't be time for you to go home before Daylight, but the rest of the legion can probably turn around and head back once we arrive."

He tucked the empty pouch back into his one intact pocket.

"The Risen are obedient slaves. Somteh doesn't need living soldiers now."

— CHAPTER FORTY —

The entire Embalming Guild was packed into the great hall. Priests of the Atamonen, city government, and every discipline of science crowded in to hear the words of the Prime Embalmer. Sorreg had received the summons shortly after Kratch left her lab. He hadn't returned the rest of that day or the next, and Sorreg feared for his safety. She had no idea what kind of hierarchy existed in Berunfolk culture, but she knew from Kratch that the Prime Embalmer's first assistant, Orch, was not a person to be trifled with. She feared for her own safety as well. If she was wrong and Orch decided to betray her, Zarix wouldn't likely be lenient again. Her career would be over.

Hopefully *just* her career.

Dolen still hadn't returned, and she had given up hope of seeing him again. Now, seated on the edge of the room packed with hundreds of her fellow guild members, she had never felt so alone.

The position of her seat was no accident. The last time the science wing met, she had been seated at Zarix's right hand as he trumpeted her success. This time she sat last in rank among the Senior Embalmers, her view of the dais where Zarix sat partially obstructed by one of the many columns that held up the domed ceiling of the huge chamber. Zarix had freed her after her apparent change of heart in his chambers, but clearly he still felt she deserved a comeuppance. She couldn't have cared less about his approval. At least she got a seat. Behind her the room was crowded with Junior Embalmers and the lucky staff members invited to hear the Prime speak, standing room only.

Arched doorways opened off the sides of the long hall, and gas lamps cast shadows from high above. High on the wall behind the podium, a stained-glass window depicted Ata Lashka raising the dead, arms outstretched, beaming down from above. In Daylight, the scene would glow like a halo around a speaker's head. It glowed now as well, from torches on the wall outside the window. Only Risen were strong enough to make the climb up the high cliff to light them, and their glow was a sign that tonight's meeting held special importance.

So many people. Too many. Sorreg perched on the edge of her seat, willing the event to start so it could be over.

From a small door behind the dais, Zarix entered, and the room erupted in applause. He took the stage and, after a few moments of beaming at the adoring crowd, held up his hands for quiet.

"My fellow Embalmers, welcome to this night of all nights."

His smile made Sorreg itch.

"In generations to come, scholars and scientists will look back on this night and know that this was the moment the world changed. Fathers will tell their sons, and everyone will say they were here, they saw the miracle for themselves. But only you, my learned Embalmers, will truly be able to say, 'I was there. When Prime Embalmer Zarix saved the world, I was there.'"

Sorreg rolled her eyes. Despite her fears about his intentions, the man had a gift for oration. It almost made up for his questionable skill in medicine, though he was surely aware of that. He'd made a practice of surrounding himself with great scientists and taking credit for their work.

"Despite all our successes—the peace treaty that made us safe from the beasts of Beneath, and the Red Spore which returned our Risen to their rightful place as protectors of the living—we, the scientists of Somteh, have long failed at our most important mission. We are but one of two intelligent species on Ert, yet our friends the Berunfolk must still cower in fear from the light of the Atamonen. We have failed to share the glory of our gods with them, as the Atamonen have commanded."

They did? Sorreg wasn't much on religion, but she couldn't remember any such commandment from the priests.

"Tonight, that will change."

With a crash, the doors on the sides of the hall all opened at once, and Berunfolk filed in. They poured through the doors, surrounding the Embalmers, and filling the stage around Zarix. All of them wore Embalmer's cloaks, their clawed hands hidden in the folds of the sleeves.

I don't like this.

Sorreg breathed slowly through her nose, fighting the panic welling up inside her. Too many people, too close. She'd never been one for crowds, and this chamber hadn't been designed to hold so many at once. She tried to focus on Zarix's words, booming over the crowd as the Berunfolk took their places all around the hall.

"The Eyes of the Atamonen have never looked upon the Beneathers with love. Indeed, the shining light from the heavens melts the very flesh from the backs of the lowly creatures of shadow, and so they have hidden away in the dark tunnels, hating us because they could not share the favor of our gods. But with the blessing of the Atamonen, I have found a solution to their plight!"

All around the room, the Berunfolk opened their cloaks, each pulling out a brown, leathery egg.

Oh, gods. It's a demonstration.

"I have developed a compound that will protect them from the glorious light of the Eyes so that they may walk under the open sky like men, instead of scuttling beneath the ground like vermin. The long years of Daylight will open to those from Beneath, and with this, the years of darkness will cease to hold danger for us. The love of the Atamonen will carry us through, as we remember together the days of shining light!"

Movement jostled Sorreg's elbow, and she glared up at the Berunman who had sidled up to her chair. With a start, she recognized Kratch.

"Watch. Put on when Kratch say," he whispered, dropping something into her lap.

He backed away, returning to his place in line.

Sorreg peeked at what he'd dropped. It was like thick fabric, but smooth and clear. She touched the soft edges and realized what it was.

A hood. One of the filters they used when handling dangerous, fume-emitting plants or spore-forming fungi. Made from the gills of some underwater creature, its wearer was protected from poisonous air.

Heart pounding, she grasped the hood's edges. In the front of the hall, Zarix raised his arms.

"In the years to come, you'll remember you were here. You are the witnesses to the new world. A world of light! A world without fear! The world the Atamonen intended for us, the humans of Ert."

Sorreg glanced at Kratch. He nodded.

Each Berunfolk in the hall raised their egg.

Don't do it, Sorreg silently beseeched them. *He's tricked you. It won't protect you from the light. It's poison, and you will all die.* But she sat frozen in her seat, heart pounding in her ears.

Kratch's voice jolted her hands. "Now."

She lunged for him, intending to throw the hood over his head and protect him from the poison she knew was in those eggs. Zarix had betrayed the Berunfolk. He wasn't going to cure them. He was going to kill them all, and everyone here would be witness.

Kratch shoved her back. "Not Kratch. Sorreg. Now. Now!"

One of his tentacles whipped out of his sleeve and wrapped around the hood, pulling it over Sorreg's head. She tugged the neck strap tight by long habit trained into her by emergency drills.

All around the room, the eggs dropped.

"Welcome to the new world!" Zarix yelled, fists raised in triumph.

Green gas flowed from the ruptured eggs. Kratch grabbed Sorreg by the shoulders and dragged her to the doorway.

Sorreg watched in horror through the blurry, clear eyes of the hood as every human grabbed their throats, eyes wide. Blood poured from their noses. They clawed at their faces, gagging up red foam. From the front of the hall, Zarix's laugher turned to a choked gurgle.

Kratch pulled Sorreg from the massacre with a tentacle wrapped around her neck, keeping the hood secure.

"Big Man think he trick Berun," he said as they cleared the doorway. "Berun trick Big Man instead."

— CHAPTER FORTY-ONE —

R ayli stood in the arena, surrounded by her clan. All of
Tornado would fight tonight, and the crowd was noisier
than usual. The announcer's voice was barely audible over
their excited buzzing.

"You're in for a treat tonight, folks, though I hope those of you in
the front brought your wet weather gear! Things are going to get
messy in the arena!"

The command from Blubberlips had come as he'd finished
painting Rayli with her signature red dye. Tonight, it wasn't the
usual fight to kill. Tonight, he'd left them with one word.

"Survive."

It was the most ominous instruction he'd ever given them.

Nightfell was nearly over. The gladiator battles would end, and
Rayli knew her time as a commodity was drawing to a close. By
the next Nightfell, her owners would be long dead. No one cared if
Clan Tornado's fighters were around to be preserved for a century
of sleep. No one cared if they were torn apart tonight for the
pleasure of a bloodthirsty crowd. The money they earned on these
final battles would keep Blubberlips happy for the rest of his days.
To him, nothing else mattered.

Survive.

She looked over to the huge doorway, behind which lurked
whatever monster they were going to fight. Its bars had been

covered with some kind of thick material, and she couldn't see anything inside. In the middle of the arena, a large, square shape was covered with cloth. Something underneath it rattled, scraping at the edges.

The torches around the edge of the arena were high out of reach as usual, but four freestanding torch racks had been added around the far walls. Between them, waist-high piles of fist-size, black spheres lined the edges of the circle. Rayli counted ten piles between each set of torches. Forty piles of...whatever they were. She looked at the pile closest behind her. Each round thing was wrapped in dark cloth, its end twisted into a stem about as long as her finger. Wrapped like that, the things looked like giant berries from a shroom forest.

The announcer's ladder descended, and the smarmy man climbed down with his bodyguards.

"I bet you're all wondering what's in store for our proud gladiators tonight, right?"

A roar from the crowd.

He strode to one of the piles and picked up a wrapped sphere.

"All right, stand back!"

The crowd laughed as the gladiators moved away from him. He sauntered to one of the torches and touched the end of the cloth stem to the fire. It fizzed into flame, and the announcer hurled the lit thing high into the air, up to the level of the watching crowd.

As Clan Tornado watched, the thing exploded in a burst of spark and flame.

Rayli's stomach churned. The gladiators were all freshly embalmed, soaked in the flammable preserving herbs. They suffused her skin, her lungs, even her hair.

And the arena was lined with explosives.

"Exciting, huh?" the announcer cried. "But why would our brave fighters want to be anywhere near something so dangerous?"

He nodded, and the bodyguards ripped the cloth cover from the small cage in the middle of the arena.

The things inside were knee high. Pale yellow, they looked like something that belonged under the depths of the ocean. Four long, spindly legs ended in feet spiked with pairs of claws. Their heads boasted thick jaws lined with razor teeth. Over their wide, blue eyes and flat ears perched two strange antennae tipped with glowing blue lights which matched those at the end of their long, thin tails. In the dark, those lights would surely act as lures, beckoning prey to those sharp teeth.

But they were so small. Even without weapons, surely these five little creatures were nothing to fear.

From the door behind the clan, another beast was led in. Rayli's heart squeezed to recognize a ghote, like the ones she and Dolen had raised on their ranch in a life that now seemed like nothing more than a dream she'd once had. The docile creature strained back against the guard, who dragged it forward as it bleated in fear.

The guard grabbed the ghote and hurled it into the cage with the five yellow creatures. A howling blur of yellow chitin and whirling blue light filled the cage.

In three seconds, all that remained of the ghote were a few scraps of bloody hair.

The five yellow creatures, frenzied with the kill, pounded against the bars with bloody claws.

"And there you have it, folks!" the announcer shouted. "Behind that door," he gestured to the covered gate on the other side of the arena, "a hundred hungry puyorin beasts are just waiting to pour out and meet Clan Tornado for dinner!"

Laughter from the crowd.

"We'll start them out slowly, what do you think?"

The announcer and his guards shimmied up the ladder.

Rock, Scar, and Rayli huddled in the middle of the clan. Rayli felt Carrol's shaking hand on her back. The woman was nowhere near ready for this fight. Her new left arm barely functioned.

"All right," Rayli said. "Those of you who aren't quick, stay by the piles of explosives. That's Carrol, Jawbone, Outlaw, and Skeet." The slower gladiators nodded. "Who's got steady hands?"

A couple of fighters volunteered, and Rayli assigned them to man the torches.

"Once they're lit, we don't have much time. We'll try to get them into groups, and you guys throw the bombs, okay? Yell before you throw." She looked at her teammates. "Nobody burns tonight."

The announcer's voice boomed over the crowd.

"Is everybody ready?"

The roar was deafening.

"All right then, let's..."

Rayli glanced up toward the announcer's stage in the middle of the sloping rows of seats that surrounded the arena. It was dark up there, and she couldn't see anything, but he didn't start talking again.

"Okay, to your stations, everybody."

Rayli, Rock, and Scar moved toward the cage of angry beasts in the center. "We take these out first, then see how many at a time come through the door."

All around them, the crowd noise changed. A strange green fog drifted down from above.

"Remember. The command was survive." As if they could possibly have forgotten.

Something fell over the edge of the arena. The gladiators scattered. From the far side, something else fell, toppling over the wall and landing with a hard thump in the sand.

It's people. They're falling out of their seats.

Rayli and the clan watched as the front rows of the crowd clutched their throats, hacking up bloody foam. The two people who had fallen rolled in the sand, gasping for air, eyes bulging.

In minutes, the arena fell silent except for the banging of the beasts in the cage. Bodies hung over the edge of the arena walls, dripping blood from their noses and mouths, twitching as they died.

"Tornado, to me!" Rock yelled, and the gladiators gathered in the sand.

"Survive," Rayli whispered, grabbing Carrol's hand.

They bolted for the barred doorway that led back to their quarters. Together they heaved it open and raced out of the arena before the dead crowd could Rise.

— CHAPTER FORTY-TWO —

Dolen peered around the cliff edge.

"Peaceful, huh?" The legion commander shook his head. "Doesn't look too peaceful."

The city around Somteh was in flames. Berunfolk and humans darted between burning homes and businesses, and the screams that rolled across the plains suggested the humans weren't winning. A few giant beasts that reminded Dolen of the drillers that had chased him to his death in the mountains tromped among the wreckage, flinging bodies with huge front claws. In the flickering light, Dolen would swear that the beasts were being ridden by Berunfolk.

"I have no idea," Dolen stammered. "When I left, everything was fine." *Well, not fine. But nothing like this.* The Risen uprisings were over, and there was peace with the Berunfolk. Risen were slaves to the Red Spore, but there was no fighting. On the surface, it would have looked perfect.

"Clearly something changed." The commander turned to his troops. "Look alive, hundred and third! It's time to save the city."

Dolen shrank back to his new Risen friends. Borl offered a sword to Dolen and pulled the bow from his back. "Here. You'll need a weapon. You're not Legion, but stick near us if you can."

They assumed Dolen was heading into the city with them. He looked over the plain to the far-off mountains. If he ran, maybe he could find his way to a village before the end of Nightfell. Somewhere he'd be preserved. If he was lucky. If there was a village nearby that hadn't been attacked.

And if he didn't make it, he'd rot on the road.

He took the sword. "If we can take the city back, there should be some Embalmers still alive, right? Someone to preserve us?"

The man shrugged. "It's our only chance. But either way, we're going in. It's our duty."

Was that the Red Spore talking? Looking around as the Legion raised weapons and shields, preparing to charge into battle for a city that wasn't their home, Dolen didn't think so. These were soldiers. The Red Spore didn't make them want to fight. This was what they did. He prayed they did it well.

"I don't know how to use this," Dolen said, holding the sword out in front of him. "I'm not a fighter."

His friend grinned. "You are now. Just swing it at anything that's not human. The big beasts are tough, so go for the leg joints. The Beneathers, you just have to try to cut off their heads. Quickest way. They're only brave in big numbers."

"Hundred-third Kamteh ready!" the commander boomed.

"Ready!" the legion shouted in unison, starting a call-and-response.

"Who do we fight for?"

"Humans! Humans!"

"What's the night for?"

"Humans! Humans!"

"What's the light for?"

"Humans! Humans!"

"Hundred-third Kamteh—attack!"

They poured around the cliff, forming a phalanx heading into the burning city. Arrows from the archers in back sailed up and over the Risen in the lead, finding targets among the Berunfolk that turned to meet them. The huge beasts lumbered over, and Dolen hung back as the legion raced past him. His new Risen friends ducked past the grasping claws, scaling straight up the creatures' legs and beheading the Berunfolk on top. Instantly the beasts reared up, flinging the Risen from their backs. They seemed to go crazy without their riders, flailing without direction. The living soldiers cut them down, leg joint by leg joint, until the creatures scrambled on the ground. A swift downward stroke of a sword and the beasts went limp.

Dolen followed the soldiers as they cut a path through the city. He stayed well clear of the burning buildings, holding his sword out in front of him, praying to the Atamonen that he wouldn't have to use it.

The screaming had mostly stopped. As they moved down the main road, groups of soldiers broke off to attack small bands of Berunfolk who either died under the flashing blades or retreated into the night.

Up ahead, the cliff loomed. Hundreds of windows looked down over this plain. Weeks ago, when Dolen had first arrived, he had been awed by the sight of the glowing pattern up the sheer cliff face, the soft glow of lamps and gas lights like flickering beacons in the night.

Now the city was on fire.

Not all of it. But pockets of flame licked out windows on the west side of the cliff, smoke billowing out into the air. Dolen watched as someone appeared in one of those burning windows. The person blocked the flames for a moment with their shadow, then leapt from the sill. They didn't scream as they fell.

There will be nothing left. This is it for the city. And this is it for us.

No embalming in Somteh. No preservation for the Risen or the newly deceased. But maybe if there were survivors, they could take the dead to another town.

And Sorreg is in there somewhere.

He hadn't been able to save Rayli. He'd left her, promising he'd be back, and never returned. But maybe he could help the person who'd tried to help him. And burning, to a Risen, was the fastest way to reach Ata Lashka when their service was finished. Better to burn than to rot.

You heard the words. Ata Lashka had spoken from the box in the tunnel. He didn't understand any of it, but he knew it was a message.

He followed the Kamteh elite legion, pounding down the main thoroughfare toward the cliff entrance. Berunfolk stood guard, killing the civilians who tried to escape. The legion cut them down and pushed their way in.

Smoke burned Dolen's eyes. The air was thick with it, heavy and green.

The soldiers stumbled and fell to their knees before him, ripping off their helmets. In the main entry hall of Somteh, the living members of the elite hundred-third Legion choked, spewing bloody froth from their noses and mouths.

The eggs.

Dolen had seen this in the tunnels. The toxin brought by Orch, the Prime Embalmer's Berunfolk assistant.

It was free in the city. It was everywhere.

The Risen soldiers and Dolen formed a wide circle around the dying men, unable to help except to keep them from being trampled by Somteh citizens racing blindly for the exit. All of them had blood caked around their mouths and noses.

All of them were Risen.

With a sinking heart, Dolen realized the entire cliff must have been permeated with the toxin. Somteh was dead. The panicked people might not even realize it, but all of them were Risen, and the place was eerily quiet. He remembered the man from the tunnel who died this way, lungs dissolved by the poison, unable to speak or even whisper.

"What's happening here?"

Dolen answered the Risen soldier. "It's a poison, a gas. When they Rise, they'll have no lungs left. They won't be able to talk."

"But I'm breathing it in." The soldier drove his knife into the eye of a Berunfolk that tried to rush past him, kicking the body away as it twitched. "Why isn't it working on me?"

"No idea. Some things seem to work different on Risen." He thought about the empty herb packet in his pocket, the soothing steam that coated his throat with embalming herbs. "But I think it's the embalming. Our lungs are protected. It can't hurt us."

They protected their brethren until, one by one, the legion soldiers Rose.

Borl approached his commander. "Sir, the city has been poisoned. You and the rest of the Legion are now Corpseguard. I'm sorry, but your voice will not return. Given the situation, I ask to assume command of the legion as Corpse-captain."

The commander looked at his troops, staggering to their feet, already reaching for the weapons they had dropped as they died.

He nodded.

"Hundred-third, move out!" Borl commanded.

The Corpseguard legion headed deeper into the city. Dolen watched them go, then turned and raced for the hidden tunnel that would take him up to Sorreg's lab. If she were there, she'd be Risen and confused. He knew all about that.

"I'm coming, Sorreg," he muttered, darting into the dark, low doorway.

— CHAPTER FORTY-THREE —

Sorreg followed Kratch through low passages used by Berunfolk, safe from the chaos of the main hallways.

Zarix's gas was everywhere.

Sorreg tugged at the neck of the hood again, feeling it securely stuck to her skin. She was still processing what had happened.

Zarix had made the gas in the eggs, using some method only he knew to dissolve the embryos inside. He'd claimed to be creating a medication that would allow Berunfolk to walk freely in the light. As she thought about it, he probably had actually made it, or had someone else do it for him. But then he'd changed the formula. The gathering in the great hall was supposed to be a demonstration of his power, where the unsuspecting Berunfolk would drop the fragile, gas-filled eggs, releasing what they thought would be their salvation but would actually be their death. He probably had the eggs sent all through the tunnels, laughing at the idea of mothers trying to help their children and killing them all instead.

The Berunfolk were one step ahead.

It had to be Orch. Zarix had underestimated his assistant. Orch must have known all along and manipulated the eggs on her own, turning Zarix's Berunfolk-killing toxin into something that only killed humans.

Sorreg stopped to catch her breath on a rough-cut stairway. These back tunnels were only used by Kratch and his people, and the stairs were steep. Kratch had said her lab should be safe for the moment, and they were headed there to wait out the worst of the fighting. She had wanted to bolt straight outside, but he'd shaken his head.

"Surface not safe. Berun attack there, too."

So they'd climbed, staying away from the main corridors where people died and Berunfolk rampaged.

The hood's gill filters protected her, but the interior fogged easily. With each breath she took it became more opaque. Sweat poured off her brow and dripped into her eyes, but she couldn't remove the hood to wipe it away. She squinted against the salt and started up behind Kratch again.

When did he know?

She remembered the odd look on his face when she'd told him what she learned. He wasn't shocked that Zarix was going to betray them. He'd known then—she was sure of that now. And perhaps his knowledge had saved her life. She'd trusted him with what she thought was a secret, tried to help him save himself and his family. In return, when the time was right, he saved her instead. The truce in Somteh was long gone, but between Sorreg and Kratch, there was trust.

Finally, they emerged into the animal room behind Sorreg's lab. Kratch left her cowering behind the cages while he checked to make sure the door was closed. Finally he returned.

"Lab safe. No fighting here."

She still dared not remove the hood. The green gas had thinned as they climbed, but she had no idea how they were dispersing it. More could pour through the ventilation system at any time.

Wonder where they got that idea? The evil of the Red Spore discovery kept spreading with every thought.

Sorreg plopped down on a stool at the back of her lab, hooded head in her hands.

"I'm sorry, Kratch. Everyone is dying. Your people and mine. It's worse than it's ever been, and I didn't see it coming."

He cocked his head to the side. "Sorreg knew. Sorreg tell Kratch. But Kratch already know. Could not stop Orch. Could only save Sorreg."

"I didn't know in time." She looked up into his strange red eyes. "Thank you, Kratch. You saved my life."

He gave the little snort that passed for a laugh. "Sorreg would save Kratch." He glanced toward the door. "Not safe yet. Must leave. Must go high to mountains. Hide long time."

The enormity of the destruction hit her. Somteh was lost. He was right; she had to leave. "If I can get out of here, I'll try and make it to Kamteh. Nightfell will be over soon, and the surface will be safe for me." Her stomach sank. "It will, won't it? Zarix didn't actually make a cure that lets you walk in the light?"

Kratch gave the laugh again. "No cure. Berun stay in dark." Under his cloak, the tentacles snaked around, making his shoulders bulge in strange ripples. "But no Kamteh. Orch make many more death eggs. On way to Kamteh already."

Sweet Ata. It wasn't just Somteh. Ert's capital, the teeming city of Kamteh was about to die just like Somteh.

"When?"

He shrugged. "Leave now. Kamteh days through tunnel."

"Everyone will die. I have to warn them." Sorreg leapt to her feet. "Can we get up to my apartment? I need to get supplies. I have to try to get there before the eggs do."

The tentacle was soft on her arm. "Sorreg will die. Monsters on land. Berun in tunnel. Death eggs guarded by many." He released her. "Sorreg go to home. Get things. Go to high mountain. Only chance."

She stood in her lab, looking over her life's work.

What would become of the science? The medicines she'd hoped to create? Without Somteh, who would embalm the dead? She shivered, picturing the death eggs in a city like Kamteh. Without the capital and its armies of living and Risen, who would be left to care?

Zarix, you fool. You arrogant, ignorant, bigoted fool. You've doomed us all. In a generation, all that would be left of humans might be a smattering of tiny villages high in the cold mountains, scraping out subsistence and huddling in fear when the Eyes closed.

"Sorreg, is that you?"

She spun around at the voice.

"Dolen! You're alive!" She rushed to her assistant and threw her arms around him, only realizing a moment later how unnerving that must be for him, with her in the alien fume hood. She quickly let go and stepped back. "Sorry. I'm sorry about that. I'm just so glad to see someone I know. Someone alive."

He chuckled. "Well, alive depends on how you look at it."

"Right now, I see a human that's not foaming blood out his nose, gasping for air on the ground. That's enough for me."

She filled him in on the conclave in the great hall, Zarix's betrayal, and the Berunfolk's double-cross. Dolen shared a look with Kratch, who gave one of his tentacle shrugs.

"War with human. Has always been since humans come."

The stool creaked as Sorreg sank back down onto it. "It doesn't have to be. We proved that here. Even if Zarix never meant it, we still made it happen. It could have worked."

"Could have," Kratch agreed. "Didn't. Not ready."

The comment surprised Sorreg. "What do you mean, not ready?"

Kratch blinked. "Berun not ready. Humans not ready. Still too much hate."

But not here. Not in this room. Sorreg marveled at the little group for a moment. Kratch had never hesitated to save her. Even though it meant betraying his own kind, the threat of such wanton destruction was enough for him to set species considerations aside. Did he really think that sometime in the future, humans and Berunfolk could live in peace? Did she?

And Dolen… She smiled. He'd accepted Kratch from the very beginning. Maybe Kratch was right. Maybe somewhere, someday there could be peace. But not here, and not now. Not while the death eggs existed.

Dolen filled them in on his adventure in the tunnels. He seemed about to say something more, but glanced at Kratch and paused before resuming. "I met up with a legion of soldiers from Kamteh, all of whom died as soon as they marched into the city. A couple of them were already Risen, so those guys can still talk, but the ones whose lungs got melted are pretty unhappy about the whole situation." He shot a look at Sorreg. "And the ones who Rose before they arrived here already felt the effects of the Red Spore. It's already growing in the wild."

I always wanted to change the world, but I never wanted it to be like this.

"A legion of soldiers?"

Dolen nodded. "Elites. They sent them when there were still Risen uprisings here. Now they're down there fighting Berunfolk, just like they did at home."

Sorreg shot up from her seat and raced to her desk. After a few moments of cursing as she opened drawer after drawer, she pulled out a large, folded sheet of paper and opened it onto the surface, motioning for Kratch and Dolen to come take a look.

"Here's Somteh," she said, pointing to the city on the creased map. Her finger traced a line along the edge of the mountains. "And here's Kamteh. When did the death eggs leave?"

"Today. Eggs already gone." Kratch peered at the map.

"And they're going through the tunnels? Through the mountains?"

The Berunman nodded.

"Why not travel across the plain? It would be so much faster."

His brown cloak rippled in a shrug. "Berun like tunnels. Tunnels home."

She flipped the map around. "Show me. Draw a line where the tunnels go."

From the depths of his cloak, Kratch produced a pencil and traced a line, clearly understanding Sorreg's train of thought. "All under here. Not safe for human. Berun and monsters." He lifted the pencil in the middle of a jagged set of peaks. "Here. Tunnel end here." He circled a place. "Go through open valley. Then here." He circled again. "Back into tunnels. This part open, but always shade on edge of mountain. Safe for Berun even in light time."

Sorreg flipped the map back again. "Then that's where we'll ambush them. We cannot let those eggs get to Kamteh." She looked up with haunted eyes. "This is the failure of the Embalmers of Somteh. And from what I saw downstairs, I'm the last living member of that Guild. It's my problem, and I will fix it as best I can."

She turned to Dolen. "You say that whole fighting legion is Risen now?"

He nodded.

"Then go get them. We have a week of Nightfell left. Time enough to save Kamteh and the world."

— CHAPTER FORTY-FOUR —

Rayli looked down at Blubberlips lying in a foamy puddle of blood. As she watched, he blinked and stirred, reaching for his throat on the sticky ground.

"Does it hurt?" she asked. "Did it hurt to die, you disgusting worm?"

He rolled over and looked up at her, fear in his eyes.

Rayli smiled. "Hard to talk when your lungs are splattered down your chin."

Rock's voice jolted Rayli from her vindictive trance. "Hey, come on. We need to get the weapons and get out of here."

They'd shut the gate behind them in case the hundreds of dead fans decided to stagger down into the arena when they Rose, but Rayli remembered the confusion of waking up after a bloody, painful death. Most of them would likely just mill around in the stands until someone told them what to do.

"Get up," she said to Blubberlips, and he leapt to his feet.

Oh, yes. He's got it, too. How the tables have turned.

"Here's what I want you to do." She stood right in front of him, smelling the metallic scent of coagulating blood. "I want you to go and sit in my cell. I want you to wait there. No matter what anyone tells you to do, all you're going to do is wait there. You won't let anyone embalm you. You'll fight them if they try. You sit, and you rot. That's what you do. Nod if you understand."

He nodded and raced away down the corridor.

It was possible that someone would try to embalm him after the end of Nightfell, but he'd be well on the way to decay by then, and basically worthless after a week of bloating. It would have to do.

"Red, we need to go. Here." Rock tossed her a sword—a good blade of solid chitin, not one of the cheap, blunt practice swords. She tucked it into her leather strap. Still half covered in the red dye of combat, she followed him though the hallways, pausing at every turn. Carrol was right behind her.

"We stick together, and we figure out what's going on here," Rock said. "It sounds like fighting up there, and I smell smoke. We figure it out, and we make a plan."

They had no idea what was going on. Everyone in the stands had just suddenly died, choking and gagging on blood. Whether it was some science experiment gone wrong or a deliberate attack on living humans, the old instinct of the Risen to protect the living kicked in. They didn't deserve it, but Ata Lashka's command fueled their intentions.

Down the long, rough-cut stone halls they crept. The door at the end was locked, but the guard who held the keys was Risen and mute now, and he followed Rock's order to unlock the door. Clan Tornado, all twenty gladiators, climbed a stairway into chaos.

Newly Risen raced down the hallways pursued by Berunfolk. Though the Risen were stronger by far, these humans were terrified and confused. As a group of Berunfolk lit small torches to throw at the Risen, Tornado leapt out behind them and slaughtered the Beneathers easily.

"Risen, to me!" Rock shouted, and the obedient people fell in behind the clan.

They fought their way up three more levels, killing Berunfolk and gaining Risen, useless though they mostly were. None of them could talk, all were blood-soaked and death-addled, but in a few of them the confusion was already turning to anger. They could use anger.

Up ahead, the sound of battle clattered down the main stairway. Rock and Scar led the charge up and out into the main thoroughfare of Somteh. Long trade halls stretched off on each side of the wide, gaslit hallway. In peacetime, the halls would've been full of goods for sale: textiles made here in the city, spices from across the continent, and embalmed dead awaiting another Nightfell to Rise and serve. Today those halls were mostly in flames.

A clanging of weapons came from the south end. Metal on chitin, from the sound of it. Whoever was fighting, that was the place to be. Tornado raced down the wide corridor toward the noise.

They found a pitched battle. Soldiers in Kamteh uniforms cut a swath through disorganized ranks of Berunfolk. Creatures Rayli had faced in the gladiator pits fought for the Beneather side, and she and her clan lunged to action.

All that time in the pits, I thought I was wasting my time. Turns out I was training to save the city.

They whirled into battle, cutting down monster and Berunfolk alike. No living humans fought with them. She saw no one alive at all, just these Risen soldiers who couldn't even grunt as they fought, blood drying on their chins and noses. They'd been alive when they arrived here.

"Hey, who are you?"

Most of them had been alive. The soldier addressing Rayli had no blood on his face—none of his own, anyway. And he could talk, so he'd been dead before that gas had hit. She'd never been happier to be Risen.

"I'm Red. We're trained fighters. What in the rotting tomb is going on here?"

The man shook his head, firing an arrow at a fleeing Berunman. "We don't know. Met some guy on the road who said Somteh was at peace with the Berunfolk here. Looks like he lied. Led us into a massacre."

She shook her head. "It was true until about an hour ago. Then this gas came out of nowhere and the Beneathers attacked." She noticed him looking her over and realized she still wore her gladiator costume, such as it was. "I'm a gladiator of Clan Tornado, and you can keep your eyes to yourself."

He snapped his gaze away from her bare flesh.

"So what are we doing here? How many Beneathers are coming up from those tunnels?" he asked her.

"No idea."

She looked across the hallway, hazy with smoke. A figure holding a sword in front of him, waving it like a flag, emerged from a small tunnel entrance. The set of his shoulders made Rayli's heart lurch for a moment.

But it couldn't be. Not after a hundred years.

"Rayli?"

The voice cut into her soul. The last time she'd heard it, she'd been lying on her bed in their tiny ranch house, wracked with the agony of a childbirth that had ended in her death.

"Dolen, I'm here!"

They rushed together through the smoke and haze. All around them swords crashed and arrows flew.

He looked exactly the same as when he'd gone off to try and save her life. He hadn't aged a day.

He didn't return because he died trying to save you. And you died trying to have his child.

They stopped two feet away from each other, staring into matching pairs of gray eyes.

"It's you. Rayli, it's you! They said you were dead."

She grinned. "I was. I am."

"No, but..." Dolen shook his head. "Why are you dressed like that? Why are you dyed all red?"

"Long story. And it doesn't matter. Nothing matters now. You found me, Dolen. You came back to me."

She fell into his arms, skin against skin. The battle around them fell away into a slow-motion murmur. Her head lay on his shoulder, and Rayli was instantly transported back to the first time he held her, when they were young and the world was full of promise.

She knew in that long ago moment that Dolen was her anchor, her light in a storm, the steadfast mountain that would always protect her from the fiercest winter storms. A hundred years had passed, and nothing had changed. His heart pounded in her ears, and the distant, hollow feeling she'd gotten used to was replaced by the feeling of his pulse in time with hers. "Never leave me again," she murmured, and he kissed the top of her head, just the way he had that first time. The smooth stone of his amulet pressed into her flesh as they clung together.

And the dark shadow lifted from her mind.

— CHAPTER FORTY-FIVE —

T hey gathered in Sorreg's office. Dolen had clutched his wife's hand all the way up the back staircase, afraid to let go in case she disappeared into his memory again. But Rayli was real. Different. Stronger in body, of course, since she was Risen like him. But stronger in spirit as well. The red dye over half her hair and face made her look fierce. That was what they needed now. She'd brought another gladiator, an older woman she introduced as Carrol, and Dolen brought Borl from the hundred and third legion. They'd crept through the quiet upper staircase to Sorreg's lab to find her and Kratch listing supplies and gathering lab equipment.

Borl rushed in, weapon raised. Dolen jumped between him and Kratch before the sword could fall on the cowering Berunman.

"No, this is Kratch. He's our friend. The only one we trust."

Borl's eyes narrowed. "I thought you trusted them all."

Sorreg's voice was muffled inside the hood. "I vouch for Kratch. I forbid you to hurt him, and I charge you with his protection."

The soldier immediately lowered his sword.

"Now let's get all this sorted out."

Dolen made the introductions. When Sorreg heard Rayli's name, she thew her arms around the surprised gladiator. "Oh, my dear, I can't tell you how happy it makes me to find you alive. Dolen was crushed when the records said you were decommissioned."

The woman snorted. "Sent to the fighting pits, you mean. But I'm here, and that's what matters." She turned to Dolen and pointed at his chest. "And I want a rune like that."

Sorreg's eyes narrowed. "Why?"

"There's a thing they did to us. Some kind of red dust first, then a slime they put inside my skull. It made me into a slave and took my Lightshaper power away. But when I hugged Dolen and that rune necklace touched my skin, the dark cloud lifted out of my brain." She held her hand out and Dolen pulled the necklace over his head. He winced as the cloud immediately descended. How had Rayli survived like this? It was the only silver lining to the thought of her being gone—that she would never have become a slave to the Red Spore. Looking over at her now, barely dressed, dyed like a barbarian—he shivered and turned his mind away.

Rayli held up her hand. Light from the gas lamp in the hall jumped into the air. She made it dance, tracing the Rune of Ata Lashka that hung around her neck now before dissipating it into a shower of sparks with a snap of her fingers.

"You've been practicing," Dolen said.

"I'm stronger in every way," Rayli said. "Seems when you feed dead Risen bodies to other Risen, we inherit their strength. Guessing some of the mystery meat came from other Risen Lightshapers." She turned to Sorreg. "You look like a science person. You know anything about that?"

Sorreg hadn't raised her head since the Red Spore was mentioned. "We know a little about it, yes."

Kratch spoke up from the corner where he still eyed Borl. "Berun know. Highest order leaders drink dead corpse blood. Get Shadowshape power. More blood, more shadows."

Everyone goggled at him. "You do?" Sorreg's hood was fogged from the inside. "Your leaders drink their blood and steal their power?"

Dolen cringed back at the tentacle movement under the cloak. "Every weapon counts."

"Well, I want a rune like this," Rayli said, handing the rune necklace back to Dolen. "What can I use?"

From one of the lab benches, Sorreg retrieved a pot of ink and a small brush. "If it's just the rune, try painting it on your skin."

Dolen took the brush from her and shaped the rune in the center of Rayli's chest. In the old days on the ranch, she wouldn't have dreamed of allowing such an intimate act to happen in front of other people. Now she stood with hands on hips, watching to make sure he didn't miss a line.

He pulled the brush away and they waited.

"Nothing." Rayli frowned down at her chest. "Is it right? Every corner?"

Carrol peered at it. "It looks perfect to me."

Sorreg blinked behind the clear hood. "It's not the rune. It's the stone."

They turned to look at her.

"The stone. It's mirrorstone. The original Red Spore culture was grown on mirrorstone that was tainted with Risen blood. The pure stone must be acting as some kind of blocker. Some antidote." She breathed in. "A cure."

Rayli strode down to the line of stones on the lab benches. "Which one is it?" She held up a clean piece of stone. "This one?" A smile settled on her lips. "Yeah, it's this one. I can feel it."

She broke off a small piece and looked around. "I don't really want a necklace I could lose." She fished in drawers until she found a sharp knife.

While Dolen and the rest of the group looked on wide-eyed, she cut a slice in her abdomen. Straight-faced, she broke off a small, sharp shard of the mirrorstone and shoved it into the wound. "You got a needle and thread?"

Sorreg found some suture and sewed the wound shut with shaking hands. "Does it work?"

Rayli's fingers traced the uneven stitching. "What kind of Embalmer are you? Yes, it works."

"Me next," Carrol said, and Borl lined up behind her.

"Wait." Sorreg held up the knife. "This is science. We need to know how small a piece will work to counter the Red Spore. This will save the Risen forever. There will be no more slaves as long as we have the stone."

They broke off a tiny sliver, barely bigger than the needle, and pushed it into Carrol's belly. Almost immediately she sighed. "I feel it. The cloud is lifting." She turned to Sorreg. "Try it. Tell me to do something."

"Raise your right hand."

Carrol grinned, arms at her side. "That's my good arm, and I still didn't lift it. Experiment successful."

Borl got a similar shard, and Dolen as well, in case he ever lost the amulet. Sorreg broke off one more, handing it to Kratch.

"I won't live forever, and I don't want to wake up a slave. No one should have to endure that. I'm so sorry that it's happened."

Dolen and Rayli held Sorreg's arms as Kratch coated the shard in slime. Rayli almost let go when the tentacle emerged from his sleeve, but she held on at a look from Dolen.

"Clean first. Sorreg not dead yet." He shoved the needle of mirrorstone into the soft skin of Sorreg's belly. She grunted against the pain, hissing into the hood. When it was deep in the tissue, the tentacle changed color around one of the slime-emitting suckers, and he smeared a different yellow slime over the small wound. Sorreg's breathing eased, and she tucked her shirt in, covering the sticky wound.

"All right," she said. "Here's where we stand. There's a shipment of death eggs headed to Kamteh in the tunnels. We need to gather supplies for the trek, including cold weather gear for everyone, especially the Risen." She blinked. "Which is almost everyone, I suppose. We'll head overland and reach the opening in the tunnel here." She pointed to a circle on the map. "If the legion will go with us, we can stop the shipment here. Fight them in the tunnel and either bury the eggs in the snow to freeze, or maybe I can find a way to inactivate the gas before we break them and release it." She sighed. "If only we had some way to bring that tunnel down around them. Bury the whole shipment under the mountain."

Rayli smiled. "I think I might know a way."

— CHAPTER FORTY-SIX —

Rayli and Carrol found the rest of Clan Tornado in the Textile Hall, finishing off a swarm of Berunfolk who controlled several beasts armed with four sharp pincers each. When the Berunfolk died, Tornado made quick work of the directionless beasts.

Rayli called them over and explained the plan.

"There's a lot going on here, but this is what's needed. I'm taking a legion of soldiers out to the mountains to stop the poison that killed everyone here from getting to Kamteh. I need help to gather supplies for the journey, and then the rest of you can stay here to defend the city, or what's left of it."

Rock frowned. "Where you go, we go. Tornado stays together."

"Ordinarily, yes," Rayli said. "But if we manage this, there's a very good chance none of us will make it back before the end of Nightfell. We'll fall somewhere in the plains and be scavenged or rot. I won't have that for you, and we can't leave the city defenseless. Most of the new-Risen are just normal people. They have no idea how to fight. You'll have to help them hold the city, and I think we also need to collapse as many of the tunnels as we can find to stop the flow of Beneathers so we're not facing so many."

Rock scowled, but without mirrorstone, he couldn't disobey Rayli's command. They moved out into the hallway. Smoke still choked the air, and Berunfolk were setting Risen on fire everywhere they could find them, hacking their legs so they couldn't run.

"We can't save them all," Rayli called back as her clan muttered, wanting to help those in need, "and remember that a lot of those folks probably bet on your grisly deaths in the arena. Maybe just a few hours ago." This admonition worked, and the clan stayed in formation behind her. They didn't realize she and Carrol were immune to the spore and wouldn't respond to direct command, but so far Rock, their usual leader, didn't argue.

The staircase that led to the gladiator pits was tucked behind the knocked-over remains of a large, potted fungus, its planter shattered. When they reached the bottom, they found the door as they had left it: closed but not locked. The Risen guard was nowhere in sight, but Blubberlips was right where they had left him, sitting in Rayli's cell. She met his eyes as she passed by. *I could free him. Let him go try his luck upstairs.* But she remembered the feel of his fingers on her skin, smearing red paint before her battles, laughing at her shame. "You're doing a great job in there," she said. "Keep it up." She ducked in and grabbed her shirt and loose pants, pulling them on over her ridiculous fighting costume. He watched her with rage in his expression.

Depending on the timing, he might be salvageable to embalm, especially in the dryness of this cave. She hoped that without even a sip of embalming herb, the gasses in his gut would make him bloat and explode before that. *A girl can only dream.*

She thanked the Atamonen that Dolen hadn't insisted on coming with her for this part of the plan. When she finally had time to tell him all about her time since they'd parted, she planned to offer a slightly edited version of what went on in the arena. He didn't need to see this for himself.

The clan gathered all the weapons they could find, shoving them into rolled blankets and duffel bags they found in the medical supply room. Rayli counted off three gladiators to help Carrol drag those bags to the stairwell and defend it. The remaining twelve she directed to grab the rest of the blankets, doing the math in her head.

"Four. We're down four since we got out of here."

Rock sighed. "We're very flammable." He and the others all had scorch marks, now that Rayli had time to look.

They stopped at the closed gate to the arena, listening to the noise inside. The rattle of bars and an angry screeching told her the puyorin, those vicious little beasts, had likely not escaped from the cage in the middle of the sand. It felt like a century since the announcer had boasted of a hundred more waiting behind the far gate, which must still be holding, or this area would be overrun with Berunfolk already fleeing through that passage.

They peered through the bars. A few Risen milled around the sand, staying away from the rattling cage in the middle. Still more sat up high in the stands, clearly baffled by the change in everyone around them. Rayli remembered that a newly Risen often didn't realize they had died. These would wonder why everyone around them had gray eyes.

"You, up there!" she yelled to someone in the stands. "Push that ladder down so these people can get out of this hole." The man did as ordered, and for the first time, Rayli was glad of the spore. As a Risen under its effect, it was truly horrible—but freed from its tyranny, she had to admit it was useful. She wasn't certain that Dolen's boss, Sorreg, had been responsible for the creation of it, but her relief when the mirrorstone cure proved effective was suspicious.

When the ladder hit the ground, she had a change of heart. The stands were still nearly a quarter full, as people hesitated at the sound of the fighting outside.

"Everyone come on down here!" she called. "One by one, all of you come down and wait over there!" She pointed to an empty patch of sand.

While they obediently complied, she and the rest of Clan Tornado carefully gathered the huge piles of explosives, putting them into bags and wrapping the corners of blankets up to make parcels. Individually, the bundles weren't powerful, but together she hoped they could bring down a mountain. They dragged the explosives out through Clan Tornado's entry door and up to where Carrol and the rest waited.

"You guys stay here," she said to them. "There's one more thing I need to do. Carrol, come with me, please."

She and her friend trudged back down the hall. She paused at the entry to the arena, where the remains of the crowd still stood on the sand. She closed the gate from her side, securing it in place and peering through the close-set bars.

"You there in the blue," she called through. "Yes, you." She paused and smiled. It was the announcer, his smirk wiped away in a thick smear of blood on his chin. "Welcome to Clan Bloodthirsty. I'm sorry I can't place bets on this, the final Last Man Standing battle, but I suspect it will be a quick one. Announcer-man, go open the cage in the middle of the arena. Good luck, Clan Bloodthirsty. I'm counting on you to make a good show, though no one will be here to watch. But you should absolutely clap for each other. Go on! Let's hear that Somteh Arena spirit!"

They applauded as the announcer approached the cage.

He turned as he walked, terror in his eyes.

"Don't want to fight in the arena?" Rayli smiled. "I didn't want to, either. But nobody gave Red a choice. Do it right now."

He lifted the gate, and the enraged puyorin swarmed him. The crowd clapped, unable to disobey the order as the first of them fell to the hungry jaws.

"You could have given them weapons," Carrol said.

"Might have made it last longer," Rayli agreed, "but there's no one to watch. It doesn't need to be a big show."

Carrol scowled. Rayli ignored it, purposely missing her point in a way the other woman couldn't fail to notice.

The applause turned to the sound of snapping bones and tearing flesh which died away as they left the arena gate and walked back down the hallway. Rayli grabbed a guttering torch, holding it well away from her. It cast long shadows on the rough-hewn stone of the tunnel.

On the long shelf, the trophy heads at the back of the line were rotted, truly dead. Rayli passed between them, watching decay in reverse as the heads grew less desiccated. Lips at the end were thick and slack, and those closer in were firm and mobile. Thick, greasy tongues protruded less. Eyes went from absent to jelly, to mostly intact under fluttering eyelids. Every clan was represented. She stopped at the top of the line. Grappler was there, but not Flint or Backhand, who would be on another clan's shelf. Her heart bled for them, but there was no time to find them all. The Star Clan woman and man that Rayli had killed in the last clan-on-clan battle were there, though the Star woman had no eyes. Tod's head stared at her, and she remembered cutting it from his shoulders when the spore had first made her a slave. She had apologized every day when she passed him here, though he could not answer or offer forgiveness. The first unfortunates from Rayli's Last Man Standing battle that had won her the place in the clan were there as well. She stopped at Blue, the frightened young man who hadn't made it out of that first fight.

"I'm so sorry, my friends," she said. "I can't get you new bodies. I can't get you out of here. The gladiator fights are over, and all the living in this wretched city are dead. Berunfolk are destroying them, and soon this place could be overrun as well. The only thing I can do is free you with fire. Those of you who can, if you're okay with this, please blink twice."

Down the row of heads, every eye that still had a working lid blinked once, and then again.

Rayli raised the torch.

"May Ata Lashka welcome you. You have served the living well. Go to your rest."

She raised the torch and stood back, honoring the dead by watching as the flames consumed those who had been forced to be her enemies.

— CHAPTER FORTY-SEVEN —

The group who gathered in Sorreg's lab for final preparations could not have been more disparate. Rayli stood to one side, along with a bunch of barely clad gladiators from her clan. Dolen tried to equate the strong, determined woman in red dye who stood before him with the gentle wife he'd known for years, and came up short. Rayli had always been as tough as a rancher had to be, but this woman had a fierceness he wouldn't have believed. *Death changes us all.* The gladiators ranged in size and shape from a couple of hulking men down to Carrol, the older woman that Rayli shielded just like Dolen shielded Kratch. They all smelled of smoke and bristled with weapons. The cache of explosives they'd brought took up one whole corner of the lab.

Borl represented his Kamteh elite legion of soldiers, all Corpseguard now. The rest of the Legion was still below, fighting Berunfolk back into the tunnels to retake what was left of the dead city. Most of the soldiers were mute from the gas, and all were obedient to commands. Dolen considered sharing the mirrorstone secret but decided to hold off until the world was safe from the death egg threat. Soldiers were obedient by training, but it couldn't hurt to keep them spore-obedient a bit longer. Lives could depend on it.

And now you sound like the Prime Embalmer.

Sorreg herself stood with Kratch, who had turned back to the huge pile of supplies he had scavenged for the journey.

"All right," she said, words slightly muffled in the clear hood, "it's time to get out of here." She turned to Rayli. "Most of your clan is staying behind, right?"

She nodded. "They'll take some of the explosives and collapse the tunnels leading up to the city from below to secure what's left. There are probably some live people still out on the plains, which is good, because we're almost out of Nightfell. When the clan goes down, someone will need to take care of them."

Part of the supplies Sorreg and Kratch had brought included embalming herbs and the linen wraps used to enshroud the dead. A detailed list of instructions accompanied that package, but whatever they managed to do with the bodies should hold them until reinforcements from Kamteh could arrive. Any Risen left intact after this battle would be heroes of Somteh and eventually preserved with exquisite care for their next Rising. Carrol wasn't happy to be left behind here, but one of her arms wasn't fully functional, and she admitted she wouldn't be as much use as the legion soldiers out in the mountains. Clan Tornado would stay here and fight for the city that had cheered for their destruction. No one had ordered them to do it. No spore mandated it. But Risen served the living, and were honored and preserved in death. Since the days of the Atamonen, it had always been so.

The legion knew they might not return. If everything went perfectly according to plan, and Kratch's estimate of how fast the death egg caravan would travel through the tunnels under the mountains proved correct, they might have time to race for Kamteh before the Eyes opened and they fell lifeless. If not, as long as Sorreg survived, she would send another legion to retrieve them wherever they fell and return them for further embalming. Their supplies included enough herbs to preserve them inside and out for the next week until the job was done.

Dolen and Rayli were coming on the mission, along with Kratch, who would not be dissuaded. He insisted that Sorreg might need him, though she had expressed doubts about her own usefulness on the journey.

The location of the ambush was on the way to Kamteh. As the only surviving member of Somteh's Embalming Guild, the responsibility of reporting Zarix's betrayal to the Supreme Embalmer in the capital city fell to Sorreg. She would see the death eggs destroyed and continue to the city. She hadn't said what she planned after that, and Dolen hadn't asked.

Won't matter to me. If we ever see her again, she'll be Risen like us, a century from now.

Dolen and Rayli would stay with the legion and hope for a better Nightfell next time, together.

The door to the lab burst open, and the gladiators spun to face it, weapons raised.

A Risen man stood there, eyes wild. His left arm hung limp, and the back of his hair was singed off. But his black beard was intact, though caked with dried blood, and Sorreg murmured his name in shock.

"Zarix..."

He stumbled in and slammed the door behind him.

"Stop where you are."

The former Prime Embalmer froze, obedient to Sorreg's command.

"As ranking Guild officer, I have assumed control of the city. You will serve the living as Ata Lashka has commanded."

His eyes narrowed, but no sound escaped his flapping lips, and he stood where he had been ordered.

"I like you better when you can't talk," Sorreg said.

He kept glancing over his shoulder at the closed door.

"Were you chased here? Are there Berunfolk after you?"

He couldn't talk, but shrugged, eyes still on fire. He made a charade of writing on his hand, and Sorreg nodded for Dolen to take him paper and pen.

The pen was awkward in his hand as he scrawled a message. *Help me.*

She laughed, fogging up the fume hood. "Help you what? Help you kill another city? Help you make another load of poison to destroy every human on the planet?" She frowned. "But it's a good question. Who besides you knows how to make the death eggs? Does Orch know?"

Zarix shook his head and wrote, *Secret. Only I know. Orch changed what I created.*

"Ever the egomaniac," Sorreg snorted. "But you're certain? Without you, the death eggs can't be recreated? Did you write the formula for creating them down anywhere?"

Another head shake.

"No, you wouldn't, would you? Afraid someone would steal it from you, like you stole from everyone else." She sighed. "But that's good. Even if Orch isn't with the caravan when we destroy it, she won't be able to make more on her own. This secret dies with you. And you're coming with us to Kamteh. The Supreme Embalmer will decide your punishment."

The look on his face was almost worth it. But Dolen had seen the dead; nothing was truly worth the destruction of a whole city, even one as dirty as Somteh.

They distributed the explosives. Most would go on a couple of handcarts procured from other labs, while some would stay here with the clan to collapse the tunnels. They packed plenty of small stones to heat for the final part of the journey into the snowy mountains and donned travel cloaks before descending the back staircase.

Smoke hung in the main halls of the once-proud city. The colorful awnings that had hung above stalls selling the wares of a continent hung in tatters. Bodies littered the floors, both Berunfolk and Risen too damaged to stand. The party stepped over these, hurrying to the entry hall.

"Hundred-third, to me!" Borl shouted, and his legion formed up. "Report!"

One of the soldiers who had already been Corpseguard before arriving approached. "There's still fighting on the south and west ends, but it's died down a lot. Living survivors are being kept outside in a warehouse, and Risen survivors are holding position in the tunnels. Somteh is not secure, but the worst appears to be over."

Borl nodded. "The legion marches with me. Clan Tornado will take over the city's defenses. We march to save Kamteh."

Rayli hugged each gladiator, speaking to each in turn. The big man called Rock laid his forehead against hers just long enough for Dolen to raise an eyebrow. "Take care of them. All of them," Rayli said. The man turned to Dolen as Rayli moved down the line.

"You're Dolen. I've heard a lot about you." He held out a hand, and Dolen shook it. "She'd given up ever seeing you again. I'm so glad she found you."

"And you must be Rock," Dolen replied. "Thanks for taking care of her."

Rock laughed. "She didn't need much taking care of."

They watched Rayli hugging Carrol for the longest time. The two women shared whispered words.

"All right, Tornado," Rock shouted. "Let's go take back this city!"

The horde of leather-clad warriors ran screaming into the halls. Rayli returned to Dolen. No tears marked her cheeks, but he was sure they would have if Risen could cry.

"They'll be all right," he murmured. "Next Nightfell we'll come back here and see them again."

She turned to him. "They're good people. The best."

Along with Sorreg, Kratch, a still-seething but ironically obedient Prime Embalmer, and the Kamteh hundred and third elite legion, they headed out into the starlit night.

— CHAPTER FORTY-EIGHT —

T hey waited above the pass, pulling fire-warmed stones from the edge of the campfire that had burned for hours. Rayli exchanged the cooling stones in her cloak for the warm replacements, keeping her distance from the open flame. Their campsite overlooked a shadowed path between two high peaks. Even if the Eyes were open and bright, the path would be dark enough for Berunfolk to use; now it was nearly as dark as the openings to the tunnels on each end, where the carts of death eggs would travel on their way to Kamteh. From Rayli's vantage point, she could see right down the steep scramble to the flat lane below, and into the mouth of the explosive-rigged cave. A long cloth fuse led from the cave to just below where she sat. As soon as the Berun arrived, she would shape the light from the fire behind her, igniting the fuse leading to the piles of explosives deep in the cave. Rayli's crew would have a few moments to back away to safety before the far mountain buried the death eggs and the Berunfolk who transported them.

The legion grew restless. Kratch assured them that this was the path his kinsmen would follow. He waited alone down there now in the tunnel, alert for their approach. Even during the darkness when the surface was safe for them, the Berunfolk kept to their ways, preferring the security of walls around them and stone overhead. And yet, monsters from below roamed the surface. In the six days of travel to bring the party from Somteh's cliff to this snowy mountain, the legion had lost six fighters to the beasts that roamed under the stars. Nothing had attacked since they'd arrived at the pass hours before.

Rayli breathed in the cold, clean air. Mountains smelled like home.

When she had died a century before, she had taken her last breaths in the dawn, the hour when the Eyes of the Atamonen opened one by one, flooding the Ert with light. The Risen stayed awake until the final Eye opened, but Rayli died just before Ata Marska looked down upon the world, and she had not had time to Rise in her home. She awoke in Somteh, confused and devastated, with a scar on her belly where the child had been cut from her in the moments after her death. She and Carrol had been planning a trip to Rayli's home to scour the records and see if the child had lived, but Carrol's death and their sale to the gladiator pits ended that hope. On the road to this mission, Dolen had told her what he knew: only that the boy was born alive and taken to the Kamteh orphanage. He'd told her all about his journey from their little ranch up to find the herbs that might have saved her life. She'd listened to his tale, how he'd come to find her, been hired by the Embalmer's Guild. How he'd ventured deep into the tunnels and found the voice of Ata Lashka. Dolen wasn't prone to fancy, but she suspected this last was some sort of waking dream, brought on by long hours alone in the dark.

Wrapped in Dolen's arms, sitting on a rock overlooking the pass below, she thought about their baby.

"We had a son," she said, fingers wrapped around a heat stone.

"I know," Dolen replied. "Next Nightfell we'll go to Kamteh and search the records. If he survived, his grandchildren would be alive right now. Probably in their sixties. By next time, his great-great-grandchildren might still be alive. It will take some doing, but we'll find them. Kamteh will know what became of him, and he might have even known who we were and where he came from."

What a thought. My son may have known my name. Known that I died to bring him into the world.

"We would have named him Marten, after your father," she said.

Dolen laughed. "We'll be sure to tell my father that, if we can find him next time."

Stars crept across the heavens as they sat in silence, watching for Kratch to emerge with the early warning of the caravan's approach. Behind them, the legion was quiet, even those few who were dead before arriving at Somteh and could still speak.

"The world will be different next time," Dolen continued. "It's different now than when we lived. Who knows what will change?"

"Maybe there will be peace with the Berunfolk. Your friend Kratch seems to think it's possible."

Dolen kissed the top of her head "It would have been possible if Zarix hadn't betrayed them."

The Prime Embalmer had hovered around Sorreg for the entire journey, pulling the small cart in which she slept as the tireless Risen plodded on. He kept writing his repentance on any paper he could find, begging her not to tell his superior in the capital what he'd done. Sorreg swore to deliver his body to the Supreme Embalmer for justice and would not be swayed.

Dolen vouched for Sorreg and the Berunman, but Rayli was still skeptical. The whole plan came down to trust. Weeks in the gladiator pits had robbed Rayli of that particular luxury. She'd seen how quickly humans would turn on one another, and now their lives depended on a Berunman's commitment to some far-off peace.

No one seemed concerned that this could all be a trap. When Kratch had agreed to betray his people, Dolen and Sorreg believed him. *They know him. You don't.* And early in the journey, she'd cornered him when no one else was looking, demanding to know why he'd sacrifice his people's chance to eliminate the humans once and for all.

"Room for both," he'd said.

"I don't buy it," she countered, but then followed his gaze.

Sorreg was walking ahead of them.

"That's it? One human treats you like you're not garbage, and you're willing to do this to save us all?"

He blinked at her then. "Human and Berun count with same number. You want big number, you start count at one." He gave her a moment to process that thought. "When eggs drop and gas come, Sorreg try to save Kratch, not Sorreg. Big number start counting with one."

"Not all Berunfolk think like you do," Rayli said.

Kratch shrugged. "Not all humans kill like you."

She started to retort, but closed her mouth. He was right. She was a killer. Other humans made her what she was now. There were times in the pit when she would have happily killed every bloodthirsty person in those stands, screaming for a good show, for more blood. But one decent human was enough for Kratch to see the potential in all of them.

Maybe we should all be more like Kratch.

Movement below the high ridge drew her mind back to the present.

Kratch raced from the tunnel's mouth, cloak streaming behind him.

"They're coming!" Dolen called back to Sorreg and the waiting Legion.

Below, Kratch scaled the steep cliff face, ignoring the ropes the Legion had secured to aid their own ascent. The Berunman wasn't even winded when he reached the party.

"They come. Whole Berun army to kill at Kamteh. Wait. Be ready."

Sorreg put the last of the dry wood on the fire, and the blaze made deep shadows in the jagged stones around them. Rayli would use the light from that fire to light the end of the fuse below. Sorreg pulled on the fume hood, battered now, but still functional, just in case any of the death egg gas escaped from the blast that would bring down the mountain.

They had to time it perfectly, and it was better a moment late than a moment early. Too late, and some of the caravan would escape into the open path below. The legion stood ready to kill any Berunfolk that made it out before the explosion. If death eggs were ruptured in the open sky, the gas would dissipate harmlessly in time. But too early, and some of the egg-laden carts might avoid it on the inside. Any intact eggs could be re-routed and might pop up anywhere. Without Zarix, even Orch couldn't make more, but if any survived, another Berunfolk might figure out the formula. This was the moment to destroy them forever.

The legion joined Rayli and Dolen on the edge of the cliff. They left a clear path for her to seize the light of the fire and send it down the end of the fuse. It lay just at the edge of her range, but she had practiced. She could do it.

Kratch appeared beside them.

"Wait," he said, eyes closed. "Wait." He made the odd, guttural sounds of Berun language, and Rayli realized he was counting. "Almost..."

His eyes snapped open. "Fire now."

She raised her hands, pulling the light from the campfire into her power. The gift of Ata Runi flared bright in her heart. She shaped the light into an arrow of fire, hurling it off the edge. Every eye watched it fall.

Perfect hit.

The light fizzled out right on the end of the fuse, which ignited in a small shower of sparks.

She watched it burn as it inched closer to the mouth of the tunnel. The piles of explosives nearest the opening would blow first, then those deeper in as the chain reaction set them off. Once the first pile blew, no force would stop them.

A pair of red eyes appeared in the tunnel, followed by three more. Five more. Ten more.

Hurry, hurry.

The fuse burned on, approaching the cave entrance. Rayli held her breath as the race for the lives of humanity sizzled across the path, burning fuse heading for the first Berunfolk scouting the open skies beyond the tunnel while the army followed with the wagons behind.

With a puff of smoke, the fuse died.

Ata Runi, no!

Rayli reached for the fire behind her and shaped the light again, but her arrow of flame fell far short, dissipating in a few twirls of useless sparks at the edge of her range.

"I can't light it!" she cried. "It's too far!"

From both sides, the call went up.

"Hundred-third, to arms!"

The legion poured over the edge, weapons ready.

Rayli and Dolen looked at each other, nodded, and leapt down the steep hillside into battle.

— CHAPTER FORTY-NINE —

Dolen skidded down the hill, drawing the sword he barely knew how to swing. In the pass ahead, the legion sprang into battle. Arrows flew over the heads of the spearmen in front, and shocked Berunfolk fell with grunting gasps.

Ahead of Dolen, Rayli charged into the fray, sword high over her head. He hung back, knowing that in a clustered group he was as dangerous to his allies as he might be to the enemy.

The legion fought with the strength of the Risen. If the caravan had been only Berunfolk, the battle would have been a slaughter.

But the Berunfolk had allies.

Dolen scrambled part of the way back up the hill, straining to see into the tunnel. Four carts of death eggs stood in the mouth of it, and the Berun drivers cut the traces of the huge skitters that had pulled them. The beasts plunged forward, plowing into the Legion, scattering them with sweeps of their claws.

The carts are right there. If I could light the explosives...

"Fire!" he yelled up the hill to where Sorreg and Kratch waited. "Throw me fire!" They disappeared from the edge.

He watched the battle. The four skitters bristled with arrows from the legion but did not fall. He heard Rayli's scream of rage. She leapt onto the back of one of the beasts, standing on its shoulders and plunging her sword straight down behind its head. As it crumpled to the ground, she jumped off, rolling to safety and springing back to her feet, sword dripping green ichor. Like a creature possessed, she raced toward another, shrieking her rage.

Dolen's jaw dropped. She'd told him a little about her gladiator training, and the monsters she had fought in the arena, but even then, Dolen couldn't imagine her doing such things. Now it played out before him as his sweet, kind wife, mother of the child he'd never known, cut a path of destruction through her enemies.

"Dolen, here!"

He looked up at Sorreg's voice and stepped aside as she tossed a thick, burning plank down to him. They had cut up the carts they'd used to bring the explosives to make Rayli's fire, as there was nothing in these mountains to burn. He grabbed the plank, holding the burning end away from him as he turned toward the mouth of the tunnel.

A legion of soldiers and a hundred Berunfolk stood between him and his target.

He skirted around to the edge of the pass, dodging the backswing of a soldier's sword. A cloaked Berunman knocked into his back, and he spun around, brandishing the plank before him. The Beneather hissed, claws bared. Its tentacles waved out the neck hole of its cloak, filling the air with a sour smell. The creature jumped back when he swung the plank. Before Dolen could stop his swing, the creature was on him, ripping the front of his shirt, scoring three huge gashes in the skin of his chest. He flung the creature away just as a soldier spun around. The Corpseguard plunged his sword into the Berunman's neck, favoring Dolen with a grim smile before turning back to the rest of the battle.

Dolen took a deep breath. The plank-torch still burned in his hands. It cast a long shadow across the cliff wall ahead of him.

That shadow moved.

Swallowing the dim starlight, it peeled itself from the stone, coalescing into a solid being of darkness. Four arms with razor claws sprung from its form as it plowed into the battle, sending soldiers and Berunfolk crashing into the narrow walls of the pass.

It formed a head. Eyes of obsidian focused on Dolen.

He raised the burning plank and screamed his own war cry.

The shadow beast reared back.

"Light always beats shadow!" Dolen yelled, holding the plank high.

The shadow leapt. It flew over the raging battle straight at Dolen. He backed away, still holding the torch, as the creature landed right on top of him. He crouched, expecting to be crushed by its weight, but instead of bone-breaking mass, Dolen felt a pressure in his ears. Darkness swirled around him, sucking the breath from his lungs. His eyes bulged in their sockets. The shadow monster wrapped around him, sucking the light from the air and the flame from the torch. It guttered out with a wet, gulping noise, leaving Dolen inside the roiling, angry darkness.

— CHAPTER FIFTY —

Sorreg stood at the top of the short cliff, watching the battle below. She had never felt so useless.

The legion fought below her. Even Dolen, the lab assistant, had jumped into the fray. Yet here she stood, paralyzed as their plan fizzled away, devastated by a fuse that died halfway to its target.

"Sorreg leave now," Kratch said, pulling at her coat. "Cannot stay."

She stood firm, helpless to tear her eyes from the carnage.

Dolen's voice called up from below. "Fire! Throw me fire!"

The campfire Rayli had used still burned behind Sorreg. She ran to it and grabbed a plank alight at one end, dragging it from the flames. *Please stay lit.* She hurled it over the edge. "Dolen, here!"

It tumbled down the hill, and Sorreg blew out a sigh as Dolen picked it up, still burning, and headed into the battle.

"Wear hood." Kratch was next to her, holding up the fume hood.

"We're too far, and the wind is blowing away from us," Sorreg said. "Even if the eggs rupture, the gas won't come up here."

She felt a presence behind her and turned to see Zarix. All the pain of the last few weeks flowed over her. She saw again the Risen man pulling his hair from his head, white wisps fluttering to the ground. Dolen's hands around the prisoner's neck, strangling him as commanded.

He wasn't beholden to the spore then, with his mirrorstone amulet protecting him. He realized what he was doing. A chill froze her to the spot. Why had he obeyed? *Because he was afraid. He saw what was happening and had to play along.* Zarix had turned Dolen into a killer. Somehow that was so much worse than if it had been the Red Spore.

She remembered the wet gasps of the conclave, all her fellow Embalmers falling to the death eggs. The smell of blood. The eyes of the newly Risen. Green, heavy gas, and the smell of smoke in her city. All because of one man.

"This is your legacy." Her voice could cut through rock. "You did this." She waved a hand toward the battle. "We had peace. Maybe it wouldn't have lasted. Maybe the Berunfolk would have turned on us eventually. Who knows? But even if they did, we had a fighting chance. Until you had to be the hero. Had to trick them. Zarix, the genius. Zarix, savior of Somteh."

He backed away and she followed, staring into his silent face.

"You thought they were stupid. You thought your own assistant wouldn't know what you were doing. Berunfolk are the masters of the natural world. Kratch can do things with a wave of his tentacle that you and I can only dream of." She glanced at the Berunman who still held out her fume hood. "The medicines we could have developed together...the cures! The science we could have made!" She raked her hands through her hair. "They will never trust a word we say again, nor should they. Even if we win here today, even if those brave soldiers manage to kill every last Berunfolk down there, we've still lost. The war between our peoples will never end. Millions will die on both sides, for generations to come, because Prime Embalmer Zarix thought he could take their whole world."

"Sorreg should..."

She whirled on Kratch, cutting him off. "What? What should I do?"

"Should run," Kratch finished.

She peered over the edge.

A shadow rose on the far cliff wall from the mouth of the tunnel. She watched it claw through scores of fighters until it zeroed in on the brightest light in the valley: Dolen's torch. The beast flew across the battle, enveloping him in darkness. The burning plank winked out, and Dolen disappeared in the swirling black mist of its body.

"What is that thing?" she whispered.

"Human shape light," Kratch said. "Berun shape shadow."

The shadow monster stood, leaving Dolen's still body on the bare rock. It turned back to the battle.

Despite the strong opposition, the legion was holding strong. They were pushing the fighters back into the tunnel where the carts still stood.

We could still do it.

If they could trigger the explosion, the eggs could still be destroyed. The distant city that knew nothing of the death that waited in this dim mountain pass might yet be saved. It would cost the lives of the legion, burying them here in the frozen mountains forever, but all of them had known the risk when they charged down the hill. Every Corpseguard soldier was prepared to die for Kamteh and the human world.

They need fire. They need it to come to them.

She spun around. Kratch still held out the fume hood, eyes pleading for her to save herself.

The Risen Zarix continued gaping at her, voiceless and guilty.

She calculated the distance. It was their only chance.

A smile creased her lips as she faced her former mentor. "Prime Embalmer Zarix, you wanted to save the world."

For the first time, she was unashamed of the Red Spore that made Risen into obedient slaves.

"Now's your big chance."

— CHAPTER FIFTY-ONE —

Rayli screamed in the tunnel mouth. From atop a bucking skitter, she watched a shadow fly across the battle and engulf her husband, snuffing out the fire he was trying to bring her. She plunged her sword down into the skitter's neck and leapt clear as it fell beneath her.

Across the cavern, the other two skitters went down under similar blows from legion soldiers who had watched her. Four carts full of eggs sat further in the tunnel, right next to the deepest pile of explosives. Dolen had been bringing her the necessary fire.

And Dolen had fallen.

Her eyes swept the scene. Every Berunfolk was fighting, claws darting out to lacerate the soldiers, dodging their weapons.

Every Berunfolk except one.

They all looked alike to her, but this small one wore robes trimmed in gold, with the same emblems as Sorreg's, proclaiming her as part of the Embalmer's Guild. Orch, the Prime Embalmer's assistant. It had to be her. She stood in a dark corner, eyes closed, hands and disgusting tentacles waving complex runes front of her.

Shadowshaper.

Rayli longed to fight Orch with light, but the faint phosphorescence in the cave was nowhere near enough for her to shape. She had other tools. Clan Tornado had made her a gladiator. Without a sound, Rayli lunged.

Orch's eyes opened as Rayli's sword buried itself to the hilt in her chest. The glowing red eyes flickered, and tentacles flailed, spewing slime into the air. Shadows writhed in the cavern, jittering as Orch's control wavered. Rayli twisted the sword, dodging a flood of green ichor that pulsed from Orch's chest. The Berunwoman's jaw opened and closed, and she dropped, the red glow winking out, and the flickering shadows fading away.

Rayli pulled her sword from the Berunwoman's body and spun back toward the cave opening. The shadow monster shuddered and froze. It crystallized in the cold air, darkness turned into black snowflakes of ash that drifted to the muddy, bloodstained ground.

Dolen!

Berunfolk backed into her as the legion outside pushed them into the cave. She shoved forward, cutting every cloaked figure that moved, but there were too many.

She retreated, skirting around behind the bulk of the battle, then pushed forward at the edge of the fight. Dim starlight reached her, but too many warring bodies stood between her and the place where Dolen had fallen.

The tunnel mouth was a natural cave ringed with jagged teeth of rock. She climbed up the edge, searching the darkness for the shape of her husband.

He lay far out across the pass, halfway between Rayli's perch on the edge of the tunnel mouth and the steep cliff that led up to Sorreg's fire. The glow of it was much too far for Rayli to pull and shape.

Kill them all. It was all she could think of. Even if every soldier were cut to pieces here, if Sorreg was left on that hill, she could bury them all.

She glanced back to Dolen. He was intact, but the shadow beast had wrapped itself around him. Rayli's power shaped light, and the Berunfolk's shaped darkness. Rayli's power could kill a Risen if it enveloped one. If the shadows came from the same gift, perhaps they could kill as well. Dolen wasn't moving. *Please, Ata Runi. Don't let the darkness take him.*

The glow above them brightened. Rayli looked up to see an orange blaze headed for the cliff edge.

It was shaped like a man. A tall, thin man on fire.

The burning form ran to the edge of the cliff and tumbled over without a scream. Rayli watched the man fall, bouncing off the sharp rocks all the way down, blazing against the snowy gray stones. He crashed to the valley floor in a fiery heap.

Rayli climbed higher, above the whirling claws and blades below, hanging onto the lip of the tunnel's entrance with her legs wrapped around a jutting stone.

Closer. Come closer.

She reached out, but the burning man was too far.

Get up, she willed across the pass.

The fiery figure struggled to rise, but his legs had broken in the fall. He crawled forward, inching toward the battle.

From behind her she heard a Berunwoman's voice. "Get the eggs! Retreat!"

She turned to see Berunfolk rushing toward the carts. If they moved them down the tunnel, the battle was lost.

Across the pass, the burning man crawled, bringing his light closer and closer, inch by agonizing inch.

And halfway between them, Dolen stirred.

He sat up, shaking his head. The light from the burning form glinted off the necklace that hung on his chest.

"Dolen! The light!" Rayli screamed across the bloody ground.

Dolen lurched to his feet, looking for the source of the reflection. He grabbed the mirrorstone necklace, the shining rune of Ata Lashka, and aimed it toward Rayli.

The reflected light shone like a beacon across the battlefield. Rayli grabbed it and shaped it into a ball of fire.

"Hundred-third, retreat!" she yelled, but there was no time.

As the flame dropped from her hands, she let go of the rock. The blast shattered the air, ripping down the tunnel. Explosion after explosion lit the darkness, their power flinging Rayli out of the tunnel and across the pass.

She thumped to the ground as a rumble echoed across the little valley.

In a rush of white, the tunnel collapsed. An avalanche poured down from the mountain, burying the death eggs, the Berunfolk, and the retreating hundred and third Kamteh legion under a wall of ice and snow.

— CHAPTER FIFTY-TWO —

They left the legion buried in the mountainside.

Dolen hated to do it, but they all knew the chances of the damaged Risen making it back to a city were slim.

"They're frozen," Sorreg said. "It's four days until Daybreak. Even if we dug them out and they could all walk, we wouldn't make it to Kamteh in time. They're safe here until I can send a party to dig them out."

The four of them stood on the hillside looking down over the avalanche. No sign of the Legion remained, but they were Risen. Quick to freeze, but also quick to awaken. They weren't embalmed well, so staying here in the ice would preserve them better anyway.

Rayli nodded. "We should stay here, too. Send a party for all of us."

Sorreg's eyes fell, and Dolen could almost feel the wave of loneliness pouring off her. She'd still have Kratch for a little while until the light drove him underground, but Kamteh was five days away.

"We could go most of the way with you. If we stay in the mountains instead of down on the plain, it should be safe."

Sorreg's face lit up. "Would you do that? I was thinking maybe I'd camp here until it's light, but I'd rather get closer to Kamteh if we can. I burned the map with everything else in the bonfire."

The map, and the Prime Embalmer.

All that remained of the man was a charred skeleton. It seemed unfair that he be released to the Atamonen when so many others had been cut down by his folly, but the gods would know what to do with him. After the blast, his burning body was still crawling toward Rayli, just as Sorreg had commanded him. Dolen had to scoop up Rayli from where the explosion catapulted her and carry her away until Zarix burned past the point of movement.

With a last look toward the collapsed tunnel and the lost legion, they gathered what remained of their things and set off toward Kamteh.

Dolen looked out over the snow-filled valley. Kamteh was nowhere in sight, though its faint glow had been visible across the mountains for a few hours. Another high wall of peaks rose beyond the valley, but surely the city was just on the other side. Dolen had lived in the mountains his whole life, but these were different than his home, more rugged and vertical, full of dead end valleys and impassable crevasses.

He blinked, realizing what he was seeing.

"Kratch, you have to get underground. It's almost dawn."

Dolen looked to the sky. All the stars still shone down, the constellations he'd navigated by when he was alive. But the edge of the Mushroom and the Shepherd's Crook were dim because the sky had begun to glow. In the hour before the Eyes fully opened, the Atamonen peeked through their lids. He could see them now, eight faint circles of light in the purple sky. The red ball of Ata Lashka, the only Eye that moved, had almost set behind the mountain. How long had the Eyes been peeking? How long before they opened fully, snapping to full, shining life as Dolen's soul flowed back to them and his body fell limp in the snow? In less than an hour, it would happen. This was their only warning. Soon, in one instant, the world would be bathed in light, and the Risen would crumple to the ground wherever they stood, falling into the deep, instant sleep of the dead until the Eyes closed again in ninety years, and those whose bodies were still functional popped back into wakefulness, as if no time had passed at all.

But Kratch was in danger. He was wrapped up against the cold, but his exposed face would blister in the light. It was time for him to return to Beneath, to his people, to the long years of deprivation as they scrambled for food in the darkness below.

Dolen had worried about Kratch. He'd betrayed his people, destroying their chance to rid the world of humans. If any of the Berunfolk survivors from the battle had recognized him, he could be in danger when he returned to the tunnels.

But Kratch wasn't worried. He flapped the Somteh lab assistant garment he still wore. "They see human robes, not Kratch. Smell explosives, not Kratch."

The little Berunman peered at the sky now.

"Kratch go. Almost burn."

Dolen crouched in front of him. "Thank you, Kratch. Without you, Kamteh would be dead. I don't know what Sorreg will be able to do, but I know she'll fight for your people. Someday there will be peace again." He smiled. "Tell your children about us. Tell your grandchildren. The next time we wake up, maybe we'll meet them."

The chitinous face couldn't smile, but the eyes glowed with warmth. "Kratch not forget. Dead man friend." He held out his claws, and Dolen wrapped his hand gently around them in a strange, sharp handshake.

Kratch turned to Rayli. "Dead woman strong. Take care of dead man."

Rayli grinned. "You know I will. Take care of yourself, Kratch."

Tears spilled down Sorreg's cheeks, and Dolen took Rayli's hand. She nodded, and they moved away, leaving the scientist and the Berunman to their private farewell.

"She might still see him sometimes," Rayli said. Her cheeks were slack, and Dolen thought she might be sniffling along with Sorreg if she were able to make tears. "If she stays in a city, they might find a way to meet."

Dolen chuckled. "They're not some secret, star-crossed lovers." He shuddered at the thought. *Tentacles. No way.*

"No, not lovers," Rayli agreed. "But she loves him. And he loves her. They saved each other's lives. Kratch stood with her against his own people, and she would have sacrificed her career, her whole life, to save him. I don't think she has any other friends besides him."

"And us," Dolen said.

Rayli glanced at the sky. "Yes, us, for maybe fifteen more minutes. Then the next time we see each other, we'll all be Risen."

The mirrorstone under Dolen's coat was warm against his chest. "But we won't be slaves."

Sorreg returned, and Rayli held the Embalmer close as she sobbed. Finally they pulled apart, and Sorreg wiped her face.

"You must think I'm so weak."

Rayli smiled. "I think you're stronger than I am."

In the purple, pre-dawn light, Sorreg's eyes glittered like the fading stars. "I can't carry you when you sleep. But if you bury yourselves in snow, I'll mark the spot and come back for you as soon as I get to Kamteh and get some help."

"We should go a little higher," Dolen said. "Make sure we're above the melt line when it warms up here."

They all hugged one more time.

"I'll see you again," Sorreg whispered. "I'll take good care of you, and next time, we'll all wake up together."

With one final squeeze, Dolen and Rayli broke away from Sorreg and looked up the hill. They climbed with the strength of the Risen and settled on an icy ledge high above the path where Sorreg squinted up at them. They waved at her and watched her piling stones into a little cairn right below the spot where they would freeze.

Snow was piled up on the ledge, and they dug a small cavern in it, ducking inside and burying themselves in freezing powder. They wrapped their arms around each other and pulled the last covering of snow over their heads.

"Any minute now, the Eyes will open," Dolen whispered, his face pressed against Rayli's cheek. "We won't even know."

"And an instant later, to us, we'll wake up somewhere else," she agreed.

"I'm so sorry, Rayli. I'm so sorry I didn't come back to save you." He felt her smile, and her arms around him tighten.

"But you did. You came back and saved us all."

He remembered the talking box in the tunnel, the final words of Ata Lashka to her people. "Live well, in service and hope," he repeated, mimicking the sounds his god had said, though he didn't understand the words.

"I love you forever, Dol—"

— EPILOGUE —

Sorreg sat in the candlelit room, alone with the dead. A sweet smell of herbs perfumed the air, and carved runes on the walls gave the protection of the gods in this sacred space. Two bodies lay before her, eyes closed, faces calm and peaceful.

It had taken hours to scrub the dye from Rayli's blonde hair, and a faint pink tint remained on one side. Sorreg smoothed a thick ointment over the dead woman's scalp and massaged it into the long, thick tresses. A different ointment made her face shine in the flickering light, and Sorreg used a ghote-wool applicator to make sure she got every fold of both ears and the insides of her nostrils. A special healing cream would help the battle scars heal over the long years of sleep. By the time Rayli awoke, she would look even more beautiful than she did now.

Sorreg said the prayers as she wrapped layers of oil-soaked cloth around Rayli's body, tight over her crossed limbs.

"Sleep well, friend. I'll see you next time."

Once Rayli was complete, Sorreg turned her attention to Dolen, lying next to his enshrouded wife.

She thanked the gods she'd been able to find them. When she had arrived at Kamteh, the city was already beginning to repair the damage of ten long years of constant attacks by the Berunfolk. She'd stumbled in, exhausted, dehydrated, and starving after four days alone, lost in the hills, and been taken straight to the Medical

Embalmers. The emblem of her office got her first-rate care, and Kamteh's Senior Embalmers made sure she recovered quickly.

As the only surviving Embalmer from Somteh, she told the grave tale of the city. All the way here, she had debated what to say. Zarix was dead forever, burning out his final moments to prevent another massacre. He would never see true justice for the destruction of their city and the lives his hubris had cost. She could have left his legacy intact, paid for with his unwilling sacrifice, but lies and deception had caused enough damage. She told the story exactly as it happened, including her part in the creation of the Red Spore. Zarix was gone, and Orch was gone, and the death egg recipe was lost with them. The cities of the world were safe for now. Treachery on both sides had cost countless lives, human and Berunfolk alike. The truth would have to be enough.

She drew the best map she could to the location of the stone cairn beneath the frozen bodies of Dolen and Rayli. It took a week for the team to retrieve them, and they were nearly thawed by the time they arrived. The map to the legion who slept under the avalanche was a lot less certain, but she was confident they'd be found soon.

Dolen lay on her table now, in the embalming room under the city of Kamteh. Soon she would leave here and return to her home, to rebuild the Guild from the ruins. Teams were already on their way to try to preserve the thousands who'd died in the egg attack and lay unembalmed. Many would rot before they got there, but at least Rayli's clan friends were already well treated. They would be fine until the team arrived to wrap them for the long sleep.

Sorreg repeated the embalming process for Dolen, with the same care. She hadn't embalmed a body for years, focusing instead on medical research, but the old movements and chants came back from her early training. The prayers calmed her, even if she doubted their ability to grant favor from gods she didn't believe in.

A letter lay open next to her, written on tanned hide to survive years under wrapping. She glanced at it one more time.

Dolen and Rayli,

I hope that when you awaken, I'll be beside you, ready for a new decade of adventure. But you will rest here in the Hall of Heroes, and I return soon to Somteh, so in case we never meet again, I wanted you to know what I have learned.

Your son survived. He was adopted by a family of artisans in the Potter's Guild, and lived to old age, well respected. He was put to the flames upon his death but left three children, your grandchildren. Two sons, both potters like their father, had seven more children between them. One of your great-granddaughters is an Embalming Apprentice, and I intend to watch over her career. I'm taking her to Somteh where I can train her myself. Your other granddaughter had no children. She entered the Embalmer's Guild and was expected to excel in the art of preservation, but she had a bit of her grandmother's gladiator spirit and rebelled against the Guild's strict confines. She left the city and, as far as I have learned, trained with the barbarian tribes, and possibly even the Berunfolk, in the distant desert. She currently travels the country on her own, with a select group of apprentices who are learning her secrets. I believe you have met her. Her name is Naren'da, and she once traveled with your father among her band. I hope to find her sometime and let her know how her grandfather and grandmother saved the world.

Rest well, my friends. I will find you next time.

Yours dearly,

Sorreg

She folded the hide and placed it under Dolen's hand, crossing his arms over his chest. The wrapping soothed her, though tears wet her cheeks by the time she was finished.

"May the peace of the Atamonen hold you until you Rise again."

The final words of the process echoed across the chamber, and Sorreg stood. Two apprentices waited outside the embalming room to carry the dead to the alcove where they would be cared for until they Rose again. The young men saluted Sorreg with fingers over their lips, and she ascended the stairs, passing through the elaborate guild hall. Frescoes of the Atamonen adorned the high ceiling in bright colors, and mosaics of rare tiles were edged in gold and silver on the walls. Sunlight from the Eyes streamed in through high, open windows, and Sorreg breathed in the sweet desert air.

Kamteh's Supreme Embalmer had charged her with rebuilding Somteh, naming her Interim Prime until a new one could be elected. Hundreds of people who were outside the city during the death egg attack had survived the battle and were already salvaging what they could from the ruins of their homes. The cliff city's interior had burned, but stone walls held firm, and like the dead beneath this majestic hall, Somteh would rise again.

Sorreg's caravan would leave tomorrow for the ten-day march across the plains. Other Embalmers from all divisions were eager to prove themselves far from the strict rules of Kamteh. Artisans, builders, and tradesmen would accompany them, along with a regiment of soldiers in case any Berunfolk still prowled the empty tunnels. The death egg gas would be long gone, blown away in the hot wind that scoured the desolate halls. One day soon, the city's banners would fly again in the endless sunlight.

She would never see darkness again. By next Nightfell, her life would be long over. It felt strange to hope for an early death, but if she lived to old age and infirmity, she would not be allowed to Rise and meet her friends again. Her fingers traced the needle of mirrorstone under the skin of her belly. If she Rose, she would be ready.

So far, she had not shared the secret of overcoming the Red Spore. Kamteh, too, had experienced Risen uprisings, and so many good people had been staked out to rot here, far more than at home. The peace of the spore had saved so many, but at the price of their free will. For now, she kept the knowledge to herself. In time, she would share it, but Zarix had taught her to trust no one. She'd learned his lesson far too late.

She repeated the words Kratch had whispered to her at their parting. "Leave city. East one day. Rock that looks like mushroom. Kratch wait." They would have to keep their meetings secret, but with his help, their work could continue. The peace between Berunfolk and human was only shared by two, but it was a start.

The huge outer doors of the Embalmers' Guild were closed. On the walls above the doorframe, a mural depicted the Atamonen bestowing their gifts upon the world. In the center stood Ata Lashka, dressed in a golden tunic, arms outstretched, giving life to the dead who worshiped at her feet. Upon the doors themselves was a painted mosaic of living men and women receiving the light of the gods, which fell into their outstretched hands like raindrops, dispelling the monstrous shadows that lurked below them, grasping at their feet from beneath. The doors were so tall that when Sorreg reached them, the shadows at the bottom of the mosaic were all she could see. They reached for her with glowing red eyes.

Every Nightfell, darkness tried to claim the world. The living and the dead strove together, holding it back until light returned from the sky.

Someday we will not fear the darkness. Some day we will find a way to live with our shadows instead of fighting them.

Sorreg took a deep breath, opened the doors, and stepped out into the sunlight.

— ACKNOWLEDGEMENTS —

This novel comes to you from a comic book world by way of a card game. When Jeremy Mohler approached my husband and me about creating a card game set in the comic world of Nightfell, I quickly realized there were miles of tunnels to explore beneath the dark surface of Berun. The epic war between humans and Beneathers, between the light of the Atamonen gods and the dark of the Kisamonen, had been going on for centuries before the events of Nicolás R. Giacondino's graphic novel began. I knew there was a novel in the backstory of this amazing world, and ideas followed questions in my mind.

I've written in existing game worlds before. It's a unique position for a fantasy author to be constrained by the canon of a fully fleshed-out world while examining some new aspect that has yet to be completely formed. Riding on the rails of someone else's vision gives a unique perspective, and it's a trip I love to take. So I happily signed on to create the backstory of not only the Lost Legion of the comics, but the origin of the Corpseguard as we know and love them today. With Nicolás's welcome guidance, I created the ancient scientific wonder of Somteh's history, and the people who paved the way for all of Berun as it came to be.

Deepest thanks to Jeremy and Nicolás for trusting me to become the godmother of Berun.

Thanks to Alana Joli Abbott, editorial coordinator and developmental editor, for shaping up the rough edges of this story.

Thanks to Scott Colby for smoothing the passages in copyediting.

Thanks to Mikael Brodu and Nicolás R. Giacondino for making it look beautiful.

Thanks to my agent, Alice Speilburg, who has the Eye of the Atamonen shining down on my work.

Thanks to Nik Everhart and Grant Striemer, the first to venture to Somteh, and to Grant for giving Rayli her mad gladiator skills.

Thanks to all the Nightfell fans who are making the jump from comics to novels.

And as always, thanks to Andrew Vogel for the thankless job of being an author's husband. Who knew boardgaming would lead to the world of the Corpseguard?

— ABOUT THE AUTHOR —

D.W. Vogel is a veterinarian, cancer survivor, marathon runner, board game developer, and speculative fiction author. Her science fiction Horizon Arc series is available from Future House Publishing, along with the game world fantasy, Super Dungeon: The Forgotten King. She is also the author of the feminist fantasy Flamewalker, and co-author of Five Minutes to Success: Master the Craft of Writing. Her short stories are available in many anthologies, and she is represented by Alice Speilburg Literary.